FOREVER ROAD

Library of Congress Control Number: 2017951039
Vintage ISBN: 978-0-692-89183-4

Book cover design by CalMedia Enterprises
Printed in the United States of America

For pink elephants and summer,
thank you Jenny.

I have dreamed of you so much that you are no longer real.
Is there still time for me to reach your breathing body, to kiss
your mouth and make your dear voice come alive again?

I have dreamed of you so much that my arms, grown used to
being crossed on my chest as I hugged your shadow, would
perhaps not bend to the shape of your body. For faced with the
real form of what has haunted me and governed me for so
many days and years, I would surely become a shadow.

O scales of feeling.

I have dreamed of you so much that surely there is no more
time for me to wake up. I sleep on my feet prey to all the forms
of life and love, and you, the only one who counts for me today,
I can no more touch your face and lips than touch the lips and
face of some passerby.

I have dreamed of you so much, have walked so much, talked so
much, slept so much with your phantom, that perhaps the only thing
left for me is to become a phantom among phantoms, a shadow a
hundred times more shadow than the shadow that moves and goes
on moving, brightly, over the sundial of your life.

Robert Dresnos

FOREVER ROAD

As Emma sat on the rock behind her family's weathered barn, memories of summer rushed back. It was odd to find the world around her continuing with its business as if what she'd been through had never occurred. She looked out at the familiar landscape. The single lonely road that transformed the rolling hills into a neighborhood wound gently to the horizon, the drone of crickets hummed across the land with a mocking aloofness, and the long strands of yellow grass danced idly with the wind. The rabbits in the meadows hardly even knew—let alone cared—that summer was gone. She looked to the sky where the sun continued its endless journey. Life carried on with a slow-moving, unbridled certainty.

She sat still and breathed deeply, without energy, while what must have been her last few tears trickled down her cheek and fell to her dusty forearm. He had stolen a piece of her soul, and like a thief in the night was leaving her life as suddenly as he'd entered it. She closed her eyes and thought back to the moment it all began.

∞   ∞   ∞

Early June's moderate temperatures were just beginning to make way for summer's rolling heat. Most of the birds, frogs, and other critters occupying her family's five acres had already borne the burden of new offspring, but late bloomers still sang their mating calls—one final effort in the struggle dividing the included from the excluded. A din of birdcalls erupted from the surrounding trees.

Emma stood listening outside her blue-trimmed country home before her attention shifted and she stepped to the worn path connecting her house with the road. Striding down one side of the dirt trail her family called a driveway, she pushed past giant oleanders with their dehydrated white and pink flower buds. On the other side, a gully bordered a purling stream.

Across the stream rose an unfinished wooden barn bleached yellow by the sun, and beyond the barn was an open field extending to the hills that bordered the valley. The field was dense with wild wheat and littered with competing plants that offered a shimmering fierceness in the morning and a golden tranquility around dusk. The public road ran tangent to the open field until both ceded to the hazy distance.

Emma knew that if she looked closely enough she could make out her neighbor's house. This was her destination today, but because she lived on five acres it was a hike just to reach the beaten roadway. She took little notice as she passed the bushes and the barn, or crossed the miniature bridge marking the end of her driveway; instead the final leg of the journey fixed her thoughts.

The sign for Forester Road was weathered, its white lettering more closely resembling "Forever Rd." It was designated for the entire public, but only the ten-or-so families living directly off it and perhaps an occasional guest ever put it to use. Because of its lack of traffic, the asphalt was badly neglected and had developed extensive potholes over the years. Emma weaved around them efficiently, her frustration compounding as she drew closer to her destination. How exactly she was "volunteered" into the service of her neighbor, she didn't know. Waiving the details, her parents settled the matter with a punctuality of decision only parents could summon: she *was* going to help him with things around his house. For her final high-school summer, she was bound by service four days a week. Her brooding was lessened only by the fact that the old man had agreed to pay for her efforts.

As she approached, she looked up to inspect the yard. It was simple, and not well-maintained, but it *almost* had a quality of elegance, as if it were quaint at one point before being abandoned as a lost cause. She'd never paid it much mind, but now she noticed that the double-boarded fence at the entrance was broken. The wood was sun-scorched, the planks fading more quickly than they could be repainted. Inside the yard was a small carport with a galvanized roof. Two run-down trucks smelling of oil rested underneath; she wouldn't be surprised if neither ran. The property was significantly smaller than any other on the road, as if during the settlement of the surrounding area the old man had come along and managed to greedily mediate for his own little piece. A dirt pathway led to the small house where two rockers rested under the shade of an awning, the final features ornamenting the tiny parcel of land.

She reached the door and knocked. After pausing for a long moment, she knocked again with an accompanying, "Mr. O'Sullivan?"

Another ribbon of silence followed before she heard a muffled yell from inside and then the creak of the door as it opened slightly. Mr. O'Sullivan peeked through the crack.

"What?"

She hesitated, "Well, I'm *supposed* to help you today." *Remember?* Her tone was less than cordial in return, and she knew she wasn't winning the initial argument to be allowed inside.

Although Mr. O'Sullivan, or Greggory as he would later insist, was her closest neighbor by proximity, she had never been inside his house. In fact, she'd barely spoken to him in her entire time living there. When she was with her parents at the grocery store or in town doing odd chores, a courteous wave or simple "hello" had always sufficed to be rid of the cranky buzzard. To her surprise, the crack in the door widened until she could fit her body through.

She stepped into the dark foyer and looked at the old man. One of the few streaks of light daring to penetrate the transom highlighted his ragged hair. His countenance appeared ancient: sunken eyes, a large nose, and an endless expanse of wrinkles. Behind his knitted eyebrows and tight grin, he had a bitter, fixed expression as if angrily confronting death. He must have known what she saw, because he pushed his eyebrows together into an even tighter knot. She forced an apologetic smile and lowered her gaze to tattered clothes a size too large for his waning body. Blue veins crawled over the backs of his hands and knuckles, the vessels more prominent than the feeble bones underneath. She could feel his gaze burn into her. There was no way in hell he was going to offer a handshake, so they just stood as the silence of galaxies separated them.

"So..." she finally managed, before scanning the foyer.

From the few times she'd seen him, she assumed Greggory lived in rooms laden with tasseled drapes, antiques, and claw-footed tables, but there were none in sight. Only an umbrella rack stood nearby—no umbrella—and the adjacent room was equally plain.

He led her through the living room and into the kitchen: tattered armchair, yellowed appliances, sawdust near the refinished window, a wooden table with two wooden chairs.

Greggory walked to the sapphire flame of the stove, and just as he placed his bony hand on the kettle it began to whistle. She inhaled deeply, catching the scents of spice and vanilla. After taking the time to steep and pour himself a mug of tea, he turned and watched Emma from the opposite end of the kitchen. His gaze was no longer derisive, but it also wasn't hospitable. It was a stare of unfamiliarity. He didn't shirk from her returning gaze but instead watched her carefully, tentatively, as if he was trying to make up his mind. A current of impatience ran down her spine.

He took a small sip before finally saying diplomatically, "I guess I should show you the house."

By "showing" her, he merely retraced their short steps and gave names to each room. "This is the kitchen, the front room, and…" he led her towards the back of the house, midway down the hall, "…the bathroom." Then, with a raised finger to add to the formality of his request, "I ask that you don't go beyond here." Two closed doors remained at the end of the hallway, presumably bedrooms, but Emma was uninterested in discovering any mysteries within. She replied simply, "All right."

"Good." He led her from the hallway, "You can also help with some things outside if you want to stay here for more hours."

More hours? Hilarious. She nodded politely as if considering.

The living room, kitchen, bathroom, some dusty cupboards and closets, and a few other miscellaneous objects—oh, and the option to do to some things outside if she felt inclined—would compose the grounds for her cleaning. *Shouldn't take too long*, she determined thankfully.

Back in the kitchen, he grabbed his mug of tea but once again omitted an offer to share.

"So," the single word returned, "should I start then?"

His focus returned to her.

"What? No. No, this is a bad time for me." *A bad time?* "— Hmm. Wednesday?"

"Come back Wednesday?" she replied to ensure she'd heard correctly.

"Good. I'll pay you for an hour today, at whatever the market price is."

"Oh, you don—" she couldn't quite finish before Greggory shooed her out the door.

"All this, just have a lot to do—you and with Reid coming."

He closed the door behind her.

She walked back down the lonely road as quickly as she had arrived, and with similar frustration—this time at being forced *from* the house. What an inconsiderate, bitter old man. Didn't even tell her who Reid *was*. She wasn't one to use profanity, but *Old Fuck* ambled to the front of her thoughts. He even managed to spoil her resentment. As she walked, Emma could see the heat rising on the pavement. Mirages rose and rippled in the near distance.

GREGGORY

Should I have given her tea? was the first thought to cross his mind. *Next time.* Admittedly he was flustered by how she watched his movements and stared at his decrepit face. It struck him, reminded him how weak he'd become. He never used to be so weak.

He dumped what was left in the mug down the kitchen drain; although Earl Grey with vanilla was his vice, occasionally Greggory needed something a bit stronger to quell his thoughts. In the far reaches of the kitchen rested a dusty bottle of scotch. Yes, she had struck him.

His wrinkled hands reached for a cabinet above the refrigerator. His old bones cracked as they stretched, no longer built for such a task. With more exertion than he expected, his soft palm reached the bottle. Greggory ran his fingertips along the dusty glass surface to reveal the molasses liquid within its half-empty container. The house was quiet now. In his only scotch glass he poured half way, no ice. With drink in hand, he went to rest in the chair in the living room.

No, he never used to be so feeble, vulnerable, alone. But the way she watched reminded him of what he'd become. He sipped to steady his nerves.

∞   ∞   ∞

While the events defining the man he would become occurred later in his adulthood, what he himself considered the beginning occurred well before.

He lived with his parents in suburban Boston. Their residence was surrounded by daunting-yet-warm New England style homes that gazed down from each side of the street with their steep rooves and narrow eaves. The architecture was most often paired with a coastal setting, but for Greggory it was associated more with the never-ending gray skies, as if in some symbiotic relationship—house evolving with weather and weather with house. Along with the houses, the vivid autumnal colors—leaves rustling against the cement and swirling into a torrent of color like some Leonid Afremov painting—and the snow (relentless rather than jovial) gave Greggory a sense of home. Thoughts of such things brought him to his childhood, and he would often reminisce about the market some miles off towards the coast, his favorite sandwich shop, or sitting on the dock with his friends watching the fishing boats tug along with their lucky and disastrous stories.

He was young, just beginning to broaden his shoulders as he transitioned to adulthood. His medium champagne hair came as a bit of a surprise; his mother's hair was auburn and his father's dark. Whatever genetic variables played into his hair came as a stroke of luck, since it complemented his gray eyes and gave him the luxury of being perceived as older and more refined. The Irish slenderness came from his mother's side, but his perfect posture was instilled by his father. His energy levels were extraordinary, and Greggory was determined to inject significance in the largest of contexts into his life.

His parents had witnessed a great depression and two world wars, his father even participating in the second. As a result, they attempted to inculcate moderation, hard work, and (above all) patriotism. His parent's jingoish push, however, repelled Greggory. He secretly kept whimsical and philosophical fantasies that could have easily turned him into a beatnik.

That secret capriciousness caused him to shift his life's focus from one goal to the next over the most minor inclinations. The one steady enterprise remained his love of women. He combined his charm and boyishly handsome looks with devilish motives to attract the fairer sex, and having been born with healthy and robust traits—including that unique champagne hair—he just happened to be especially successful. Greggory accidently discovered this ability well after he graduated from high school, when he was in his early twenties.

Samson's Bar and Grill was a small shack on the fringe of town. Boat nets and harpoons more picturesque than functional hung from the wooden gray slats outside, while nautical maps and ship's wheels lined the interior. He'd made a habit of visiting for the seafood sandwich and fried potatoes.

He would sit in the bright red booths of the restaurant and peer out at the hustle of the restaurant's dealings. It wasn't long before he discovered the place was—practically speaking—run by the only full-time waitress there, Sarah Boehn. She was an older gal, in her late thirties or early forties, and was able to operate the place with the sole help of a cook in the back. She sat guests, took orders, stayed late to balance the logs, and, while he ate, came over to chat.

Sarah Boehn—strong and confident, with womanly curves, and being desirable even with a tiny bit of fat around her stomach. Her sexuality stemmed from how she strutted with her strong, stout legs and voluptuous ass. Apart from her generous womanly characteristics, what he was most attracted to were her high cheekbones and sharp nose. They were mischievous, enigmatic traits that gave her a vaguely snobbish quality of unattainability. But contrary to what one might first think of her, she was always nice enough to seek simple conversation, even with Greggory. She had a smile that pulled slightly to the right when she laughed, and her eyelids always squinted in disbelief when his tales reached their peak. When Greggory later reconsidered her memory, he appreciated that she had clearly been more snake charmer than snake; she'd known exactly what was happening in the long, slow string of events leading to the outcome of their relations. At the time he often noticed her hovering around him as she strode about the restaurant, but upon leaving would brush away the idea as an adolescent dream.

Then one night when he came in late, perhaps ten minutes before close, she finally struck him, inflicted darts of passion that would last longer than her ephemeral body. She quelled his apologies for arriving just before the kitchen closed, and even offered free coffee. She kept a stern eye on him from a corner of the restaurant until he finished, and then came over and casually suggested that he stay and talk. He hadn't intended to linger, but because she'd been kind about his late arrival he felt obliged. She refilled his coffee and asked him about his life. Their banter persisted long enough for the cook to finish preparing for the next day, so she released him in that unique tone of both boss and comrade, "Adios Cesar, te veo mañana."

They were alone. She dissolved the business formality by sliding into the booth across from him. Only the generational ritual remained, but that too began to melt away as they shared drinks and she touched his forearm with the tips of her fingers. Finally he established a vague awareness of what was happening, seeing it align with his childish fantasies. After their synchronous outbursts fell to silence a few times over, he locked eyes with her before shirking away, embarrassed. Her all-knowing smirk caused his fingers to tremble in his lap. His heart lapped in his chest.

On the third repetition of catch and release, laugh and eye contact, she yanked the line. Without waiting for protest or consent, she lifted herself and grabbed him loosely by his wrist. Maintaining her easy, confident posture, she led him to the close confines of the kitchen. Once there, her eyes pinned him to the stainless steel countertop.

A motherly whisper, "Hey?" and then she pulled his chin up with two fingers to force him to look at her. She smiled before proceeding.

∞   ∞   ∞

For months he continued the affair, slinking in and out of the dark blur of the night to meet her after Samson's closed, and eventually at her own apartment. Once he was allowed, he always preferred her lonely, single-bedroom apartment to Samson's. The kitchen and living room of the place were almost indistinguishable, separated only by linoleum tile in the kitchen and a couch facing an old television with a tiny screen in the living room. The cupboards and cabinets were wooden, furnished with cream-colored appliances, and the walls were plain save for a painting of a scarred fisherman standing in front of a dock. The painting could easily have been hung at Samson's, but somehow it bled through to her personal life.

In those early days of his youth, lying complacently naked next to her in bed, he would have enjoyed staying wrapped in her arms indefinitely. She would stroke his hair and offer soft kisses with warm affection until morning came when she hastily jumped from bed to throw on clothes, remembering she had something to do. To this day he couldn't properly decide whether she was merely lonely or had some womanly intentions he didn't understand, but once they stopped fooling around (a gradual decline over many months) there was no sadness or resentment from either. In fact, if he'd seen her longer than a brief passing-by during that time—which he hadn't—he expected they would have embraced and begun chatting like longtime friends.

As unseemly as it was, his relationship with Sarah allowed him to develop his charm. Near the end of their time together,

Greggory was already meeting other girls, one after another. Although he wasn't especially discriminating, they tended to be women more towards his own age with the same desperate ideals of a novice lover. Granted, many of the girls upon whom he planted his wandering eye held no illusions about what was happening, but some expected more only to become injured by his swift absence after he got what he wanted.

His noncommittal nature with these women in combination with his parents' push to have him do something respectable with his life eventually resulted in a sudden surge of moral guilt, which in turn led him to decide that structure was the solution to his wanderlust.

His answer came in the form of an advertisement for volunteer work in impoverished nations. The pamphlet had lain flat in the junk pile, ready to be discarded any day. Still, the young black children on the cover, in tattered clothes and holding on with nothing more than broad smiles, spurred him to pick it up. He looked at the photograph on the front and found it more believable that their clothes weren't quite in shreds, their impoverished bodies not quite skin and bones. They were no longer a typical in-your-face advertisement creating infested guilt like a horrible blowjob. No, these people were real and relatable. Hope and maybe a bit of rash determination aroused him to call the number at the bottom.

EMMA

Because Emma didn't own a car, spending time with her friends, with anybody, was often difficult. Forget the possibility of dating, distance alone squelched that endeavor, but to add she was perhaps more introverted than most. The majority of her leisure was spent in solitude: just her, nature, and her thoughts. Even though this isolation slung her into depression at times, she mostly enjoyed, or learned to enjoy, the time alone.

During her summer afternoons, when not helping Greggory, she explored river outlets bubbling from her family's property, read behind the horseless barn, or went on brisk hikes up and around the surrounding hills. As the sun's rays began to cast long shadows over the valley, she would sit in a tight, still ball— legs tucked between her arms—and watch the day conclude. Of her many vantage points, Emma was most often lured to one location in particular: the top of the hill across the street. The hill might not have been the tallest in the area, but it was the most accessible. Furthermore, it held a mystery that had captivated her since the previous year.

As she climbed one of the tattered trails beginning at the deserted lot across the street, she remembered why she hadn't made the trek in some time. The yellow strands of cheatgrass—

or maybe they were foxtails—always wove into her socks. Even though she stayed on the matted parts of twined grass, those inexhaustible burdens always managed to collect. Only after a good fifteen minutes, cutting back and forth, wading through unkept footpaths, did she reach the summit where the yellow fibers gave way to red rocks and hard Indian dirt.

The peak of the hill had a flat circumference of about twenty-five feet. Off to one edge stood a coast live oak that leaned outward. The cabled roots protruded and clung into the flat topsoil. Its limbs fanned out like an umbrella. It was the only tree for at least a half-mile in all directions.

Upon reaching the tree, Emma took a seat in the shade and began picking at the needles in her socks. With each tug the coarse filaments popped away.

Once contented (relenting to the fact that many would remain), she peeked slyly like a detective in the direction of the tree trunk. She eased into the topic, anxious at the possibility that her memories had become mired and deformed during the time away. To her relief she identified the carving about five feet up in the bole. Now that she had confirmation it survived, she stood and inspected the marks more candidly. On her previous visit, she remembered being unable to decipher the blurred lettering. As she stared at the shaved wood—hoping she'd gain some ability she hadn't previously possessed—she came to the same indeterminable conclusion: *Initials? An "S" or a "B"?* All she could make out with certainty was the slanted plus sign separating the letters. She passed her fingers over the shallow markings.

Emma was intrigued by the carving. It was mysterious and romantic. On and on she wondered whom the letters represented. Different faces came to mind as her imagination flared.

After five or so thoughtful, idle kicks while standing there pondering the marking, she realized she wasn't poking at the dirt at all, but rather something with a finer-grained texture more like sandpaper. She looked down. The ground was uniform, almost smooth. She felt it again with her toe. Yes, definitely not dirt. She squatted and rubbed her index and middle fingers over the area.

Once she was certain of the object's size, she began digging around the corners, outlining its width like an archeologist sectioning off a dinosaur bone. When the layers proved too tough for her fingers, she picked up a nearby stick. Eventually chunks broke apart and she could exhume the object with more authority. It wasn't big, maybe the size of a book, and she deduced it had to be a box of some sort—treasure chest. She had to stop twice as her arms tired, but using the stick like a lever she finally popped the thing out.

In her hands she held the object. It was light and smelled of mulched leaves. Upon inspection, vein-like markings covered the top. The grooves were largely faded, but she pieced together a Nordic design of intricate trees and pinecones. She guessed the box would likely be valuable had the weather not damaged it entirely. Her eyes followed the lines closely, consciously ignoring the portions splintered and damaged by rain and clay-oven heat over the years.

Emma was duly excited by the discovery, but her eyes widened when she lifted the cracked lid and found two small pendants threaded by one thin, golden chain. Even though they were old, both were preserved well by the enclosure.

The first she picked up was presumably the older of the two. Aside from being tarnished and slightly warped at the bottom, its oval shape remained intact. The pendant was as thin as a dime and had a smooth, unadulterated back. Inside the dotted border was a pressed image of an elephant wearing exotic tapestries. It looked like a token from one of those machines at carnivals where you put two quarters in, crank the knob, and out pops a pressed penny of the Virgin Mary, though this appeared to be created by hand. The baroque design betrayed the expertise of the jeweler, and the delicate amber and pink colors glinting from the gold offered a quality of piousness.

The second pendant was sculpted and polished from variolite, and simple in design. The pockmarks of the stone ranged from dry moss to emerald green and flashed its shades when she turned it in the light. The polygonal shape resembled a Hindu elephant. The thin chain torqued through a small cave at the point where the elephant's trunk touched the base of its head, causing it to hang sideways.

Although both featured elephants, they didn't appear to belong together. Yet, there they were. If anything, Emma became more intrigued at their differences. Each held a uniqueness that brought about a flood of questions to her fantastical answers.

At reexamining the site, at discovering treasure, excitement washed over her. The items probably weren't worth much money, but with the box they were another three puzzle pieces, undoubtedly relating to the carving in some great mystery ready to be revealed. She felt like Sherlock Holmes. With the small pendants in her palm, she studied them with close scrutiny, and only when she felt assured that she could recall the details did she tuck the pendants away and follow the trail down to her house.

∞   ∞   ∞

The next week while idly twiddling the items with her thumbs in bed, Emma realized she was almost late for her meeting with Greggory. In a stroke of luck, if she could call it such, she glanced at the clock and jumped out of bed: 2:52. *2:52!* She had scheduled to meet the old man at three, and he wasn't keen on people being late for appointments. She'd already had the misfortune of receiving a brusque scolding herself. Upon arrival that day, he'd made a general remark about how people who didn't follow through with their commitments weren't trustworthy enough to keep around. She bowed her head and nodded in agreement, but his rigid demeanor remained for the rest of the afternoon.

With complete strangers, his reactions were more severe. She recalled a package being delivered to the house—how he placed the order without internet she had no clue—and when the UPS driver delivered the small cardboard box, Greggory calmly laid into him about how late he was and how their customer service was next to shit and how a company allowing such a lack of effort was fucked (paraphrased) and would fail sooner than later. The delivery man took the brunt of the irate rambling rather gracefully in her opinion, but nonetheless he left silently defeated. Afterwards Emma stared at Greggory wide-eyed from the front room, her mouth hanging in disbelief. He skulked past her and into the back rooms with the small package tucked under an arm, and only later did he offer a hushed apology about his *slight* overreaction.

With that scolding fresh in her mind, she hid away the box with the pendants and headed out the door.

Emma learned in those early weeks that it had been her parents who threw her into this servitude. It clarified why he never appeared to need help, and why her assigned cleaning tasks were quite easy in comparison with some of his own projects. When she first arrived, he was in the process of replacing the kitchen window and fixing the siding of the house. He was always physically preoccupied with some usually strenuous task, and to top it off, the way he acted towards her suggested he didn't care for the company.

She considered not returning at all (I mean fuck, nobody wants to be around *that*, right?), but the pain she saw in his eyes, or perhaps simply saving herself from her parents' harassment if they found she ditched, convinced her to continue the effort and return regularly and on time. She would walk over from her house, down the hot pavement, to help him for a few hours before being asked to leave right on cue.

A stroke of luck came when he offered her, and would continue to offer her, tea as soon as she arrived. At first she thought it was a trick and politely declined, but after a few such overtures she accepted with skeptical hesitation. Soon, he began planting a full mug on the kitchen table for her without a word, and eventually he inserted small talk, forged with awkward, out-of-practice niceties.

Her initial lamentations slowly wore down to acceptance. They both understood that he was difficult—there was no question about that—but she found herself conversing with the old man more often regardless. Gathering that he hadn't had somebody to talk with in a long time, she would experience his ramblings from time to time. Most often he would recall his old life in Boston, but every so often she would listen to him speak about his travels to South America. "I remember when I was in a place called Manaus, and this little boy came up to me waving an action figure in one hand and a dirty palm for money in the other. Little did I know his brother or friend or whatever he was was pickpocketing me from behind. Little bastard. Gotta watch out for them Brazilians—clever devils. They have muddy rivers and endless rainforests. I don't know about now with all the logging, but back then there wasn't logging in the least. Yes, muddy waters and pink dolphins—it's true—yes, pink dolphins." Then something would click in his brain and he would conclude, "Anyways, that was a long time ago. You did all right cleaning today. Here..." He'd hand her the day's pay and ask her to schedule her next appointment. As if he was managing a tight schedule, he'd put on his reading glasses, squint at the calendar on the fridge, and mark the time she suggested.

Up to that point, none of her suggestions had been turned away, but after she tried for Tuesday he rejected it: "Tuesday doesn't work. I have to pick up my grandson Reid from the airport. Friday work for you?" A hint of anxiety slipped into his words.

"Your *grandson*?" The words flew out automatically. Not that Greggory couldn't have had children, but he never spoke of them. Through all their small banter, he omitted, left out, failed to even suggest, that he had children, and so grandchildren seemed impossible. The news dizzied her.

After his confirmation—"Yes, grandson"—she continued to stare until he led her out of his house.

How old is he? Does he look like Greggory? Do my parent's know about him? They probably do. Hmmmf.

Greggory certainly hadn't revealed much, only his grandson's name: Reid. *Or was it Reed? Dammit.*

GREGGORY

After reading the pamphlet detailing the volunteer work, vigorous but rewarding, he dialed the number and an operator transferred his call to the office lines. The recruiter took his information and scheduled an interview at their nearest office, which was serendipitously located in Boston.

Although small, the building was neat and well-kept. Dark mahogany desks sat strategically to the left of the entrance, easily the first thing to catch the eyes of people passing the building's tall windows. A nest of desks situated towards the back was arranged to maximize the illusion of space, and bright portraits of smiling children lined the walls. The workers wore suits like bankers, and offered fixed expressions as they gave resolute answers over the phone, "Mhm, yes."

A woman approached him already knowing who he was. They shook hands, and she led him to her desk amongst the nest. They sat and discussed everything he should expect while volunteering in a small settlement far removed from society.

Each topic was covered quickly and concluded with her asking, "Any questions?"

When his few questions were answered, she would go to her file cabinet and withdraw the next bundle of paperwork, then continue on. After everything was said and done, she prepared a series of contracts and waivers, which he signed without reading.

There wasn't much to do in the weeks leading to his departure. Greggory was left biding his time at his parents' home until he boarded the plane in late spring. His flight went from Boston to Miami to Eduardo Gomes International Airport in Manaus, Brazil. The heavy, oppressive air hit him as soon as he stepped off the plane. During his taxi ride to the agency's local headquarters, he peered out at the tall skyscrapers in the middle of the new city, and at the *favelas*—built on top of each other in a wall of color—on the outskirts. This initial sightseeing was quickly replaced when his attention was forced back inside the cab.

He tried communicating with the driver in the smattering of Portuguese he'd picked up in the intensive learning courses he enrolled in back home, but failed miserably in relaying anything of value. In the dim yellow glow of the window he stared back at his lamenting reflection, trying to recall the correct conjugations, verbs, and sentence structures to get him to the part of the city where he needed to be.

It took several tries, but whatever he said on his final attempt must have sparked recognition, because the driver shook his index finger in the air and let out the exclamation, "Oooeww!"

They sped along the crowded streets, passing a blur of maple faces in business suits and rags alike, until the taxi turned down an alley and stopped. Streaks of black soot and grime trailed the length of the faded pink building next to them. The smell of sewage invaded the confines of the cab. As he scrambled out of the vehicle, the stench suffocated his senses and a ball knotted in his throat. He suppressed the urge to vomit while he inspected the building. It was much smaller than the headquarters in Boston, but a sign in the corner of the window suggested that this was, indeed, the place. He couldn't see inside because sun-stained yellow blinds blocked his view, but he'd come too far to turn back now. With a drawn-out exhale, he waved the driver away and stepped inside. No wooden desks, no telephones, no file cabinets, no portraits of children. Only two plastic chairs—unoccupied—and a front counter with a bell.

He studied the sign taped on the counter, *Toca a campainha para obter assistência,* then tapped the bell twice to let them know he was here. After a long moment, a fat woman hobbled her way from the back, not attempting to conceal the look of inconvenience plastered across her face. A bead of sweat slung from her temple.

"My name's Greggory—Greggory O'Sullivan. I'm supposed to check in here?"

Breathing heavily, she looked down at a small sheet of paper and thumbed through the lettering with her sausage fingers. She mumbled to herself, things he couldn't pick up, before trying to speak with him in Portuguese—also things he couldn't pick up. Even after his studies and initial feelings of confidence while he listened to these slow, immaculately pronounced sentences over his cassette player, he had difficulties picking up what she was saying. As with the taxi driver, they began a back-and-forth wash of broken English and Portuguese. They advanced in baby steps. She pronounced her sentences slowly with her fat lips. From the jumble, he picked out a few words: *Colônia Antônio Aleixo.* This was the city where he was told to catch a boat that would take him upriver. Then came another: *táxi.* He tried to confirm her instructions, but she only repeated her sentence. When he agreed to take a taxi to the city she nodded cheerfully. As he was turning to leave, she repeated "Reimburst *taxi,*" as if it would lead to an epiphany or jolt of excitement on his part. "Ahh, reimbursed." He smiled and stepped outside.

The headquarters was far from the commercial district, in a location where it proved much more difficult to hail another taxi. He stood on the curb waiting, his body feeling heavy, while he peered down the empty street in both directions. The sounds of honking and sirens echoed in the distance. The humidity and scent of sewage pressed onto him. He couldn't shake the image of the fat lady inside pointing and laughing at him from behind the counter.

The moments dragged for what seemed like an eternity until another cab came zipping down the alley as if by accident. He flagged it with a wave, and fortunately the man stopped. Greggory clambered in, and the driver introduced himself as Rafael. In his best Portuguese, he instructed Rafael of his destination. The tires made a quick screech as they picked up speed, and soon he and Rafael were weaving in and out of traffic. Rafael conversed in spirited Portuguese as they snaked their way through the city.

He was a lively fellow, Rafael. He responded in animation, flailing his hands at the traffic, at the city, at Greggory's American accent. Dark hair poked up through the collar of his shirt, and beads of sweat leapt from his body as he assaulted the air with his gestures. Although Greggory understood only a handful of words, finding them in small bits like panning for specks of gold in piles of dark soil, he nodded and smiled in affirmation like a polite guest.

In the hour-and-a-half drive north, they escaped the city to a more rural setting. Every few miles they'd pass rundown communities. Glimpses of shanties patched together with plywood, metal sheeting, and cardboard appeared alongside the road. Rafael never ceased his fervent gibbering. The roadside became bare, and soon there were no dwellings. Not that Greggory had ever been to Oklahoma, but the landscape oddly reminded him of the place: its open expanse of pale yellow grass and a deserted road carving into the distance. But on the horizon he could see Amazonian trees, and eventually their cab made it to them. They passed a few errant trees, and then entered a thick cave of jungle. Their artery of travel became bumpier, and the air even more oppressive. Greggory craned his neck to see the top, but his view was blocked by a canopy of hanging limbs and splayed leaves. Then the tunnel closed around them entirely, taking much of the daylight. Rafael turned down an unmarked dirt road, and finally the car stopped.

Looking back to stare at him, a fretted word popped into Greggory's head: *robbed*.

"Okay, we here—friend," Rafael concluded, making it clear he was waiting for payment instead.

Greggory looked around, almost disappointed at not being robbed. His brows furrowed in confusion. "We're here?"

Rafael pointed somewhere in the wilderness, almost simultaneously as he stated the total fare for the trip. Distracted with trying to determine the location, Greggory took out his wallet and handed Rafael a wad of foreign currency. To where Rafael pointed, he could see a makeshift dock composed of sparse, waterlogged planks that barely extended past the muddy shore.

"This is it? *Colônia Antônio Aleixo?*—Where's the boat?"

Rafael only shrugged.

Greggory grabbed his few belongings and exited the vehicle in a trance.

He went to the driver's window, trying one last time to confirm, but Rafael explained very little—"This it."—a shrug, and then he jetted off. Mud flung from the rear tires as the car propelled down the dirt road and out of sight.

What. In. The. Fuck. He should have just turned around when he saw the shoddy pink headquarters, but he was raised by his parents—stay resolute. He made his way to the dock and stood to wait. His movements became heavy. His thoughts lumbered.

Maybe fifteen, maybe thirty, maybe forty-five minutes passed while he stood on the muddy shore, where he allowed swarms of insects to feed on him. The heat intensified, and

Greggory's shirt darkened with patches of sweat. Soon his mind warred: should he turn around and start walking to the nearest town? He considered and reconsidered, and just as he had come to a decision he heard a high-pitch buzz coming from downstream. A boat came whirring around the riverbend, led by the loud rumbling of an outboard motor. Relief flooded him. *Thank you Rafael!*

The boat, however, never really stopped as it came closer; rather it just hovered around the floating dock. Beckoning with an outstretched hand, the captain of the three-man crew urged him—in a similar impatient Brazilian tone as Rafael—to hop aboard. Greggory grabbed his backpack and suitcase and made his legs move. It was quite possible to misstep on a loose board and tumble into the river, but he made it down the broken, splintered dock and leapt for the boat, landing like a gymnast on board.

The captain took a moment to pop his head above the boat's wheel and smile at him. He had greasy black hair, almond skin, and a smile revealing missing teeth. The enthusiasm in the young captain's eyes immediately imposed the urge to trust him in the most severe circumstances and not at all in the most casual ones. But the glance at each other was short, and the captain reverted his attention back to the river quickly. He hollered instructions over the roar of the engine, and the two crewmen jumped to action in one coordinated motion.

The burnt-sienna waves pushed away from the boat at a steady clip as they maneuvered upstream. He stood at the railing watching the water as he was led deeper into the jungle. For some time he watched the water push away from their small vessel, but after several hours he became bored and pulled out the notebook. By midafternoon, when their craft stopped for supplies, Greggory understood that his journey would take longer than he originally anticipated. One stop became two, and then four, and the boat continued to stop every morning and night as the journey became a trip measured in days.

He occupied the time by doing anything he could. During breaks at shore, he ventured to the beach to haul in açaí palms. Although ill-versed in Portuguese, Greggory listened to the captain speak of the legends of the jungle. While he was prone to impassioned mood swings like those of a child, the captain's eyebrows always twisted with seriousness when he spoke of the shamanistic theology imbuing the land.

The rhythm of listening to stories and watching the ruddy river pass by was just becoming familiar and almost comfortable when Greggory's travels with the captain ended. He was told to wait for the next boat, while his home of four days pushed out from shore without him. As before, he stood amongst a cloud of insects, apprehensively waiting until the river spit out another broken boat. He spent the next five days traveling up the river, jumping from one boat to another. The trepidation he felt at being left stranded solidified and melted in a perpetual cycle; once on board, boredom took both their places. The shorelines remained a camouflaged backdrop of trees that passed the same way hour after hour. The smell of gasoline and the miasma of the river led him to a sensitivity that would thereafter cause a bout of nausea every time he was around open water. At one point, his stomach churned so violently, the unstable ache became so unsteady, that he rushed to the rails to vomit. After the incident, he twisted his neck towards two crewmen who spoke in whispers to themselves, just out of earshot from him. They were all smiles and laughs. He nodded their way with a tight-lipped frown, to which they turned their backs and continued their conversation in private.

The boats propelled him so deep into the Amazon that the waters turned emerald green. It was a pleasant surprise until the river vacillated back and forth in color with the same regularity as his nausea. Only after a long time did he realize that his journal entries slipped under the same blanket of boredom.

May 28th
I nearly killed myself trying to jump from a broken dock onto a
tiny tin boat while here in Brazil. To be honest, I felt rather
adventurist.
A young lad is helping me to the camp where I am to meet my
caboclo tribe. He is quite young, 13? A few of his teeth are missing, but
it somehow makes his big smile warmer. I got to wondering if he would
do this his whole life or if this is just temporary.
His crew doesn't talk much, hell they have their backs turned most
of the time looking down at the water. I try to see what they see, but the
water is too murky past the surface.

June 2nd
Ebb flow, ebb flow. Brown water. I don't know why everybody
around here refuses to look at me. I'm going to die here.

The trees against the shoreline grew thicker, almost impenetrable. The incessant buzz of insects continued indefinitely. The turbid shores, for all their drear, became an odd respite.

June 5th
I've become a savage here. I need land.

And as if answering his call, the boat stopped. But rather than ordering Greggory to wait, with a point of their fingers the crew signaled that he had arrived. In a flurry of excitement he climbed over the metal siding, waded to shore, and marched to firmer ground. The boat rocked in an awkward circle then spewed off towards its next destination unaffected. He continued onward, passing ferns and long tails of moss, into the dense cover of trees.

The recruiter in Boston had told him about the settlement, describing it as a hamlet of sorts, but upon his arrival it was smaller than he imagined—more a camp than a village. He had to blink to adjust to the darkness. With the exception of a few rays beaming like spears through the foliage, the clearing was devoid of light. Pillars of tree trunks, rectangular and gray with shadow, rose around him like gothic towers. Wooden structures with palm roofs were scattered throughout, intermixed with canopy tents. A few of the more landscaped huts had potted plants in front, placed strategically to receive the most sunlight at midday. In the middle of the glade was a large, airy building with a fire pit at its center. On the walls hung an array of fish, along with limp corpses of dead game; swollen sacks of different fruits and grains leaned against the building's siding. Supporting dusty demijohns and clay pots was a nearby structure with shelves that resembled a closet. A scent of rich dirt, decomposition, and tree sap mixed with the faint, nearly undetectable (but nonetheless unmistakable) aroma of shit, coming almost certainly from the outhouses on the fringe of the camp.

Back in the States he'd found that *caboclos* means "people having copper-colored skin," and in Manaus he found it meant "hillbillies." Whatever the case, he had reached a small settlement of thirty or forty of them. The first caboclo he saw was heading somewhere in an easy stroll with her woven basket in hand. She noticed him and came to introduce herself as Gledope. *Gedewpa?* She wore faded jeans, a Rolling Stones tee, a pink ribbon in her hair, and a gracious smile.

When word got out, it felt as if the entire camp rushed from their huts to greet him. They all wore grungy jeans and shirts. The only variation came with their shoes: some donned sandals, others sneakers. As he introduced himself to each, they nodded and grinned widely.

He ambitiously repeated each of their names and then introduced himself again, trying to avoid becoming "Tret" for the next nine months.

After greeting, each villager would offer a cheerful "Bye, Tret!" before leaving to attend to daily tasks. Before he had time to exhale—something he was beginning to do a lot here in Brazil—he heard in perfect English, "Hey, I'm Leila."

He whipped around to find two women standing before him.

"Hi. I'm Greg," he returned.

"Yes, we had word you were coming but didn't know if and when you'd arrive."

Her armpits were stained with sweat and both her face and arms were covered in mud. The mixture of the encampment and the rancidity from the lack of shower seethed from her skin in an invisible cloud. She wore a deep cotton V-neck revealing her breasts, and on her wrist dangled a series of colorful bracelets. Her eyes were severe, and she shot him a devious smirk with thin, haughty lips—that were emphasized by her jet-black hair and stout nose. She gave him the immediate feeling that she could get away with anything, good or bad. Some part of her reminded him of Sarah Boehn. She was filthy and raw, but he found something about her attractive.

And then there was the girl blending into the background behind her. She was less dirty, with a long face and big blue eyes that she hid with a downward gaze. Her nose was round with thick nostrils, like those of a Polack. Not quite pasty, her complexion was washed. Her lips were pale, and in combination with her lankiness, she stood there like dreary apparition. Only a tint of rosiness filled her cheeks with life.

Greggory found it difficult to focus on her, especially with Leila so vivid before him, but a single pendant hugging the skin between her collar bones caught his eye. It was delicate, the size of a quarter, and as the shimmer bounced to catch his eye he noticed the shape of an elephant.

EMMA

Friday was a long way off, and it felt even longer sitting in her lonely house with only a rampant imagination for company. Tiptoeing around as if the carpet were hallowed grounds, she waited impatiently for the temperature to drop so she could relieve some of the long hours outside. From time to time she'd glance at the clock. Maybe her parents would come home early from work. It was so long ago that they had time for her, back when her father still called her Peeks—a name she earned after a surly game of peek-a-boo at the ripe age of three.

In her girlhood, she and her father would go fishing and camping. Even though the activities were traditionally more father-son, neither seemed to mind. They'd drive for half-an-hour, listening to blues on the radio, until a secluded lake appeared as if by accident. At the lake they'd set their fishing poles, and Emma would watch the still line for signs of a catch. She'd drink a grape-juice box while her father nursed a beer, and together they'd share sharp white cheddar cheese and thick cuts of French bread. Her father always seemed happy just to listen as she reeled away her loose thoughts about the world.

She knew her father loved her. But after they moved to the country when she was eleven, he had to work longer hours.

Eventually they stopped talking with the familial intimacy she once enjoyed. Soon they were speaking two languages until the day came when they stopped talking altogether. Although there were times when she could have made an effort, she came to the decision that it was best to remain silent.

Emma dated the final severing of their bond to their first and only trip following the move onto Forester. It came as a shock, since they'd each had such an exceptional experience. They were still unpacking in the new house, and to placate a traumatized daughter he loaded up the camping gear and they hit the road, as they had so many times before. They began by driving down the California coast. Fog largely obstructed the view, but the slow forward motion, the windy roads curving back and forth, allowed them to talk. They listened to the blues tracks of her fishing youth, his large, hairy hands fumbling with the CD player after each series of songs. They camped among the redwoods, eavesdropped on the whistling of chilly coastal headwinds—"Redwoods receive ninety percent of their water from fog," she learned from one of the signs at a campsite. Her father brought two tents, but Emma chose to sleep in his for fear of being killed by the ravenous animals looming nearby. She huddled in a corner while her father blocked the entrance, his long, hackled snores and choked breaths comforting her to sleep.

A few times they pulled to the side of the road around dusk to try to "catch a good one," as her father would say. Mostly though, they caught the sunset behind gray bands of clouds hovering on the horizon of the ocean. Then, just before darkness overtook the land completely, they'd drop by the nearest town— quaint, white-boarded structures that were roughened by the salty air—and have burgers with fries.

The highlight of the trip was to be a small tourist city in southern California. They'd seen it advertised in a brochure. They pictured white beaches, grand architecture, and sublime food. Emma could just taste the cheeseburgers and tacos offered by such an exquisite place.

The main drag, however, was crowded as they rolled into the downtown area, and the refuge of the beach offered little relief. Near the wharf, a group of college students caught her attention. Emma still remembered them a bit too clearly: a fat guy wearing a tight "Stay Calm, Fuck On" shirt with a cigarette tucked behind his ear, a gangly one with long, dirty blonde bangs that he'd constantly swipe out of his vision, and a girl in mini-jean shorts and a bathing-suit top. Next to the line of families walking up and down the concrete pier, they leaned against the wooden railing, cussing dirty jokes and doing a horrible job of concealing their containers. Their arms cradled the tall cans awkwardly against their jeans, and they took not-so-sly gulps, even for a small girl to notice. Emma still didn't know all of what was said or done, but she remembered the tug of her father's hand ripping her past the scene. When they were out of range, her father cussed under his breath and repeated to her, "The world is a good place despite what we saw, Emma." (not even using Peeks at that point). They made it halfway down the pier before they turned around and doubled back to the car.

In a desperate attempt to reconcile the experience, to save their time from being spoiled completely, they went to a nearby food truck; her father ordered tacos and Emma a burger. At a nearby bench she bit into the burger, only to find that it was greasy. Strike three. Her father shrugged sympathetically. Because of the sour taste, they cut their stay a day short and went inland to see the desert.

Leaving the city, the scenery transformed from pastel stuccos and Spanish-style adobes to a wasteland of cracked earth and desert-hardy shrubs. The desert was always on the fringes of the small towns they passed, but absent the buildings it stuck out with plain harshness. The roads were long and tedious. There were no curves, clever signs, or ocean breezes—only mileage markers indicating that the next sign of life wasn't for another 50, 80, 100 miles. They stopped for snacks and bathroom breaks at weathered gas stations with their 1970s paintjobs. At one point she suspected they might be lost by the puzzled way her father studied his map, but she never asked.

After a full day of driving, they reached an area where red and orange boulders appeared, growing like tumors from the earth. They were round and square alike, some shaped like columns and pushing up against gravity. A smattering of Joshua trees—the midget alpaca of the palm tree world—sprouted in the barren landscape. Like a territorial predator, each tree greedily held to as much space from the others as it could.

It was dark when she looked over to her father, who returned a smile and reached over to tussle her hair. She batted his hand away with a giggle but continued to watch him, trying to make sense of the still, serene moment they shared. She must have looked tired, though, because her father turned down an abandoned road so they could stop and set camp. He tried to start a fire, but his attempts were snubbed by the wind until he gave up. Instead, they sat on a log and looked up at the stars canvassing the wide-open sky. Her dad pointed to the few constellations he knew—namely the Big and Little Dippers, and not a constellation per se but the North Star as well. Gusts whipped the sleeves of his sweatshirt and began to pick up in ghostly wails as it swept across the desert. She tucked underneath his arm.

Then, for whatever inspired reason, he howled like a coyote into the air. Then again, louder. She joined him and together they howled and howled. The wind carried their cries into the air and then to nowhere. She felt like she could do that forever, just howl with her father and look up at the stars. Eventually though, her tiredness overtook her and she fell asleep against him. She only vaguely remembered being carried to the tent, where the wind snapped against the plastic fabric. It was the best night of the trip.

She recalled the memory, and many like it, as a scrap of time that had snagged and was caught, a stationary piece among the blur. It hung in her mind like a film still, helping to string together her life. Emma figured it was typical for the plot of her life to grow astray before coming back together. She wasn't resentful when her father dismissed the events upon their return, when he was forced back to his work. When the years passed she wasn't angry that he'd forgotten. On the contrary, she relished being the only one with the memory, like the lone survivor of a wreck asked to reproduce the details, even if it was just to herself. She needlessly counted her fingers to conclude that it had happened nearly seven years ago. Time flies. Seven years living here. Nearly three weeks helping Greggory. Another two days before his grandson arrived.

With that thought, her daydream melted back to the present day and to thoughts about Greggory's grandson. Her relative isolation, dating only the boy down the street for a brief time during middle school, magnified her interest in a companion. Perhaps he was tall and had long, curly thickets of hair that fell like feathers to his eyes. He'd be gifted with a strong jawline and gentle eyes, and a smile with bright white teeth. Tanned, muscular, able to hold a conversation. Her thoughts advanced intricately, and soon she conceived of him so perfectly that they began to collapse on themselves like dominoes. (Not that she didn't want him to be a Hercules or Grecian god of sorts because damn right she did, but she could never be that fortuitous.) She began countering her hopes to relieve the stress. He was probably way older than her, or maybe an infant, or married. Then with reason: *If Greggory married and had a child at thirty and that child had a child, he'd be... ten?* Yes, he was most definitely younger than her. If he carried some of Greggory's attributes, he'd have gray eyes and a long face that was prematurely wrinkled. Her vacillation on the subject continued as the days withered by. Emma kept steady to convince herself she could never be that lucky.

∞   ∞   ∞

When Friday finally arrived, she headed towards Greggory's house ten minutes early and a step quicker. She concentrated on the rusted Ford, noting it as an artifact that Greggory must be home with his grandson. Her heart picked up speed and her palms dampened.

She approached the house and just managed to catch a glimpse through the window of a tall figure walking to the back. He was certainly older than a small child. The image already clove about half the possibilities she'd previously fabricated. He had to be fifteen to thirty, but she refused to reposition herself to get a better view. Instead she walked to the door and knocked.

"Greggory, it's Emma," she chimed, before hearing footsteps from inside.

"I'm coming. I'm coming."

The door opened to Greggory checking the small-faced dial of his watch. "Twelve minutes early," he concluded, "There's tea in the kitchen."

As she passed the front room, she inhaled the spicy odor of the dark house. If there was a quality that helped lighten the house, transitioning it from somber to cozy, it was the smell. She had forgotten it in her time away.

It took reaching the kitchen for Greggory to finally mention what she'd been waiting for, "By the way, my grandson Reid's here if I didn't already tell you. You may still work your regular days." Then he tossed in, "If you're not preoccupied with other things, of course."

Just as he finished, on cue like a stage actor, Reid came walking from the shadows of the back rooms. Greggory moved to the side of the kitchen, and the corners of his lips curled to a smile.

All her preconceived notions liquefied. He was finally real, wearing a cotton shirt that perfectly followed the contours of his body, with thin lips and wavy brown hair tucked behind his ears. His six feet—maybe five ten—provided him just enough height to hover above her. And although a bit slender, the way he faced her full on, confident and direct, radiated sexuality to her curious eyes. He held out his hand, standing above her, looking right into her.

He was definitely on the positive spectrum of her many speculations, and in the instant she locked eyes with him, her lips wound into a broad, uncontrollable grin before her eyes darted away.

"Hey, I'm Reid."

His cool, impish grin, a trait that seemed his default, took control of her.

"Hey. I'm Emma. Nice to meet you," she said as she offered an awkward handshake.

His soft touch lingered slightly longer than she thought was normal. Along with the warm pads of his palm, his easy movements away from her sustained the suspicion that Reid's lifestyle was quite foreign to her own, that he had no problem attracting girls.

She forced small talk using Greggory as a referent, and after a few minutes of stop-and-go conversation, Greggory made an excuse to go to the back room to fetch her late allowance. They were left alone.

She became aware of her breathing and the murmur of her heart. She did her best to control both. Her hands shook beneath their stillness. She wondered what it took to spur a valid conversation.

After a long pause, she was just about to say something when Reid broke the silence, "Hey, you don't have to come by to help my grandpa any more. I can handle it from here out."

Her heart sank and a tide of irritation rose—just a sliver. He dropped half-an-inch from his previous position on her imaginary scale.

"I don't mind helping him. He's a nice man," she returned with a smile.

"Are you sure? I can help him with whatever now. Besides whatever you're doing, I'm sure I can handle it," he winked.

He dropped a foot. His mischievous smile came again. Moreover, something arrogant and experienced in his expression agitated her. Her jaw tensed.

"Umm... okay," she responded a bit more severely.

Without remorse, he dug himself deeper, "I was just kidding. Don't get mad."

"I'm not mad, *Reid*."

In the back of her mind she knew she was being sensitive, but she tuned it out. It was their first meeting and she was beginning to feel like a fool. All her thoughts, all the time invested on the subject, and he was turning out to be a jerk. It was as though he didn't give a single shit. Narcissistic fuck.

"Okay, just making sure," he said before becoming distracted with some mundane detail of the house.

"I'm not mad," she repeated more aggressively.

Her jaw locked shut. Reid's gaze sailed past her—outside, at nothing in particular. She refused to take her savage stare from him, hoping he would at least recognize her, her frustration.

Her heart thumped with fury, and part of her indulged in the attraction to it—*to him?* Given another three seconds she would have jumped on him either to attack or to rip off his shirt. It would have made him notice her. But it never happened because Greggory found his way back to the charged air of the room.

"All right Emma, here you go," he said, handing her a white envelope.

"Thank you Greggory, what would you like *me* to do today?"

She and Reid worked on odd jobs throughout the day, but she was careful to avoid him in the process. Every once in a while she'd sneak a furtive glance, hoping to catch him looking at her, but the day concluded without another exchange. Greggory led her outside while talking about building a shed, or something, once the window was complete. Then he patted her

on the shoulder and offered the same almost-grin he'd
attempted once before.

GREGGORY

It was she who approached him, not the other way around. Leila poked her head into his canopy tent that night as he was preparing for bed, and asked, "Skinny dipping? Now?"

The idea was absurd. He was still acclimating and tired. But, skinny dipping, with Leila, in the middle of the night? Opportunities like these didn't come around often.

"Come on man, don't be a bore," she added.

He gave her a look.

"Is anybody else going?"

"No. I tried convincing Sophia, but she's set on staying in. The caboclos are sleeping. Think of it as a little American fun." She made quotation marks with her fingers at "American," and winked, making him believe she hadn't tried very hard with the others. "Also, I have this." She waved a small flask, taunting him.

That moment solidified his initial impression of Leila. She did things because she wanted to. She was an initiator, a creator. Bold.

Although he pretended to weigh the possibilities, he was already sold. He clambered from under the covers. She smiled and gazed down at his boxers, then met his eyes again.

"Yeah, yeah. Let me put some shorts on."

She did a fist pump in victory.

Outside, the night was hot and wrapped in moisture. A worn trail carried them away from the village. No moonlight penetrated the jungle above them, and the path they walked was simply a lighter shadow between darker ones. Long, undulating howls speared through the canopy. The scents of rotting vegetation, exotic flowers, and moss suffused the air.

She wore a white tee with no bra, and her breasts pressed against the loose fabric. For some time, their breaths and the nightlife around them were the only sounds. The walk carried them deeper into the long alleyway of shadow. Eventually she whispered again.

"It's exciting to be here, right?"

He wasn't certain if she meant that exact moment or traveling to South America. "Yeah, it is. It's like the unknown." A silence.

"Like dying."

"Dying?"

"Yes, dying. Exhilarating to think about it. We just don't know. I can't wait."

There are two types of people: those excited at new possibilities, and those scared shitless. She was the former, and he was attracted to her for it. She was unpredictable. He looked over to her as she pulled ahead of him, her step quickening the closer they came to the exit.

Her demeanor changed when they cleared the jungle's edge and stepped onto shore. Grabbing his hand, she raced forward. When they were close enough to the water, she reached down to tear off her boots. Then her shirt. He did the same. Their feet squished and splat in the mud. The waves swept across the rocks and pebbled shore. They inched carefully forward until their ankles were in the water. A dark slosh fanned against the shore and then receded. Both Greggory and Leila wriggled their toes.

"Wow. This is amazing," she whispered. Moonlight jacked across the crests of the river's currents. On the other side of the channel, the thick arms of tropical trees formed a sinuous wall. The land surrounding them teemed with life: insects, birds, amphibians. The smell of the river became almost appealing at night.

"We're really going to do this, right?" She glanced over to him, a wild smile appearing.

"Yes. Well...are you sure? We could get hurt." Rocks scattered about; the harsh terrain invited hesitation. She looked him over, mockingly. He ceded. "I'm just not sure I can save you if you drown." She laughed, and pulled down her shorts, making the decision for both of them.

Standing there erect, she appeared proud, as if clothes should never really be touching her skin, as if they were mere courtesies to the ignorance of others. Then she shrieked and ran for the river. Her limbs whisked outward and crashed to the surface not too far in. Greggory chased her, ripping off his own shorts before landing in the water.

They splashed and stirred for a short while, until the icy water became too much to bear. Their teeth chattering, they were forced to the shore. They planted on the pebbles, leaned against each other. Her exhales were loud as they tried to find warmth. She stretched her arms for her shorts, where the flask of whiskey waited. After working the bottle from her clothes, she unscrewed the top and took a long gulp. Then she passed it to him to do the same.

The liquid burned, but settled in a warm ball in his stomach. He shivered. She bobbed her head as if singing a song only she could hear, and then stopped to look at him. He looked at her. They both laughed. Another round of gulps.

His body leaned into her a little deeper, and hers reciprocated. And for a few moments, they talked about something or another. Drank more whiskey. Words flowed away with the river currents. His motives became driven by his body. Leaned a bit closer, another gulp. She looked at him with a tilt of her head. But when he tried a little closer, she stood.

Leila presumably had a boyfriend in every state, maybe in every country. Men undoubtedly flocked to her. But she appeared totally unaffected, as if she didn't have the social switch that allowed her to realize that another human was interested. She didn't pick up hints, and she did *not* care. She was in it for the adventure. It made Greggory more interested.

She told him she was too damned cold, and they should head back.

The trail to camp felt shorter. Her arms waved energetically and she spoke wildly, thrilled with their decisions that night. When the camp came into view, he tried walking her to her canopy tent, but she rejected the offer. "Another time, let's do it again." With that, she kissed his cheek, and pushed him away. Well after she left, he felt the wet outline where her lips landed.

∞   ∞   ∞

The next day Greggory woke to a single beam of sunshine lighting his tent the color of creamed coffee. It was still early, but he was supposed to meet Leila and Sophia for their first formal meeting. He stretched from his position and pulled on his jeans, still groggy from the whiskey and late night.

The agency Greggory volunteered with pledged to introduce shelter and agriculture to every impoverished settlement around the globe, steering these places away from the chancy outcomes and mercurial nature of hunting and gathering. He could visualize the typed text of the paperwork iterating their mission, promoting their cause.

During the first meeting amongst the three volunteers, Leila and Sophia told him what they'd accomplished in the time before he arrived. Shelter was a nonissue; the caboclos already had reliable shelter before any volunteer ever stepped foot here.

However, there was still the issue of agriculture. The volunteers before Leila and Sophia had already found a suitable water source and had begun digging a trench to the determined plot where the crops would grow best: a soft corner of soil at the far edge of the settlement. Now, the primary focus was to connect the trench with the land before (hopefully) producing agricultural soy. A secondary objective, now speaking quietly and swiftly, was to expulse the smell of shit. Leila and Greggory did most of the talking.

But however much the real concerns took precedence during that meeting and the many similar ones to follow, Greggory nonetheless couldn't help but also search for subtle signs from Leila that they might continue where they left off.

In the days after, he carried on with the usual tactics that proved successful with his past conquests—glance at her in hopes she would catch his eye, make obvious movements close to her body when they spoke, offer childish jokes—but none seemed to work. He tried flirting with her, but she'd cut him off with a distracted comment, or simply refuse to catch onto his words.

It was late when Greggory snuck over to her tent. He didn't have a flask of whisky to seduce her, but he poked his head in and asked, "Hey, are you thinking what I'm thinking?"

She was under wool covers and lifted her head to see who it was. Her toes rocked back and forth beneath the blankets. "Depends. What are you thinking?"

"Let's go back to the river." An image flashed of touching her skin in the water.

But without hesitation, without any resentment or anger, just fatigue, she replied, "Nah, I think I'm good tonight, man. Maybe another time. Try Uyude, he's pretty cool."

Frustration shot through his body, but he cut it off quickly and replied "Okay, no biggie."

He tried again several times over the following few weeks, but each time she declined politely. Only when she needed something would she go to Greggory. "Hey, Greg, can you give me a hand here?" His body would draw close to her, he'd look her over, and she'd smile at him. "Can you bring this to Sophia for me?" He'd graze her hand and she'd wink. Each time it would re-spark his interest, and the hope that his attention might result in a favorable outcome sooner than later.

When she failed to notice him, or (more accurately) when her eyes simply glossed over his features without discerning a thing he had in mind, it only deepened his desire for her sour breath, her sweaty skin, her sensuous curves.

He felt atavistic tendencies emerge—the need to physically dominate her, to have his skin and body atop hers. But the weeks wore on without any sign of reciprocation, without a sign either way, and he spiraled. He became sensitive to the darkness. The incessant buzz of the jungle, the exaggerated cries of exotic birds, and distant sounds from animals began to bother him. Only later, when he reflected back from the advantage of his home in Boston, did he admit that his affliction rose at least partly from the tediousness of his sexual labors. At the time he convinced himself that he was merely homesick.

He needed consolation, and found it in his time with two of the caboclos: Uyude and Sedenoe. While his duties remained at the village, he began to join the two away from the dark crevices of the jungle at the choppy banks of the river. Although it was several miles from where he should be, he always permitted a reason to join them—they needed a hand hauling water, or there might be a better irrigation route he should inspect.

Often his belly grumbled from hunger when he neglected his duties at camp, and only then did he feel remorse. He would search the food storage only to find near-empty shelves. But perhaps more detrimental were those dark eyes drawn onto him. Although nobody said a word against him, he was reminded why he was here. To accommodate another three people, especially foreigners, was no easy task for the village; there was a reason they remained small.

As he drank from a flask in solitude on the fringes of the village, Sedenoe noticed and came up to pat him on the shoulder, "Bruh, everything is good." Around the flickering light of the fire pit, the group danced and played. They wore the same smiles as the day he arrived, but he imagined they also felt the same hunger in their bellies.

SEDENOE – A SIDE-NOTE

Ferns, long strands of moss, and river outlets running like trails through the land, these are what Sedenoe remembered from growing up. This was his home.

He ran into the jungle to hide his tears after his parents transitioned to *ashe*, the life-force that runs through all things. Soon, however, he became distracted by the network of paths that spread and intersected like spider webs, into a chaotic, infinite number of possibilities. It seemed to Sedenoe that some higher cause he couldn't quite name had destined him find to the trails and explore the jungle, as if everything was evenly calculated on his behalf. As a small boy he couldn't fully grasp Shaman Clarua's words, that it was his parents' time to go, that he should feel blessed the creator had chosen them. But the jungle gave him a sense that there was a reason for things.

Only surrounded by the enormous trees, the ferns draped around him like a green blanket, did he feel any sort of comfort. There, huddling near the roots at the ground, he was one small piece of a larger puzzle. Everything was connected and large, and he could feel the life-force pulsing around him. Not at first, with tears trickling from his eyes, but eventually Sedenoe began to grasp how snakes related to rodents, trees to fire, moss to water. How his parents were watching over him.

It became his habit to return to the jungle when his mind raced with emotion. After collecting wood or açaí, or when their small settlement held a ritual, he wandered in the direction of the darkness.

He was often tired from a day's work, but almost immediately focus returned to his eyes and his ears began to hear again.

Soon, he was sneaking away into the dark, dense jungle more regularly. Once inside, he became distracted the many gems the land offered: the sturdy and graceful limbs, the intricate designs on the backs of tiny frogs, the smell of jungle flowers, the flittering of birds and low growls of larger beasts.

As the years passed the trails carried him deeper still. Eventually, Sedenoe found that he'd made his way to the very edges of the world he knew. When he realized this, instead of turning back and sticking to the familiar paths, he fostered his findings and welcomed wrong turns. He crossed the line into the unknown. The world was reduced to untreaded trails and fractured moonlight.

Although not the largest—nor the smallest—amongst his peers, Sedenoe grew. His legs became iron, and muscles beneath his skin bulged and anchored his steps. He began taking on more arduous treks. He climbed higher peaks, descended deeper valleys, and often found he was flung farther than he intended. Before leaving camp for these longer excursions he packed supplies to last at least a week, and during his trips he learned to hunt, gather, find clean drinking water, create small fires.

He was still young when he saw his first white person. Sedenoe stumbled into a village far away from his own tiny settlement. It wasn't his first visit there—the little community had welcomed him into their arms once before—but this time something was different. Something was off; the air felt heavy. He wandered around until he found the source. Sitting under the shade of jungle palm thatching was the man, the *ayé*, the spirit. Sedenoe had only heard about these things, never before seeing them himself. He was bemused, and couldn't cut his gaze away, staring with frank curiosity. The sun had apparently burned the pigment straight from the spirit's skin. His eyes were the color of the water. At first, Sedenoe thought the apparition must have somehow become lost and separated from the invisible world. Only later was he convinced otherwise. The creature saw that he was different from the villagers who'd welcomed him, and beckoned Sedenoe out of interest. After a few long moments of trying to communicate, staring intently at each other, he offered Sedenoe a soft blanket and a handful of fruit wrapped in cloth. Sedenoe accepted, and when he returned home he hid the blanket away, careful not to say a word about it or his benefactor to the others.

After the interaction, it was some time before he ventured out again. The land he knew was shifting, and Sedenoe didn't fully embrace the change. His curiosity, however, eventually won out, and Sedenoe began seeking the strange people. It was easier to study them, as more white people had started to appear. Boats of them could be heard whirring upriver. Back home, Clarua told them that it was *Olodumare* screaming at them, and that they all needed to listen. But Olodumare's cries went unheard. More boats could be heard as time wore on. More and more camps of inhabitants were forced to interact.

The white people were like the spring season; all the flowers in the jungle bloomed. Unlike spring, however, they smelled awful and were often irritable (usually not directing outbursts at others, just to themselves, cursing beneath their breaths). He learned parts of their language, and when he was a little older, he began to hear the political whispers amongst them. More were coming.

This is when Sedenoe began telling his peers about his travels and what he'd overheard. Not that they hadn't already picked up on something—word traveled through the trees—but many remained silent in order to keep concern from slipping into their words.

His suggestion was interpreted as a rash idea more than a calculated gambit by his peers, but Sedenoe knew what needed to happen. It was inevitable they'd come, any one of his adventures was proof in that, so Sedenoe suggested that their settlement bring the white people. Invite them as guests. Control the input. "How are we going to invite them?" asked Clarua in a meeting.

"By allowing me to go get them."

He packed for long travel, and then set out by way of small boat, in the end making it deeper than he'd ever ventured. Around him the river held more vessels than he remembered, and the waters turned more colors: green, blue, red, yellow, brown, the silvery gray you got if you mixed chalks together. He hunted capybaras and fish, drank from the river, and filled his stomach with the land's offerings: Brazil nuts, açaí, cassava roots, cashews, chayote, and aguaje.

Eventually the trees became less dense, and the land opened up. Strange, colorful structures were erected, and a world far more foreign than he imagined popped into existence.

He never went to the heart of Manaus, but during his rambling search he was fortunate to find what he was looking for. He spoke with an enormous lady in the little language he knew, and invited the white people to the settlement. Sedenoe suspected the lady didn't understand him, and it took a few days—him sleeping in the streets—before she caught on to his invitation. Each day he awoke to crazy, loud wagons screaming as they spit down the road.

The first white person Sedenoe brought back was a lean, clean-shaven man with glasses—William. He smelled like pepper and cinnamon, and was obsessed with cacao. During the trip upriver, he watched Sedenoe and then looked at a small book, writing something Sedenoe suspected he'd forget otherwise. Sedenoe studied William in return, but logged the details in his mind. When they arrived, Sedenoe introduced William to his peers. Each villager immediately touched William's face to see if he was a man or a spirit. Shaman Clarua watched William from a distance.

William, however, did not stay but one or two days before he left again. Sedenoe interpreted William's parting words to mean he'd be back soon, but weeks passed without further signs of contact. The others thought the white people had declined their invitation—were almost relieved—until two more showed up with clothes and movable homes they called tents. One was a surfer man from California. He was experienced in the water but clumsy on land. Nearly every day there was something: he'd drop water, trip with wood in his hands, or inhale too much smoke. After each incident he'd step back, laugh, and say, "Bruh, everything is good." It was a line Sedenoe originally hated, until he later picked it up for himself.

From that point forward, the white people came and went. Sedenoe learned more of their language and customs, enjoyed their company. Early on he tried to inform the whites that his people were doing fine hunting and gathering—there was plenty of food around them if they'd only look—but he quickly learned that this answer wouldn't suffice. The visitors insisted on storing fruit, even though fruit would go bad sooner if not left on the trees. Selfishly, they hoarded Brazil nuts. They were horrible fishermen. They overate, and were often lazy. But even with their faults, Sedenoe couldn't say he didn't enjoy watching these mystic beings, these curious people.

When Greggory came, Sedenoe was initially uninterested. Soon, though, this new white man became his most beloved subject. Greggory didn't have the laid-back nature of the surfer man, or the refined manner of William, and it caused Sedenoe to put more energy into defining him. Greggory was nice, but often anxious. He looked like caught prey when he first arrived: wide eyes, disheveled hair, unwashed clothes. But often he exuded confidence, as when he attempted to court Leila, even though Leila brushed him away.

The way in which Greggory handled his feelings was the final thread to convince Sedenoe that white people were no ayé, unless they were some type of ayé Sedenoe had never heard of. Greggory was affected with Leila just as Uyude was with Lua, as most males are with females. He was just a bird doing its mating dance.

Leila was hard to get, and at some point Sedenoe suspected that Greggory would move on. She was just another female; everything was good, bruh. To help him see how vast life was, to knock him out of his unhealthy focus, Sedenoe invited Greggory to the river with him and Uyude. The three fished and walked along the shore to look at rocks. River life emerged every now and again, and the three whipped their heads to see what it was. The sun circled overhead, and they spoke to each other as best they knew how. They didn't understand each other entirely, but he was able to look right into Greggory's eyes when they spoke, understand him a little better.

The peak of Sedenoe's interest in Greggory came shortly after one of the camp's ceremonies. That's when he noticed a transition in Greggory. Sedenoe didn't know exactly what happened to spur the relationship, but suddenly Greggory acquainted himself with the one named Sophia. At first they were timid, but that soon faded. Sitting near each other, whispering to each other, smiling, and laughing. They ate their meals together, and spoke with animated lines. Sophia was sweet, but prior to Greggory she'd been a closed flower. She was shy, quiet. Around Greggory, she bloomed.

Sedenoe would have liked to point this out to Greggory, but he didn't. He watched, and listened, and waited for a conclusion. Unfortunately, Greggory never picked up the signs. Even after spending a morning or afternoon or evening with Sophia, he'd walk away and vie for Leila's attention.

Leila caught onto what was happening, that much was certain, but rather than bringing the two together she did her best to hold Greggory's loyalty. She began asking more of him, requiring him to stay around her longer. Flirting, pouting. She turned her body into his wandering eye, let herself laugh at his mild jokes, leashed him. Sedenoe caught only hints, but he could already see how it would end for the three.

Thinking back to all the people who'd come and gone, Sedenoe determined that the white people's stay was too thin to make any real *progress*. They'd arrive, spend most of their time trying to figure out what the previous group had accomplished, and then take one small step forward before leaving. They tried but were mostly a hardship on his people. That's why his people learned to celebrate when the volunteers were leaving.

In the end, Olodumare answered again. Created change again. After Greggory, Leila, and Sophia left, there were several more who came and went. Then, all of a sudden, they simply stopped coming, as if the settlement had been forgotten, as if it were a mistake they'd ever come at all. Sedenoe and his peers were grateful for the shirts, blankets, shoes, and jackets, but they also felt relief in returning to their old ways.

More boats occupied the river, and occasionally a white traveler would be offered refuge at their settlement, but his people made sure to stress, *please* do not bring any friends.

When things settled, Sedenoe returned to the rainforest to find new paths, to learn about change that accompanies time.

EMMA

She appeared reliably, always on time, to maintain the home of the wise Greggory O'Sullivan. Her dedication was influenced in part by that first meeting with Reid and in part by the pesky feelings of incompetence that gripped her. Worth noting, however, was that her efforts appeared to be paying off: Greggory had become almost... hospitable. They held longer conversations, and he allowed her to stay slightly longer with each visit.

As the relationship between them improved, her relationship with Reid worsened in direct proportion. The downhill slide continued with the very next visit, when she passed him in the front room and offered a timid "hello." He didn't hear her, or perhaps he did, but nonetheless it solidified her withdrawal and fed the silence between them. The misunderstanding of their first meeting—even though she understood that his comments were intended more lightly than she took them—hindered any chance at making amends, and future meetings only pushed them further away from each other. She repeated to herself that Reid was egotistical and heartless, and soon the two abstained from talking. Instead their eyes whirred around each other like resistant magnets.

And yet, there was also a secret enjoyment in the game. She waited to see him give ground. She waited to see him expose his weakness first.

Emma didn't know how well she stacked against his resolve, but she did her best. The most attention he ever paid her was in quick passing-bys. She would be on her hands and knees scrubbing some corner of some room when he approached from the back hallway, or from outside. His shoulders were relaxed, and his eyes locked. He would look intently at whatever was straight ahead, boring into it, and sometimes "whatever" happened to be her, or so she thought. Then he would come closer, and for an instant he was looking directly at her and past her at the same time. Her head craned downward to hide until she realized it couldn't be her he was looking at—his head would have to turn if that were the case.

As the weeks wore on, she experienced other episodes. In the kitchen, he undoubtedly acknowledged her once. She'd returned for more cleaner and found Reid at the sink drinking water, his back facing her. When his body swiveled around she saw him freeze, a fleeting moment when his eyes stopped on her and all truth spilled into his expression. But in an instant his observation hurtled over, and he walked past. When she was again alone, Emma found her hand shaking with fear that he might say something kind to her.

Through the window she watched him outside, relieving from Greggory's hands heavy supplies, tools, and bulky objects he had difficulty toting around. Greggory shook his head and cursed the intervention, always cursed the interventions, but left alone his knuckles supported the low of his back while he stretched, loosening the knots built in his muscles.

Reid wasn't a bad guy, but there was nothing there for her, as if they'd punctured a hole at the bottom of the barrel and let the water run dry.

The house became a lonely place, with the three of them trying to find a corner where they each belonged. Emma supposed Greggory could kick them both out—hell, it *was* his house, and he was far from shy—but she couldn't help thinking that he was searching for something, too.

The summer stretched on with simple avoidance defining her relationship with Reid. That trajectory would probably have continued endlessly had it not been for Greggory's intervention. She was uncertain if he knew the full extent of the disunion between her and Reid, but she understood why he took action: to gain a little much-needed time alone.

First he planted them together by asking her to do some small chore where Reid was currently doing some small chore. She initially cast it away as coincidence, but then Greggory began making excuses for leaving the room when they were all together. Perhaps due to some innate desire to mend a broken relationship, Emma considered speaking again. Words— irrelevant as they were to anything—rested on the tip of her tongue. *Say something, say anything.* Nonetheless, she remained silent just long enough for Greggory to walk back into the room, his disposition returning to disappointment.

She caught on to his gimmick easily enough, but after miscalculating how erudite his strategizing truly was she found herself forced into his hands like a chess piece. She'd finished the day's work and gone to the kitchen to let him know she was leaving. After searching the few rooms and then doubling back outside, she found him fitting together boards on the side of the house. He was startled, and began cussing under his breath, but that didn't stop his execution.

Up to that point, even with his prodding and devising at dogged lengths, she had effectively managed to ward off his attempts. But in the next few lines, she was done in.

He stood and led her to the front of the house where he stopped to wipe the sweat from his eyes. Then he faced her, revealing the deep wrinkles on his face. She watched intently as he lowered his head, his fingers bouncing together nervously. "Emma, I was curious if you could do me a favor next Friday?"

His voice was soft, but his words were strained. She imagined that he wasn't accustomed to asking for favors—nor was she especially keen to act beyond her obligations to him—but the way his head drooped, his sundered words, struck her soundly.

She was careful not to magnify his request and instead looked down at her shoes. She injected tenderness into her reply, "Yeah, sure. What is it?"

Then he looked up with a twinkle in his eye. There it was. *Swoosh. Bingo. Yahtzee, bitches.*

"Well, I was just wondering if you'd let Reid take you to the movies in town? He doesn't have very many friends, but I think he's fond of you."

Fuck. Checkmate.

Startled, she lifted her eyes to meet his. Her brows furrowed. "You think he's *fond* of me?" *Fuck fuck fuck.*

Her head became furnace hot. Greggory nodded. His grin mocked her. He'd trapped her, and he knew it. The heat caused sweat to dribble down her face as she struggled for an answer. His old hands slithered into his pockets as he waited.

She crossed her arms and managed to find a weak smile deep within her soul. She relented. "Sure. What time were you thinking?"

He tapped his jaw with his index finger before replying. "I don't know, really. How about eight? I think the last show plays at nine or nine-thirty."

"Okay. Eight forty-five, then?"

He nodded again, maintaining his grin as she turned to begin her walk down the long, pot-holed road.

REID

When word of the date floated to Reid's ears, he reprimanded his grandfather and protested the arrangement. Then, after his grandfather's rebuttal, he fled the house to reconsider his counter. He trailed the length of Forester before he connected the dots to the infallible logic of why the date should not take place.

It wasn't so much that he disliked Emma, but something had evidently set her off when they first met. She refused to acknowledge him, and eventually he came to think of her as a prude. Furthermore, his grandfather's fondness for her often blocked Reid's efforts to spend more time with him. From a distance, he watched secretly as Emma made his grandfather smile—a rare moment, Reid had learned. It was with his grandfather in mind (the old man had tried his best, after all) that Reid discussed the situation.

"Grandpa, if I wanted to go on a date with her, I would have asked her. You know that, right?"

"Maybe."

Maybe? "Maybe?"

"Yes maybe, Reid." He was looking down at his hands again. "You don't have to go if you really don't want to. I just thought it might be a good idea," before tilting his head back.

So much for logic. All he could do was roll his eyes, shake his head, and vent a stifled groan in protest. Reid resigned himself to the date.

"Good! You can take the truck."

"The red one?"

"The Ford."

The rusty Ford.

II

GREGGORY

Greggory had already been there just shy of three months. The first soy beans were finally planted a few weeks ago, but none of the small, silken leaves had yet sprouted. That's when he began hearing whispers of spirits, of *òrun,* and the need to appease them before any progress could be made. Word of a ritual began floating around the village, eventually welling into a confident and resolute announcement by Clarua that the ceremony was imminent. After the news had circulated to the corners of the camp, preparations began and the caboclos kicked off Clarua's ordinance by brewing a strange plant.

The simmering liquid was spoken about like a newborn, and people would come up periodically to ensure it was tended to as carefully as they remembered from the last time. After seeing so much attention given to a simple black pot, curiosity led

Greggory to explore the undertaking for himself. The acrid smell stung his nose; he recoiled before peering over the edge at the green leaves and small, coarse offshoots swirling like driftwood. Wisps hovered over the liquid as they tried unsuccessfully to condense into a cloud. Around the edges, pale yellow bubbles built up like spiders' eyes, climbing on themselves before dispersing.

When darkness grew, the villagers huddled around the fire and Clarua hushed the noisy chatter as he began his sermon. Greggory looked over the caboclos, then to Sophia and Leila, all of whom hung like small fish on the hooks of Clarua's grandiose performance. His eyes returned to the shaman, whose guttural bawling had amplified. Clarua's words became distorted by his roars as he went on. By the end of his speech, he closed with what Greggory could only interpret as, "Vitality ritual of time and home!" The orange glow of the fire painted Clarua's arched chest and outstretched arms while the last of his words echoed through the huts. The settlement became serenely still. Then, with perfect timing, two caboclos began to sing. Chatter once again resumed, and the festivities began.

When the elixir came his way, he coyly sniffed the concoction. It smelled less deadly, more innocuous—earthy, even. The taupe drink became enticing if only because he couldn't believe it was the same one he'd inspected just hours earlier. Greggory looked to Shaman Clarua, who returned a confident nod, and pressed his lips to the edge of the pot. Then, he proceeded to gulp down two large mouthfuls. It was more bitter than it smelled, but less horrible than he imagined.

Somebody laughing and singing in elongated hums patted him on the shoulder. It didn't take long for Greggory to realize he'd consumed ayahuasca, and it wasn't very long before the ayahuasca took effect. The psychedelic toxins rallied and jerked his body into a fugue so hazy he could only barely remember snippets of the night in their respective shades and twisting forms.

Post-event, he learned that many of the fantastic images he perceived had been streams of vomit, but even knowing this the profundity of the messages held unreasoned weight. He saw slithering snakes, coming from the shaky grayness to perch by his side. He couldn't quite discern whether he shared actual words with them, but their diamond heads arced towards him with pithy tilts. They touched on something so ancient it was impossible to forget.

Then his vision jumped to laughs echoing tightly in his head, as if bouncing off the walls of a narrow canyon. A fragment where he danced and cantillated bits of songs from the States, "American woman, staayyy awaaayyy"—a few caboclos joining in with big, gap-toothed grins and foreign accents. Shaman Clarua—oh Shaman Clarua—cheering to him before drinking two large gulps himself. The sight caused a hysterical fit as he pounded his fists to his thighs. Then he was sitting on the log as his surroundings vibrated less energetically—Sedenoe and Uyude patting each other as they sang at the crescent moon—Leila whipping her dark hair in a flurry of dance—blank faces moving around the camp in a squall of motion.

In his hysteria he lifted himself from the log, and in a blink was on the outskirts of the settlement. Another blink and he was embraced by the dark arms of the jungle. He saw the moon through a jeweled opening in the canopy. He wasn't sure if he was lost or found or somewhere in-between, or for how many hours his legs trotted along, but eventually he became aware that he didn't know where he was. He looked down to his feet and found he had lost a sandal. The crescent above offered little to light his way, and as the aftereffects of the drink began to settle and torment his body, the dark tunnel of trees appeared more eerie. The cries from unseen animals were too near.

Focusing on his breath, he pushed past his haze and tried to think—anything to escape the void of shadow that now trapped him. Led by the single sandal slapping against his heel, he marched through the soft ground of the jungle. Every few strides

Greggory looked upward through the slivered cracks in the canopy, trying to map his route with the position of the moon. Plants brushed against his calves, and small creatures scurried across his path. Fifteen minutes passed, and then a half-an-hour. Every second was filled with a subdued, gentle cadence of sounds: rainforest birds expressing their melancholy, insects desperate for food, the sleepy rush of the river. The river. He could faintly hear the river. He redirected himself towards it.

He treaded through mud and foliage for another block of time, until out of nowhere he stumbled over a mound and onto a path. He exhaled slowly and looked down the long dim channel of trees, where a light gray curtain in the distance signaled the end. He raced towards it, and was soon at the opening. Exhaustion washed over him.

He emerged beside the river at a familiar spot, not so far from the village. Before he could collapse to the rock-ribbed ground below, surrender to his exhaustion, he started at a figure in the shadows. The hunched outline remained nearly still, with the exception of the rise and fall of its back. He watched intently for it to attack—jungle cat, assassin, spirit being—but before he could turn to leave, his legs betrayed him and he stumbled over a rock at his ankle. The clatter caused his heart to knock and the shadow to stir.

After a long second of silence, it called at him, "Hello?" Even in his state, the words reached his ears, and his dilated heart quickly settled. The remnants of his fear waned, and he moved close enough to recognize her full figure. Then he could see the elephant pendant glittering in the dim moonlight. Sophia.

He asked in stupefaction, "Why are you all the way out here at night?"—trying to pronounce the words as if he were sober.

"I'm not so much a fan of the drug ceremonies. I've read about them." Her words were stern, yet there was a strain of timidness, or tiredness, in them. "What brings *you* out here? Without a sandal—" she pointed.

Embarrassed that the other still chose to cling to his foot (to disable a "barefoot" argument), he avoided the question and concealed his one-sandaled feet as best he could.

"So, you didn't drink any of the spirit juice?" He found the question funnier than she did.

"No!" then after a pause, with a note of concern he was unfamiliar with, "Did you?"

"Perhaps." Again a dodge. That was how their friendship began. He went to sit beside her, and caught her vanilla scent as he crouched down. "How often do you come out here?"

They flowed gently through conversation, feeding each other with matching transitions. Greggory had been so preoccupied with Leila that he'd almost completely forgotten about Sophia.

Moonlight lit her face. Her arms were wrapped around her knees, to take as little space as possible, and the way she spoke made Greggory listen intently. He watched her, but she refused to return his gaze. Instead, she fixed inquisitively at the water gushing downstream, the currents cartwheeling over themselves in a low rumble. Her words were soft. He was still coming down from the ayahuasca and his experience in the jungle, and didn't catch all of what she was saying, but the rhythm of her voice was soothing.

At one point they stopped talking to look up at the crystal skies. As he craned his neck backward, the speckled stars felt just out of reach. Even the dull ones were almost near enough to grasp. The horrifying creatures lurking nearby became totally and unremarkably irrelevant. Another wave of exhaustion washed over. As the temperature dropped, his body crept next to hers for warmth. With the tick of their synchronizing hearts— he later learned that a heart will, in fact, synchronize with another if close enough and you wait long enough—and the indelible painting above, he fell into a sound sleep on the muddy shore.

His head remained secure on her lap throughout the night, and by the time he woke the sun was well above the trees on the horizon. Abashed by their shared intimacy, he tried his best to remove himself without waking her. He inched away, but before he could peel off completely she stirred. She smacked her lips and squinted against the intruding light. Sheepish satisfaction crossed her face until she realized where she was. Then she frowned. He felt guilty for his attempts to flee.

He didn't remember what words were spoken between them, probably something like, "Last night was nice, but shall we head back now?" but they quickly took to the village. Caked mud cracked away from their bodies with each step. Ragged morning breaths filled the trail in front of them.

Upon their arrival, the caboclos were in good spirits. When Greggory asked Sedenoe what had happened—"Why is everybody so cheery?"—all he did was point to the garden, where a single green soy plant sprouted. It was quite the omen of good fortune.

EMMA

Friday approached, even though Emma was convinced she didn't care. Still, as Tuesday and then Wednesday passed, the thought of what top best matched her jeans crawled to the surface of her considerations. When Friday actually arrived, the hours ticking by, the dilemma of her outfit grew like a weed; you see it sprout in one place and suddenly it covers the yard. When she went to her room, the assortment of different combinations left her concluding that her wardrobe was too vapid for such an event. Eventually she settled for the most promiscuous top she could find: a low-cut black tee. Not especially promiscuous, actually, but it would have to do. She slipped into her hip-hugging jeans, frayed near the front pocket and worn to a sky blue at the knees, and tied her laces.

Emma was known to dress conservatively, so the outfit came as close as she ever got to flirtatious. She was very aware of the slit of skin lingering at her waist and the visibility of her black bra if a person had the audacity to look carefully. The cute lace panties she chose to match made her feel confident.

Ready by six o'clock, she sat patiently. The hours throbbed by until the final fragments of light through the windows disappeared. She sipped a glass of water, checked her phone again. Finally her enthusiasm began to wane, as she'd hoped would occur much earlier in the week.

Emma watched the public road from the kitchen window for signs of the truck. With a sigh she wondered what her parents were doing. She would have liked to tell them about the date, but there was never a right time to disclose the details. They always seemed so distracted.

Her thoughts transitioned to other pointless facts and her frown deepened. She stared at the water in the glass as though it might hold an answer. After meditating on the issue for some time, the liquid lit into an arrangement of prisms when the beams of an old Ford cast through the window. As if there were still time to change her mind, she had second thoughts. He had, after all, decided to go through with Greggory's unorthodox plan. She was banking he would make an excuse to escape. It was a real possibility, after all. She sighed and lifted herself.

She walked a straight line to the truck, pulled the passenger-side handle, and climbed in. With a clank the door shut, and it was settled. She granted an unconvincing grin. The truck started with a disgruntled churn, and soon the tires were crunching away from her home. A green textured pine tree that lost its scent years ago swung like a pendulum as they drove.

"Hey, do you think we could stop by the store for some candy on the way?" was how she chose to break the ongoing silence characterizing their weeks together.

"Of course," he replied with both hands on the steering wheel, looking straight ahead. His voice sounded foreign. She'd heard him speak only a word here or there, so his simple sentence hit her eardrums with an unfamiliar resonance.

REID

Down Forester, right on Stinson, and a few miles on was the most local grocery store. They pulled into the tiny parking lot and came to a stop in one of the empty slots. Aside from the three cars aligned in a row at the furthest reaches, employee vehicles, their truck was the only one occupying the lot.

The three employees watched impatiently through the large-paned windows. The store closed promptly at nine, and from outside he could make out their faces—artificially lit by the fluorescent bulbs—and deduce that they'd arrived just in time to be a nuisance. His step trailed behind Emma's.

Inside the dreary, dilapidated building was a colorful selection of goods, everything anybody could possibly need in a last-minute sort of effort: cleaners in green boxes, mechanic wrenches, dairy products, canned beans. One of the clerks greeted them with a polite, woeful, "Welcome."

"Hello, we won't be long," he assured. The kid looked at the clock before nodding. Not walking with her as much as behind her, he followed Emma to the shelves near the registers. Candy bars were arranged neatly in rows. She hunched over analyzing her possibilities before finally choosing a fun-size bag of Reese's and peanut M&M's.

"Are you getting anything?"

He browsed the options, hunching over himself, before declining.

When she went to pay, her face brightened as she recognized one of the employees leaning against his register at the checkout aisles. He was a scrawny, pale youth fitted in a black collared shirt and apron. If Justin Timberlake was goofier, less-fit, and young again you'd have nailed how this kid looked. His hair curled into itself.

"Hey Tim."

"Emma!" His face went from dread to glee in an instant, "How's your summer been?"

The teen failed to acknowledge him standing beside (behind?) her.

"Pretty good. You know, just been swimming and hanging out. I've seen Chelsea once or twice but haven't been doing too much. How about you?"

"About the same, lots of work. I wish I was doing more. Maybe some time we could go to the water holes? I hear there's one over near Fairview with a twenty-foot cliff that people jump off." He made his fingers into a stick figure jumping from his palm.

This time Tim turned to him with a questioning glance. He returned with a stony nod.

I'm not even dating her, bud.

"That sounds great. I'll call you some time."

"Okay cool. See you around, then."

"It was nice seeing you." She waved goodbye. Tim glanced at him one more time as he followed Emma outside.

Once they reached the truck, they continued down the road. Any light questions were quickly shut down with succinct responses, and after a few attempts to be friendly he stopped trying completely. In the truck he gripped the steering wheel with both hands, pursed his lips, and found his eyes widening. If he hadn't noticed Emma's mournful spirit, he could have fantasized that the date was going less than horribly. As it was though, the silence filling the space between them echoed off everything.

After fifteen minutes, they passed an errant streetlamp marking their destination: a dingy town in the middle of nowhere. The vicinage consisted of a full-sized grocery store, hair salon, bar (undoubtedly the most lucrative of the bunch), small gym, the theater, laundromat, pizza parlor, four street-lamps, one stop light, and a paved road dividing it all in half.

The theater's parking lot was a dirt yard in the back of the main drag. Ruts groomed the square plot, and walls from the backs of other building towered over them. The orange glow from a nearby streetlight cast long, patchy shadows along the ground. The truck rolled to a stop in one of the corners of the lot, and they exited with a solemn slump of their shoulders.

In their walk to the front of the building, they pushed past a trimmed hedge of privet, the white cloves smelling sweet and delicate. The bushes were dotted with white flowers and alluded to a city far away. What he would become conscious of only sometime later, after learning the perennial plants only bloom during summer, something in his brain forever-after associated the fragrant smell with something about Emma. Every year around the same time he'd catch a scent, and his brain would automatically print an image of her smile, of the loose strands of hair falling to her eyes, of the landing of skin along her neck, of the night here at the theater.

At the time they slipped by the hedge and followed the worn path through a black metal gate, an old gothic relic that didn't fit with the rest of the architecture, to a double-wide glass door at the front of the building. Four potted hyacinths—three shriveled and desiccated, the last clinging to fuchsia life—sat to the left side of the entrance, and above was a white backdrop streaked dark with soot. Black letters with the names of movies and their corresponding times were pinned to it.

"What movie do you want to see?" He asked a bit more curtly than intended.

"I don't have a preference."

Between the two outdated movies offered, he chose the action-drama over the animation.

"Actually, can we see the other one?" Emma cloyed.

He agreed, and together they entered. The polished ticket booth, presumably installed when times were better, stood unoccupied. A concessionist was sweeping the velvet carpet. With a tired smile he came over and rang them for two tickets, ten dollars. Aside from some dust in the corners and the aged equipment, the theater wasn't too bad. As they walked through the lobby to the show room, the smell of popcorn and old wood effused the air.

They were alone inside the dark cavity, but nonetheless they maintained whispers. "Sit there?" with a point of the finger. "Mhm, sure."

Shortly after, another couple's silhouettes walked in and sat near the front. Emma ripped open the bag of Reese's and slyly began popping them into her mouth. It wasn't long before the clicking hum of the projector and beaming orchestra from the speakers commenced. The off-white lights flooded the screen in a subdued flicker. He peeked over to Emma tucking the bag of candy away, noticing that she leaned against the opposite armrest, knees bent away from him. He leaned in the other direction with a frown and rested his elbow awkwardly on a cup-holder.

Due either to his own uninterest or to a preoccupation with their disastrous time together, he had difficulty following the movie. He caught only the main plot: the protagonist, a herculean mouse—always a mouse—with a scruffy tail, heading north somewhere on a train. Other than that, he remembered nothing. He sat in the uncomfortable chair with his stinging elbow and did his best to remain still and not look over to his left.

More than likely he would have stubbornly endured the situation, had she not made the next move. In the most miraculous and arbitrary of actions that could change the trajectory of their relationship (a type of moment akin to leaving thirty seconds early and avoiding a deadly collision, or walking into an aquarium gift shop and deciding to become a biologist), Emma straightened and placed her arm on the rest between them.

His gaze remained fixed ahead, but his periphery latched onto the move. Ever-so-slightly, calculated to appear casual, he straightened his body. His bent arm inched towards the middle rest until his uninjured elbow contacted and pinned there, like one of those toy birds that miraculously balances by its beak on the tip of your finger.

The minutes ticked by, and Emma's arm eventually brushed his elbow. As miniscule as the contact was, he felt it burn through the fabric of his sweater. For the first time since they'd known each other, their individual bubbles contacted. He remained petrified in this position for almost forty-five minutes. The movie continued to play unobstructed until there was no more film to run.

As soon as the lights came on, they sprang back into their own auras, slightly embarrassed by the secret intimacy. Led by the other couple holding hands, they walked out of the show room and into the lobby. The emptiness of the theater felt like a ghost town. The lights were dimmed and machines static. He couldn't help but grin as he escaped into the sharp night air.

The hyacinths had already begun drooping from the dew, as the two made their way around the corner. Nearly half of the dirt lot was sodden, puddles accumulating in various corners. There was no indication of rain. In fact, except for a lone cloud lit up by the crescent moon, the sky was clear. He suspected the Clean-N-Go Laundromat attached to the parking lot was the source. His gaze fixed upwards, and when his eyes returned, the sky melted into bleary streaks on the puddled ground. His hands sunk deep into his pockets, and he dared to glance over at Emma.

"Hey Emma, do you want to go somewhere else?" He was sincere.

Making her way to the passenger's side, she replied, "There's nothing really open now."

More from her tone than the words, his spirits deflated. All it took was that single line to suck the hope, gathered slowly like moss, from his lungs. But honestly, how naïve of him to think that their relations could change so drastically within a few hours, by an incremental touch no less. *Seriously.* He couldn't possibly be upset. Like an amnesiac coming to, his thoughts and movements in the theater gained clarity; suddenly and irrevocably they became juvenile and silly. The contact was nothing more than a sick illusion. But, somehow, it still managed to shock him more than he liked to admit. *Wow.*

"Oh, right." He dragged himself into the seat.

Emma was already curled into a sleepy ball. She presumably wasn't a night owl. Her face was hidden as she leaned against the passenger door. He put the key in the ignition, and with about five more clicks than usual, the engine groaned to a start. He wanted to remain angry and hurt, as if he were entitled to such things, but the peaceful image of her curled shadow eased his dejection. He looked over to her before pulling from the dirt lot to the road.

In the quiet night, his mind drifted to the ways he could possibly interrupt her peace, but as the truck bounced along, he methodically exhausted the ideas, like running a finger through the index of a science book, and finally determined that all his propositions were either out of reach or a great deal more obtrusive than he could partake in (intrepidly willing or otherwise).

I forgot my wallet at the theater? No, no. Just ask her to hang out? Definitely won't work. Play dead? He chuckled to himself with that one.

"What?" came her groggy voice.

"Nothin'."

The ideas dwindled until they were snipped away to nothing. Defeated, he began thinking about how much time they'd actually already spent together. Since their feud hindered all thoughts on the subject, he left her positive qualities suspended and boxed away in small compartments of his mind. He could coax them out with ease, but until now he'd had no reason to do so. She was tender with his grandpa and offered help beyond generational courtesies. She hummed and laughed to herself when she thought she was alone. Even when a hard day's work turned her into a sweaty little urchin, when her shirts began carrying lightning marks of dry sweat or her face was stale from exhaustion, she would veraciously smile, and her eyes would carve into happy crescents.

It was her eyes he thought about the most. One pupil was the normal size of a black ink droplet, but the other was always dilated slightly larger, as if the ink had started to spread. The enigma of her eyes and the fantasy of the event that could cause the characteristic—he later found it was from striking her head after a tumble into a shallow stream—drew him in. He decided he liked the asymmetry. It drove her uniqueness.

Then came some of the more typical manhood provocations, the things men wrote about, died for, obliterated nations over. Vanilla skin with a light splay of freckles around the bridge of her nose, enough to drive you crazy. She had an athletic build from so much hiking around her neighborhood. Her active physique, however, could do nothing to hide her femininity: wide hips, and the way her shirts loosely fell over her breasts. Her fragile collarbone. The tight skin planing her torso, inevitably drawing his gaze when she reached up to clean high shelves and cupboards. He'd caught himself fixating: on her simple necklaces, or her jean pockets which become the most interesting object in the world when she bent over to clean. He was always a bit embarrassed when he realized how much pleasure he took in watching her. She certainly wasn't a model, having neither the long legs nor the feathery weight, but she was beautiful.

The image of her looking at him with a coquettish little smile—from when they first met, the only time he'd seen it—caromed in his mind.

Then out of the quiet corner of the truck, the words, "Pull over," came from her curled ball and knocked him away from his fantasy.

With a startled jerk of the wheel, he responded automatically, "What? Our street is right there." He lifted one finger and pointed to Forester just ahead.

"I know. Pull over," she assured.

He pulled to the side of the road, the tires rumbling to a halt.

Only the sliver of moonlight hit their figures. Reid looked over and asked, treading lightly, "So... What's up?"

"What do you mean? I'm tired and want to take a nap."

If he was confused before, he only grew more so as she readjusted herself to boldly lean in his direction. In a modern truck there would be a center console to separate them, but as it was her body stretched across the cushion, head on his shoulder.

Although unfamiliar, her touch never felt awkward. It amended his feelings after the movie. That was why he dared not say a word, even though he knew she knew her bed was less than a minute away.

"You're a good pillow," she said without moving her head.

She continued, "So I don't know you very well Mr. Reid. Tell me a little. What is it like back where you live?" She yawned.

He paused, considering, "Well, there are a lot more people and places to be." He thought for a moment before continuing. "There are always lights on, and you can always do something at any time. Like, get something to eat for example." He held out his hand with that slightly fraudulent recollection, not certain if Emma was still awake but feeling her heavy breathing beside him. "There's this little crab shack I go to with my mom really late. I mean, it's pretty nice out there, and I'll be going to college nearby at this campus—all brick. You get an old prestigious feeling." Then, an unexpected frown crossed his face as he thought of the campus. He'd been so excited after he visited. He applied as soon as he returned home. He waited anxiously until he received word of his acceptance. His parents were all for it too, him being so close and no out-of-state tuition. It was a win-win. His next words surprised him even more. It felt as if he were looking down on himself. "I actually like it out here too, though. There's space out here. Don't get me wrong, it can be pretty boring, but there's a peace you don't get to feel where I live. I feel special out here."

"You *are* special. Sorry about earlier Reid."

Blood rushed to his cheeks at the realization she was awake and staring up at him with her green eyes. He could hear his heart thump thickly in his chest. She was always quick to avert her eyes when they were near each other, so the feeling hit hard when they finally locked onto his and stayed. It could have been a few seconds or a few minutes that he stared into those time-warping pits, but then her gaze snapped away and she curled against him. His heart continued on.

Reid shuffled down into his seat to be closer to her resting body. She was still leaning on his shoulder, but he contorted his head so his mouth hovered above her. As Emma exhaled, he inhaled, and when he exhaled, Emma inhaled. This rhythmic set of breaths pacified him, and his body became limp. With the same unhurried movements as in the theater, he moved in a bit closer to her mouth. A bit closer.

But before he could summon the courage to make the leap, Emma pulled away and sat up with a sleepy stare, clothes wrinkled into a mess and her hair tousled beautifully. "I'm ready to go home now."

Now? He looked at her in disbelief, but she adamantly returned to her unfocused, drowsy composure. Inside, he was tearing himself apart. His boastful imagination had already promised to feel her soft skin, her gentle lips, look into her eyes again, but all he let out was "Okay." *What a fool.*

He turned the key, and the engine churned but refused to turn over. He tried again, beginning to panic but still receiving the same *tss tss tss.*

With a nervous chuckle, Reid proposed half-jokingly, "Looks like we might be sleeping here tonight."

After a few more tries, Emma responded casually, "Well, I'm going to walk."

"Walk home?" he asked, almost in disbelief. "I thought it was cold? Weren't you cold earlier? And tired?"

"No, and I'm not too tired to get home."

She hopped out of the truck without hesitation. After a few more desperate tries with the key, he jumped out after her.

Not quite sure what the right words could be, he remained silent as he caught up to her. There wasn't anything else to say, really. He just fixed his gaze above at the cluster of bright stars and followed. His emphasis on stargazing, the deep craning of his neck, was his last effort to incite conversation. It never happened.

They passed his grandfather's driveway and continued towards Emma's home. The thump of feet on asphalt and the song of crickets pierced the night. It wasn't until they actually reached Emma's driveway that she directed her attention to him again.

"'Night Reid. Thanks for taking me out."

"No problem. Hope you had a good time."

"I did."

"Maybe we can hang out again sometime."

"Okay."

She gave him a long, hanging hug before turning and proceeding down the driveway.

On his walk home, he kicked at the asphalt. He thought about what happened in the truck and tried to decipher the events of the evening.

When he entered his grandfather's house, Greggory was still awake to greet him. He sat in the kitchen chair drinking tea and staring at a small picture in his hand. Only one dim light illuminated the table. His grandpa gently set down the picture and looked at him with a questioning smile.

EMMA

Had she not taken bold action, she didn't know whether they'd make amends. Although she didn't meditate on everything they said, she understood that their falling out was largely repaired. Her tired body begged for her bed. She tiptoed down the hall as to not wake her parents. Her door remained shut, leading her to believe they didn't even know she had been out. She opened it and stumbled into her room. In her sleepy stupor, she had one last thought before crashing—the kind that reveals our deepest thoughts. Had she been less tired, she would have nurtured it, tried to understand it. But instead, it remained a curious apostrophe for future nighttime philosophy: *Was he really trying to kiss me?* She touched her lips before falling onto her pillow.

GREGGORY

Greggory fully expected the affection he and Sophia shared to dismantle, or wane, or be ignored, but shortly after the night along the shore the two shared another moment. At the far edge of camp, Sophia was eating grains from a small wooden bowl. When Greggory noticed her, his feet began in her direction. He had intended to say something about what happened at the river, but as soon as he reached her all he could manage was, "Hey."

She looked up to him with a shy smile, and asked if he'd like to sit. Greggory watched her eat; she spoke between bites. Calmness settled between them, and a drumming of waves that weren't there echoed in the back of his mind. Ten minutes into the conversation, after laughs and smiles, a small speck of food hung from the corner of her mouth.

"Hey, you have a little something right there." Instead of waiting for her to get it herself, he reached over and wiped it with his thumb. She looked away, embarrassed.

"Thanks." They looked at each other, then shied away again.

An hour passed while they spoke. Caboclos were just barely seen walking around the camp. The light on the ground dimmed.

Greggory was so immersed in conversation with Sophia that he didn't notice Leila approach. He looked up with surprise; Leila looked at Sophia and smiled.

Then she directed a comment at Greggory, cutting the time with Sophia to an end: "There's a few baskets of food that still need to be hauled from that one area on the road. Do you have time to grab them with me, Greg?" The spot she referred to was about a half-mile away.

"Oh, you couldn't find Sedenoe? I thought he was going to help you today."

"I didn't ask him. C'mon man, Soph doesn't mind. Do you? Or are you two…"

Greggory looked over to Sophia, and Sophia's eyes darted away. "I don't mind if you go Greg," she replied quickly, timidly.

There was certainly the option to say "no," but he didn't. It would've been a trap to decline at this point. He felt a stripe of frustration when Leila pulled him away by his hand, but part of him indulged in her attention, her touch. Hand-in-hand she led him away from the settlement and down a trail where the baskets were.

When they reached the spot, it didn't appear that she couldn't have carried both baskets. There were only two. But there was really no reason to point this out. As they were just about standing over them, Leila cut in front of him and bent down sharply. He stuttered to a stop, standing inches behind her, the fringes of their clothes brushing.

"You know," she turned her neck to look at him, smiling devilishly, "we've gotten pretty close in the last few months."

Her eyes snapped him back to his fantasies.

"Yeah, we have, but we still haven't made it to the river again." He did his best to appear cool. She picked up one of the baskets and began towards camp.

"You're right. Maybe we could sneak off some time soon. Get into a little mischief."

As she trailed off in front of him, he watched her body. She looked behind her, catching him watching her, but instead of reprimanding him she simply smiled.

After they'd walked for a few minutes, Leila changed the subject. "But as close as I've gotten to you, I don't feel that way at all with Sophia. She's such a snooze, man."

"She's not too bad. I think she's just shy."

Leila laughed. "I guess. But I think you're in denial. She's a grandma."

"No, she's not." Automatic.

"Oh, somebody's got a crush."

"I don't have a crush."

"Yeah you do, but really I think you need a *woman*, Greg. I mean, c'mon, you can't go around dating grandmas." She winked and blew him a kiss. Then they reached the village.

EMMA

Emma heard noise in the front room. It was Sunday, so that meant her parents were running late. By now they should already be on the road, her mother to the art gallery and her father to finish a project he was unavoidably late in completing. Emma tiptoed down the hallway, trying to make it past them without notice, out the door towards Greggory's house.

"Oh, hey Emma." Her father caught her from the corner of his eye.

"Hey Dad." She walked towards him, lured.

"What're you up to?" He continued fidgeting with his tie, the warm scents of sandalwood, vetiver, and hints of amber from his cologne filling the room. Her mother moved to the kitchen, distracted.

"Going to help Greggory." *The man you're forcing me to help.* She omitted the second part, but tried to inject just a tiny bit of condescension into what she said.

"Oh, good. Glad to hear you're enjoying it." He inspected himself in the mirror. "Hey, are you going to be free tomorrow? Maybe we could drive to town for ice cream? I'll be getting off early, and your mom doesn't have any appointments, so she

89

could bring you. Maybe we'll walk around a little bit, too?" His eyes remained fixed on the mirror.

Under different circumstances, she might be thrilled that her father wanted to spend time together. But that was not now. "I've been kinda busy, Dad."

"Yeah, but don't you have time later?"

"I guess. But you know I'm supposed to help Greggory tomorrow. I wouldn't want to ditch my duties." And that part was, in fact, a little jab.

He thought for a moment: "What time are you getting off?"

"Dad, you should know these things. I get off at four." She had gone and done it: he finally looked at her.

"I don't know everything about your life, Emma." Sharper than he probably intended. "—But, you'll be available then?" Hint of apology now, eyes shying to the mirror again.

"I guess so."

"All right, we'll go at *six*. That's plenty of time to finish with the old man."

Once, they'd laughed, and joked, and had cute little grins between them, but that was more in the past. Lately, Emma couldn't unhinge the frustration. Perhaps this was misdirected or petty; she truly didn't mind helping Greggory at this point (part of her actually *enjoyed* it), but something still lingered after her father forced her into the commitment.

Emma asked if she could leave (even though she didn't need to ask, not in this family): "May I go now?"

He nodded, and she made for the door. At about the same time, her father called to her mother that they should be leaving.

TIM

Tim rode his bicycle home from work. It was late, and the blinds in his room were closed. He made his way to sit on a corner of his bed. The job grew rote after the first month; that much he accepted. Sweeping, assisting nagging customers, maintaining the men's bathroom, and restocking shelves were tasks he expected. They were a boring repetition of events spinning around like the images of a zoetrope, but he accepted them.

He jimmied off his shoes and kicked them across the floor. True, it wasn't his ideal job, but he hoped the experience would help him start a career one day. *Find a rewarding career,* his mother always told him, as if it were just around the corner. All he had to do was work hard enough, and soon—at some unspecified future date, but soon—he'd discover he was working in a *rewarding career.* Although he'd never been very popular or attractive, he hoped his work ethic and intelligence might lead to such a thing, and (if he were very lucky) even a happy marriage with children and a nice home of his own.

Still, it weighed on him. Even after the silliness of their pubescent dating, she occupied a secret corner of his heart. That he wasn't able to tell her he hadn't quite moved on—even though the feelings could sometimes be a mystery to himself—panged him. It contributed more deeply to his feelings of inability, and (worse) to his feelings of *ordinariness*.

Why she'd overlooked him so often afterwards, he had no clue. He logically determined that he was intelligent and funny and charming to a higher degree than most. What's more, he was dedicated beyond belief. And yet, he still had nothing to show for it.

As a result, he waited on the outskirts of her life anticipating the moment he could be there when she needed him most. Often he'd be trampled on, but it would be worth the wait when the day came and everything changed. Then, she would see how much they belonged together. Then, she would lean on him, if just for a moment. His drab routine towards success and a brighter future would be replaced with something tangible. Her smile would be better than a *rewarding career*.

He sighed and shifted on his bed, then smoothed a single, minute portion of his disordered hair. He wasn't quite sure why he clung to her so dearly. Nonetheless, that one moment had changed everything.

∞   ∞   ∞

Hosted by an organization called "Camp Green," his small school and two others in the area participated in a three-day camping excursion for sixth-graders. The idea was to build camaraderie and healthy friendships. The program was initially intended to instill anti-drug messages, but throughout the years it had become more recreational; slowly, the camp replaced instructional seminars with nature hikes, animal awareness training, and a large campfire at the end.

Upon arrival, the children filed out of the large mustard buses and retrieved their belongings while adults stood in a large clearing shouting names for roll call. Once everyone was accounted for, they headed like ants to their cabins, slatted bungalows set up in a circle. They were coarse with age, slumped by gravity, and weathered by the lingering ocean breezes. The scents of decay and mildew permeated the air. The dining hall, not far from the bus roundabout, once matched the cabins until it was deemed so putrid and unsafe that the camp was forced to renovate. Even after the ambitious attempts to scrub, bleach, and repaint every conceivable surface of the rectangular building, it still retained the faint smell of mold.

As advertised, the boys' sleeping commons were segregated from the girls'. Not only was this emphasized in brochures, but after an incident involving two young campers it served as a reminder to parents and teachers alike of the new, rigid values the organization had adopted. The camp and its representatives reiterated this segregation at the orientation, but their tone suggested that they were only half-convincing either themselves or their clients that they could snuff the hormonal output of growing teens. Children were having sex at such a young age these days!

When Tim thought back, he realized that the counselors would only have been in their early twenties. They were either trying to restore balance to their chaotic lives or simply didn't yet know its direction. Regardless of their own haphazard trajectories, they managed to be leaders and confidants (if only marginally) to the two hundred sixth-graders allowed on the premises of Camp Green.

What happened during the two days after his arrival was foggy, an indistinct period of adjustment and instruction. The weekend passed seemingly quickly, and already it was the final day. He awoke after a restless sleep on a lumpy mattress. Not one but three of his peers snored and farted continually throughout the night. When he lifted from the cheap cushion, his body was stiff. His right arm throbbed, and he had to blink repeatedly to convince himself he wasn't in a terrible dream. The supervising parent—all scruff and outdoorsmanlike—called names off his clipboard as he bobbed through the rooms. After every groan, he would make a tick on the roll sheet with his pencil.

Evidently Tim didn't respond loudly enough, so the burly supervisor—Richard—bent over him with a wide grin. "Hey little buddy, you Timothy?" he asked patting Tim's head, as if nurturing a wounded animal. With Tim's short shorts and oversized shirt hanging limply from his shoulder, he lifted himself, nodded, and watched the man walk away with the same energetic zeal he arrived with. The pat from Richard drew out the headache he'd held at bay.

Once everyone was accounted for, the campers were corralled and led like sheep to the dining commons. The children waited in a long line, holding out their trays for food and finding an open table to sit wherever they could. Silverware clanged together, and chatter filled the background. The pancakes looked flaccid, but were nonetheless better than expected. His mother never allowed him to eat sugar, so the sweet syrup masked any injustices to the cooking industry and warranted seconds. The milk, however, gave him a stomach ache to add to his list of ailments, so he stood to find Richard. After sweeping the room with his eyes, Tim determined that the man was nowhere to be found. He snuck away to find a bathroom.

Outside the dining commons, he followed the building around the corner. The path appeared unused. It was overgrown and grassy, with wild flowers sprouting from the dirt, making him suspect he was in the wrong place. He looked up and noticed a door slightly ajar at the far end—possibly a maintenance closet—his bathroom needs prodding him to enter nonetheless.

The room was dark and filled with a strange smoke and must. After a few blinks, he noticed two figures in the far corner. Restrained grunts similar to a pig snorting echoed from their direction.

Tim was just about to call out "Hello?" when the stench and smoke filled his lungs, causing him to cough resoundingly. The figures scurried away from what they were doing, and in their consternation directed themselves towards him.

"Hey kid, this is the counselor's office. Don't you know how to knock?" demanded a masculine voice above mumbled curses and a readjustment of his jeans.

"Shut up, Chris," came the other in sharp reprimand.

Tim couldn't make out much, but the girl counselor repositioned her shirt and came closer. She crouched beside him and squinted to read his nametag, "Hey... Timmy. Are you all right? Nothing's wrong, is it?" Her tone was delicate and forgiving, her brows furrowed with concern. He could see the perspiration on her forehead under disheveled blond hair, but nonetheless he thought she was angelic.

Tim stuttered, "N-no, but I need to go to the bathroom. My stomach hurts." By this point he was wrapping his arms around his waist.

"Oh! Let's get you to the bathroom," she exclaimed

Her soft hands clasped his, and she led him outside into the bright light. The bathroom was, in fact, close to the nebulous office, just around one more corner.

"I'll wait for you right here."

When he returned, she squatted down again and held out her hand, "Feeling better? My name's Amy by the way. Nice to formally meet you, Timmy."

"Yeah I am, thank you, Amy," squeaked his timid voice.

It would be years before Tim realized what he'd interrupted, but at the moment he hadn't made the connection and frankly didn't care.

"Well Timmy, I'm glad you found us when you did because we were just about to begin the nature hike. You remember Christopher right? He and I are going to lead it."

Chris, or Christopher as he heard Amy call him a few times, was muscular and intimidating as he leaned on anything his corpulent body could find. The first victim happened to be a post near the edge of the forest. Sixth-graders swarmed around him as they waited impatiently for the hike to commence. Chris's tight grey shirt hugged his body, and flowing blonde hair protruded from his black beanie. Tim unconsciously scowled in distaste at his well-fitted clothing. From the beginning, he didn't like Chris.

As he made his way closer to the group, he didn't recognize any of the students. Amy must have thought he was in a different group from the one he was assigned to. He began to panic as his feet dragged along, but when he was just about to say something that masculine voice broke his emotional trance and shut down his next words.

"Hey, kid. Name's Chris. Sorry if we startled you earlier." He offered his palm. Damn his kindness. Powerless to confront him, Chris being a counselor and all, Tim accepted. As they shook hands, Chris's eyes connected with Amy's for a split second, and the guy winked at her. Tim didn't like him one bit.

Refusing to allow Chris to become a hero to his misplacement, he fell in line as the mass of children formed together and set into motion. At the back of the line were Amy's alluring blue eyes. They wandered until meeting his; she waved. His eyes quickly averted, but the gesture allayed his panic. He resigned himself to partaking in the hike without protest.

The army of children assiduously advanced. Soon redwoods engulfed them, and all around a fresh, earthy smell rose from the ground like steam. A stream clicked in the distance, resting faintly on his ears like wind. He concentrated on the vein-like branches and the sunlit motes floating around him before his attention moved to the green moss painting the forest floor. They stopped on several occasions to discuss ferns or animal tracks or rings on a sawed-off tree trunk, or—his favorite—a pair of caramel-colored salamanders. Being in the middle of the line, he couldn't make out everything Chris communicated to the group, but he watched the dark-haired girl a few paces in front of him as her eyes wandered about. When she gazed right, he gazed right. When her gaze turned left, his went left. His only caution was when her head tilted upward — she was clearly clumsy, and habitually stumbled on roots and leaf litter. Fortunately her scraggly, tomboyish body always managed to catch itself before an actual tumble, but he would check downward before looking up at the tree line.

The hike was enjoyable, maybe the most enjoyable activity since he arrived, but by mid-day his feet began to drag. Exhaustion had his peers giving their heads to gravity.

They shuffled along until a narrow brown trail post indicated a checkpoint. As they passed Chris signaled to Amy that it was time for lunch. When the students saw the nod, they raced over the bridge, pushing their way to the other side like a spurting waterfall. Chris and Amy followed with quickened steps.

Tim was still lagging, focused on a slick rock near the trail as he followed the girl in his periphery. The cries in the distance caused his head to jerk up. Across the bridge Chris and Amy were already pulling plastic-wrapped sandwiches and juice boxes from their backpacks.

Only he and the clumsy brown-haired girl were still on the wrong side. He rolled his eyes at her obliviousness and followed her galumphing gait over the bridge. Then — and this part happened lightning quick — on the last wooden board she tripped and tumbled over. The wooden guardrails stopped just shy of where she flung herself, and she flopped like a ragdoll down the embankment.

She landed in the stream below, and her pack caught on sticks or rocks or whatever the hell it was caught on in the shallow currents. Years later, he could still vividly recall the panic on her submerged face as she flailed about: eyes huge, mouth etched open with terror. He guessed he held a similar expression. As her tiny body flopped with the current, she began relaying choked cries from under the water. He propelled himself down the bank, lunged as far as he dared into the current, and with a lean backwards ripped her loose. They both fell to the shallows gasping while her pack tumbled downstream.

Still clutching her, he rasped, "Are you okay?"

She burbled water before answering, "Yes." Her eyes had turned cherry red and her hands trembled.

After a pause, she also added meekly, "I could have gotten myself out. You ruined my shirt." She gave Tim a small shove and pointed to the torn collar on her shirt.

Tim sat staring at her and couldn't find any words.

In his daze he didn't remember how long it was before Amy and Chris raced over to them. First they asked if everyone was okay, and then they looked the two up and down for injuries.

"I'm okay," she restated firmly.

"Your head is bleeding. Let's get you checked," Chris addressed the girl.

Amy led Tim a short distance away, then whispered, "Hey Timmy, that was an awfully brave thing to do, jumping in the river like that."

He refused to look up at her, but in truth Tim was proud. He wasn't about to boast, but deep down he was glad *he* was the one who sprang to the rescue. He walked a little bit taller in his soaked clothes as the group looked intently to him. Already thinking of the praise he'd receive, he was cajoled back to reality by the pull of Amy's hand.

"No, Tim." She forced him to stop. "You *saved* her. She could have died."

Tim didn't know how to respond, so he kept quiet. He noticed her hand was trembling just slightly. The stark truth of her words was sobering. *Could've died?*

"Tim?" she asked, her tone once again matching her cognitive gaze.

"Yeah?"

"Can you make me a promise?"

Of course he couldn't, but he answered "Yeah" anyway.

"Without people like you in the world, it would be a dismal place. You have to promise you'll stay the same and look out for others like you did with her. Look after them, you know? Be selfless."

Look after people? People like her? Look after her? He didn't know exactly what she meant by it, but her emphasized pronunciation of the words was too sincere to reject. For a long time Tim interpreted the hefty request one way, but in the same fashion as realizing that planets spin around the sun and not the Earth, he would eventually understand that he had drastically misinterpreted the request. As it was, he made the promise.

"Okay, good. Now let's get you checked out."

That was the last time he spoke to Amy about the incident. In fact, despite the legion of whispers spreading like wildfire, nobody said a word directly to him until they reached camp. By then everybody had already somehow caught details of the rescue. No one really asked him about it—only some weird kid named Charles whom Tim recalled picking his nose while talking to him—but on the outskirts of his microcosmic bubble he caught the eyes, nods, and animated fingers in his direction. Of the gossip he overheard, there was only one attack: a snide pair of girls suggesting he pushed her in. Everyone else made him out to be a hero.

To a normal person the praise would probably have been welcomed, but to an introvert like Tim, the unstoppable scrutiny, suspicious grins, and unwelcomed glares began to wear. By the end of the day, he headed straight for his cabin and under the coarse wool covers of his thin bed. The voices outside were hushed, and he found peace in the stillness. He rested his eyes under the blanket and felt safety in his stale breath. The calmness survived for a whole twenty-eight minutes before a voice outside caught his ears.

Richard called out again, "Timmy Decker? Is our hero Timmy Decker here?"

Reluctantly, he dragged himself out from under the covers.

"Oh, here he is. Timmy, where were you? Off saving more people?" Richard gave him a playful nudge on the shoulder, making it clear he wasn't upset that Tim had departed from his assigned group. Tim returned a labored smile.

Richard announced with his usual enthusiasm that they were headed for the Camp Green Campfire, an event where all the sixth-graders gathered around a giant bonfire while counselors told stories and performed plays. Even before the events of that afternoon, Tim hadn't exactly been excited to attend. The fact that the whole goddamn place might burn down weighed as a real possibility in his mind; he didn't want to be anywhere nearby when it did. Nonetheless, he followed his group obsequiously.

There was a brief set of instructions, but they went awry as soon as the students reached the campfire. The flames burst outward, but the sixth-graders advanced closer. They were mesmerized by the mystical combustion and fought for spots on the moist ground. The blaze whipped and frolicked and snapped before dying into giant streams of smoke.

Tim's fear blew over after witnessing the seductive spectacle. He found a small patch of ground among the wave of students where his sight could remain unobstructed. He watched the bright layers of orange and yellow light up the darkness. After some time, the commotion around him subsided. The shuffling of feet and bodies quieted, and all that remained was the crackling of the fire and distant sounds of nightlife. Tim blinked.

"Hey," whispered a voice to his right.

"Hey," he responded, not taking his focus from the inferno.

"I kinda overreacted a little today," came the voice again. "Thanks for helping me."

Tim didn't need to look to know who it was. Before even seeing her, he turned ashen.

"It's okay. You were right—I didn't do much," he tried deflecting.

"Actually, I was stuck. Dumb rock or stick held me down." She watched him. Her eyes reflected bright orange. "My name's Emma."

"Mine's Tim," he turned and stuck out his palm politely.

Before they could say much else, a counselor in a feathered costume leapt over the fire.

He crouched before the crowd and scowled. A campfire story was about to commence.

Tim looked at the counselor, but from the corner of his eye he studied Emma. After all, he had the responsibility to watch over her. A burden, perhaps, but looking past her lankiness there was something attractive about her. Something about her made her attainable. She was obviously a bit reckless and clumsy, a dangerous combination, and an eye on her would be necessary.

Midway through the story, fire still popping in the background, he began to relax.

"Hey," came another whisper.

"Hey."

"My hands are cold. Can you hold them?"

There wasn't much hesitation before replying. "Okay."

She slid closer and extended both her hands. She had smooth skin. His hands glided over the grooves and indentations of her palms before locking fingers. They both smiled shyly.

As the campfire story continued, Emma leaned against him. Tim noticed Amy sitting near Chris on the outskirts of the shaking shadows. Did they lock eyes? He could have sworn they did, and he could have sworn she smiled. His head returned to the counselor telling the story, and a surprising frown spread across his face.

At the end of the trip, an intrepid camper named Jessica approached Tim to notify him that Emma like-liked him. After hearing his reply, Jessica settled they would date and went to relay the news.

GREGGORY

As awkwardly as their friendship began, Greggory and Sophia quickly found a groove. He worked vigorously during the day and spent nights by the river with her. As the wind brushed against the shore and against their bodies, they reminisced about their past lives. Greggory would sometimes skip stones along the choppy water, and a few time they summoned the courage to cannonball in. He always recalled those days with warmth. The smells of jungle and soot muted by the scent of her vanilla hair, they sat together watching the muddied currents churn and spoke about anything that crossed their minds. As time passed, Sophia's shyness unraveled.

There on the shore, he began to unleash his many adventures. He brought up the specters of his past, including the draconian side of his parents and his salaciousness with women. Of the many sinful stories, he included those with Sarah—creeping to her house late at night, or the time they snuck into a vacant theater so she could go down on him in the dark. Sophia showed no restraint in her repulsion but upheld the burden of listening, looking past his flaws and soon becoming and intimate advisor. Pulled like a magnet he found his way to her, beginning to need her acceptance as a child needs a parent's. At the end of each conversation he yearned for her reminder that "there's always time to turn things around."

One evening on the shore, he fished the notebook from his backpack and wrote Sophia's address: *18610 Spyglass Rd., Niece, California*. That night, long before they were scheduled to leave the jungle, he promised to write her.

After weeks of conversation, the topic finally arrived at Leila. Sophia nimbly filtered her disappointment, allowing him to catch only a brief glimpse of her eyes dropping in accordance with her shoulders, but in an instant she reasserted her poise and grace and advised him to consider what he really wanted. If he must tell Leila his feelings, then he ought to tell her directly and treat her right. Greggory responded with a chuckle; Leila was the last person he wanted to treat right. But he wondered deep down if the utter candidness of telling her could cut through the social theatrics of lust.

And so, two selfish desires warred against each other. He wanted to be a good person, and turned to Sophia for help. Perhaps stemming from a misconception that comes with growing into adulthood, Greggory felt time beginning to age him. He should give up the silly flings of his youth. Sophia motivated him. She could look at him with just a disciplinary raise of her eyebrow and it would bend his mental circuitry away from vulgarity. "Okay," he would agree. He'd raise his palms and be contented at her intervention.

But his second desire drove him away from Sophia's corrective installments. He wanted those dirty, secret encounters. Furthermore, the phrase "just tell her" only thickened and advanced his prurient psyche from dissenter to martyr. It rang in the back of his mind continually. Every time he saw Leila going about chores in her muddied, stale clothes, his vision was distorted by fantasies of ripping them from her body. The simple, brazen phrase Sophia helped concoct—the idea it promoted if it were effective—hooked him. When he considered the actual possibility that Leila would grant him attention (those haughty lips pursed in a smirk as she spoke), his mind involuntarily ceded to tasting her, biting her neck, running his hands along her arching back, rolling off her undergarments.

But somehow the weeks wore on without action. Four months passed more quickly than they ought, and the nine months he'd signed up for drew quickly to an end. With only one month remaining he resolved to say something, but with every opportunity his cowardice got the best of him.

In the new irrigation canal, where he and Leila worked to widen the gap of the trench, he looked over to her. She shoveled away, arms flecked with mud, her attention fixed at the rocky soil. He stood to stretch, an opportunity to tell her how badly he'd like to spend some personal time alone with her, but then she looked up with a devious little expression that caused his speech to derail and his confidence to sap. With a sigh, he continued digging.

Thirty days skipped to fifteen. They carried baskets of Brazil nuts back to camp to replenish the storage. Sweat beaded on her shoulder, and her tank-top was slightly darker from moisture. She playfully nudged an elbow into him.

"Well, if I'm happy about leaving this place," she went on, "it's because I won't have to haul any more of these damn baskets around."

"I know what you mean. These baskets, man." They laughed. "We can always ditch, you know." He winked.

"We *could*. But if we went somewhere, Ms. Grandma wouldn't be happy when she found out."

"She won't mind."

Leila winked in return and pulled in front of him on the trail. "I'm serious, she won't." But she ignored the comment and continued. He thought of Sophia.

Fifteen days jumped to five. By that point Leila *had* to know his intentions, right? She *had* to. But she never allowed the flirtation between them to play into anything more. Instead, she kept him on the line like a puppet.

On the second-to-last day, he and Leila spent the morning grooming soy plants. Crouched over the rows of green leaves, they spoke distractedly until she stopped what she was doing and changed the subject: "You know, we never made it back to the shore."

He nodded. "Yep. I was looking forward to going again."

"Me too." He thought about suggesting they should go, but the subject felt dead since the last time they'd spoken about it. She continued: "Do you consider yourself an adventurous person?"

He thought, and then nodded again.

"Would you go into the unknown, like the dark, if there was a *reward*?"

He shrugged, "Yeah, sure. Why?"

"Just wondering." Her focus returned to the plants.

On his final afternoon, it wasn't Leila but rather Sophia he went to the shore with. The easiness he'd come to know with her filtered through their words.

Different topics drifted in and out of conversation, but soon the foreignness of not quite belonging either here or there took their place. While chasing Leila, he'd taken Sophia for granted. Now, he looked at her, trying to determine what it was he felt. She looked up the long, winding shore.

They allowed the conversation and silence to ebb and flow like the river in front of them, and might have continued all evening had Sedenoe and Uyude not planned a farewell gathering. They headed back to the village almost holding hands, their time suddenly feeling short, to where his friends huddled around a campfire.

Sedenoe was the first to see them. His eyes were as large as discs, and he wore a proud smile as he announced, "We hid the black kettle widda celebration *tonic* in dat open spot in the woods." He beckoned them to the circle where the other villagers sat waiting. Leila was already amongst them at the opposite end, smiling at Greggory as he sat. Both Greggory and Sophia could have guessed they'd brewed the drink, but they didn't expect the caboclos to celebrate as last time. To their surprise, heaps of food were passed around the circle, and cauim—an alcoholic beverage made by fermenting manioc root—sat ready to drink. It was a veritable feast, especially with the village's stocks so low.

After eating, Clarua underwent his rite of announcement, concluding by thanking the three volunteers for their company. Then the atmosphere became lively. The villagers began to intone their ancestral songs. Shaman Clarua made no secret of his participation in the festivities, and led the celebration with the first four gulps of medicine. A twinge of sadness filled Greggory when he considered how quickly his time at the village had passed. Around the campfire he studied the caboclos' faces: jaunty, serious, distracted, alive. Together the group continued to sit and eat and take sips from the kettle.

When passed to him, Sophia's watching eyes dissuaded him from consuming the drink. The memory of his tawny vomit and brain degeneration (ending in a splitting headache) solidified his decision not to drink. He looked up to Sophia's smile and shrugged nonchalantly in return.

Then a familiar body writhed and danced in front of him, and he couldn't help but watch Leila twist and turn before losing sight of her amongst the others. The night grew long. The caboclos played drums and danced and sang and laughed. He shared smiles with Sophia, Sedenoe, and Leila. Leila winked before returning her attention to the music.

A short while later, they began chanting and rearing their heads back with laughter. Greggory tilted his head back and howled in accordance. When his chin returned to Earth, there in the shadowy outskirts were Leila's piercing eyes. Her sharp smirk was torturous, a pistol to his temple, and he slipped his gaze away to escape the deadly attention. Still, the words enslaving him the past week — "just tell her" — rang persistently.

She was no longer looking at him, but something had shifted in how she dealt with him, as if it being the last night changed something. She stamped her feet and rippled her body to the sound of the music. Her hands twirled in the air, wrists twisting freely. She slid them down her neck, her breasts, the curves of her body. Her torso gyrated to the steady throb of drums. She turned slowly, allowing him to see her body's profile. The gentle arch on the low of her back pushed her butt out, taunting him as it rounded flawlessly to her legs. He trained his eyes on her thighs. Every inch of her movements carried his mind—twists and turns, the steady berating of drums, *thump thump*.

His awareness of her movements broke only when she, after a deep exhalation in her self-passion, opened her eyes again and looked directly at him. Either she knew exactly what she was doing or Greggory's awe was so obvious that it caught her attention. She laughed. Without waiting for his reaction, she turned and slipped into the wilderness of shadow behind her. Struck by her play, he rose and gave chase.

He followed deeper and deeper away from the glow of the camp as he pursued her trail around the dark beams of trees. She remained on the rim of his vision, refusing to slow, but he made ground on her motion, quickening his strides in anticipation. The chase lasted for some time before she stopped—in turn causing him to stop—some twenty yards away. She let out a penetrating shrill that caromed through the pillars, then, "Come on doll. You have to work for me." Almost a whisper, just loud enough.

She pulled her white tee over her shoulders before disappearing behind one of the shadowy pillars. He made his way to the shirt lying on the ground and looked around squinting to see where she'd gone. Before he could find her, a firm hand reached out and grabbed his wrist, and she pulled him to her half-naked body.

Her tongue forced its way to his, exploring the roof of his mouth. He could taste the acrid drink on her saliva. He advanced on her body, hands moving to her bare breasts before lowering to the skin of her torso. Then he pushed forward to pin her against a tree. Her moans cut through the nightlife singing around them.

She spoke between kisses. "I know you've been watching me." Her hand slid under his shirt as he kissed her neck.

"For longer than you think," he confessed between breaths.

"Let's see then."

He grasped her wrists with one hand, lifting them above her head. His tongue made circles around her nipple, and she moaned again. Inspired, he released her hands and pushed her waist more firmly against the trunk. She gasped with enthusiasm before her body shuffled back into its trance. Her fingers ran through his hair, and she pulled when he bit delicately.

"I want you," she moaned into his ear, thrusting against him.

The tips of his fingers moved down her waist and into the dark crevice between her skin and panties. Then she smiled and her eyes knocked back. Her hips stirred, but while he was advancing she stopped him, regaining control by unbuckling his belt. "My turn." She was just about to begin that earth-shattering descent when something clicked in his brain and he stopped her short.

His mind warred as she looked up to him, begging him— doe-eyed—but he ripped himself away.

"I can't," were the only words he could manage before stepping back and turning to the darkness. Confusion crossed her face. Her arms locked downward and her palms faced out. Her lips came together in a pout: "*What?*"

He didn't respond but focused instead on increasing the distance between them. The regrets were slowly outpaced by his march. The light from camp had long vanished, and all that remained to guide him were his instincts. He had a rough sense of where he was, but concentrated all his energy in getting out safely to meet the person he realized he should have been thinking about all along.

The eerie feeling lingered before he jumped over a small mound of jungle soot and landed on a deserted stretch of road. Farther than he originally thought, he continued the rest of the way in a hurried gallop, as though he would miss his chance if he wasted just one more minute.

Once there, his frantic eyes searched the shore. The desperation in his heart lifted when he saw a slumped black shadow in their usual spot. With a sigh, he made his way to her.

They didn't exchange words for some time, communicating solely with their silence, but finally he answered her unasked question: "For the first time in my life, I didn't act entirely on my impulses. There's still time to turn things around after all." He wasn't quite sure she heard him, but then she bumped against his arm and rested her head on his shoulder. Finally, she whispered in his ear, "I'm proud of you." Those words were the finality of discussion about him and Leila.

Greggory wrapped his arm around her, and they lay back to look at the constellations above them—brilliant empyreal glory. What conversations they brought up were whispered as old lovers. Throughout the night they hummed their drifting thoughts as they held each other close. Hearing a clamor from the water, they poked their heads up to see what he would swear was a pair of pink dolphins gamboling through the currents. The rhythmic *woosshhhh* of the waves as they fanned on the shore, the somnolent stars above, Sophia's vanilla hair, eventually became too much. He ceded to the deep, contented sleep patiently waiting for him.

When he woke, milky morning sun splayed stagnant and warm against his cheek. Still transitioning from the dreamy void, he blinked several times to collect his bearings. Then memory returned from its nocturnal jaunt, and he jerked up with a start. A ways down the river, he had a boat to catch. His motion, or maybe his frantic thoughts, caused Sophia to stir and go through the same reaction. He looked at the sun—how high was it from the tree line?—and determined he still had time if they hurried.

Sophia collected her sweater, and together they headed back to the village. The others were already roused and moving about in preparation for his departure. Some said goodbye in passing. Others gave him a firm handshake. The little ones cried. Sedenoe and Uyude gave him a hug. Before they headed to the dock, they snapped a group picture with a Polaroid—Sedenoe, Uyude, Shaman Clarua, Sophia, Greggory, the children, and the late-appearing Leila. Sophia was handed the picture as the still moment of their happiness developed from its white membrane. Greggory later discovered it when he was unpacking in Boston; somehow it had made its way into his suitcase. Later, when he was much older, he'd find the picture tucked into one of his childhood books.

Determined two weeks prior to their arrival in Brazil, Sophia would stay an extra three days to support the new volunteers. Greggory would leave without her, his plane ticket already booked. His departure began with a faint whirring sound that turned into a riverboat. The cabin of the vessel was small, fitting one—maybe two—at most. Worn tires were slung from the sides to protect the hull. The railing was rusty, and mud and algae climbed up the sides from the waterline. The captain beckoned to him. Before addressing the man, Greggory checked that he had all his belongings—notebook, clothes, blanket, tooth-brush—before tightening the straps of his backpack around his shoulders and grabbing his suitcase, just as he had at the beginning of his adventure. Then he hugged the few remaining caboclos and Sophia, and carried himself to the angular riverboat to hop on board. Once there, he waved to the crowd and mouthed an intimate farewell to a single person.

Leila boarded the same boat, but her narrow eyes and withdrawn composure warned him well enough to stay away, not to confront her and apologize for leaving her alone in the jungle, not to explain that he'd come to a realization he had no control over. An apologetic frown from the distance was the best he could do.

After situating himself in a corner against the metal guardrail and preparing for the long ride ahead, the newness of being on the river kept him awake. Hours seeped by until it was evening and the sleep he'd foregone the night before began to weigh on him. His movements slowed and his body was bled of any remaining energy as the boat cut through the currents. Even with the bumpy waves, hard surface, and longing for Sophia he managed to fall into a deep slumber while they continued their journey through the night.

When he awoke it was day, perhaps even midday. A spray of cold water hit his face. The boat rocked about, adding to his confusion. They were moored at a small rickety pier while figures scurried on and off the vessel loading baskets bound by ropes, filled with cassava roots and açaí. The last of the crewmen finally hopped back onto the vessel, and the pier faded away until the river bent and they were cast out of sight.

Over the next few days, the boat made regular stops to haul in supplies. Between stops, the sun settled over them, the rays refracting off the water and shimmering into a million diamonds. Squinting became his default, and Greggory huddled in a shaded corner whenever he could. When boredom overcame his nausea on the rocking waves, he picked himself up and walked to the captain or one of the crewmen, trying to pass the time by talking to them, hoping they might pass the time telling him stories of the jungle or shaman theology or the river or their lives. He found, however, that they immediately dismissed him, pretending not to understand his Portuguese. "Sorry, no." Quickly, it became clear that he was welcomed as neither crewman nor guest—the boat was not meant for tourists, and the crew had elsewhere to be.

The third night on the river, the crew stopped again. This time they didn't go for crates or baskets or piles of food as they had, but rather moved toward a makeshift camp on the fringes of the tree-line. The men's movements were sluggish and their arms hung limply, as if they'd arrived home from a long day of work. Leila walked amongst them. Greggory didn't entirely understand what was happening, but he grabbed the blanket from his suitcase and followed these hollow beings as they drifted inland. They marched into the trees where a few huts appeared alongside large shadows of women with outstretched arms. The men disappeared into the huts, leaving Greggory and Leila to their own devices. The last of them informed the two, "We stay here tonight," before he disappeared as well. Greggory walked well away from Leila and chose a spot on the ground.

At sunrise, his body was tangled in blankets and his cheek was pressed against a thick vine. He stood and stretched, then walked to the pier where he presumed they would be leaving. When he arrived, however, the crew was nowhere to be seen. He waited fifteen minutes, and then fifteen more, for the men to appear and for his boat to continue back on the river, but the crewmen never showed.

It wasn't until late morning that the men made their way to the dock, grins peppering their faces and rested muscles reflected in their movements. Greggory asked one of them when they'd be leaving, but the man simply shrugged, explaining in three or four words that they were waiting for cargo that hadn't yet arrived. *Well, if you were to guess, when would you say we'd be leaving?* Another shrug. The men meandered around the dock, lazily carrying a few items on and off board. A small radio played music through a haze of static while they worked. From one of the crates, they pulled slender brown bottles and tilted them to their lips. Both the beer and radio were rare luxuries. The day passed, and it became obvious they weren't leaving anytime soon. Greggory was forced into another night on the jungle floor. Thoughts of Sophia lined his brain.

Morning arrived again. The day passed similarly. More bottles, more music. The crew was in high spirits, and it caused the women from the huts to come out to see what was happening. They lounged along the shore, laughing and flirting as they sat in the men's laps. Greggory watched from his vantage at the tree-line. He refused to participate, yearned to get going.

The next day Greggory woke, his body throbbing from another uncomfortable night of sleep, and immediately began in the direction of the pier. From the clearing, he could make out the sun having just jumped above the treetops. Today, there was no music or beer, only birds calling in the background. He looked around for the men, but they were nowhere to be found. Greggory presumed they were still in the huts, feeling the effects of the last two days. But then he drew closer to the pier, and noticed that something was off about the entire scene. Something should be there, but it wasn't. An object was missing, like the focal point of a painting that had been ripped away. Then it struck him: there was no boat.

It took Greggory a long moment to orient himself. The boat was gone, leaving no trace of ever stopping. His head automatically flipped to the place he'd slept and to the huts. He raced towards them, panic beginning to build. To one of the women, he asked where the crew went, and she responded easily, happily, that they'd left. "But don' worry sweech'art. Anoter will come around dust for you anda girl. Tey left your stuff over tere." She pointed to the pier, where his suitcase stood thoughtfully in the mud. He approached it, his eyes frantically scanning. He stood over the object and confirmed that, yes, his backpack was missing.

More than his change of clothes, more than his pens or toothbrush, more than the time he'd have to remain at this loose halfway point, more than even his journal entries documenting the past three-quarters of a year, his thoughts locked on the notebook containing Sophia's address, tucked safely in his backpack that was gone. *184. 18 3.* He tried recalling. *California. 18 New California. 18!*

The first two digits were all his memory afforded—couldn't even remember the city.

He clenched his palms and ran to Leila to ask in a desperate attempt if it was intermingled with her belongings. She just smirked and politely informed him that it was not.

After the incident he did a rough calculation on how long it'd take to hopscotch boats and drive to the airport, but in the end determined Sophia would be in the air by the time he arrived. A light turned off in one of the compartments of his soul.

When the evening boat arrived, despondency reflected the hollow feeling in his gut. He didn't internalize boarding the next boat. He didn't recognize that he'd switched boats three times over five days, or feel the pangs of hunger the days after that. The crews on the journey never said much after their initial interactions. He sat alone like a totem.

At the end of the journey, to everybody's almost-astonishment, he bashed his fists against the metal siding in a sudden outburst. The crew looked at him with a twitch of their heads and then whispered amongst themselves. For the final few hours on the river, he sputtered unfiltered words to himself. His fists remained clenched and his eyes sunken.

Never see her again. He would lash out at something, anything, but it usually resulted in punching into his own palms. The crew would watch him, politely omitting any commentary for fear of spreading whatever he carried.

After his flight landed in Boston, he traveled to the suburbs where his family lived. It was overcast, and while riding in the taxi he found the city dreary in its unchanged visage. The time away allowed him to notice the maturity of his mother and father, their docile smiles, gray slivers sprouting in his father's notorious dark hair, crinkles growing around his mother's once-youthful eyes and cheeks. The signs had been there, but only his time away allowed him to notice.

Over the next few weeks, he tried contacting the agency for Sophia's information. Unfortunately, the recruiter who'd signed him no longer worked with the company, and the people at the office couldn't find even his own file, let alone hers.

They suggested she might have registered through one of their contracted agencies rather than the main office. He felt they were covering for their own incompetence, but he had to try. He called the many numbers they provided, but no luck. Finally he contacted his agency again and reached a young receptionist. When he asked the same questions in a different way, she failed to relay any information he didn't already know, but in her nasal voice she provided contact information for the one person they *could* find—Leila—"if that would help."

He went through the same process again in hopes of reaching a different person who might be capable of finding the information, but once again received the same receptionist. The agency must have finally placed a memo on Greggory, for when he tried one last time he reached a new person he'd never spoken with before. She addressed him by his last name and suggested he stop calling, her voice annoyingly friendly yet completely unaccommodating: "Sorry about these things, but I can't do anything for you Mr. O'Sullivan. Sometimes the names and addresses of the people who volunteer with us are held at one our contracted agencies. We normally would have this information for you, but without a last name or birthday we can't help. We have information for a Miss Leila Briggs if you'd like that?" Sophia had become a missing person, and it was then Greggory realized he would get nowhere in discovering her contact information.

Afterwards, he often spent time alone. On one rare occasion he had the fortune of seeing Sarah Boehn in the supermarket, recalling who she was only after an intense pause. They greeted and hugged as friends might. Her skin was just beginning to hang thickly on her corpse, and the years of intense work to make ends meet showed on her face. Overall, however, she had transitioned well into maturity. They both smiled at the mischievous moments they'd shared, but both felt it was a long time ago.

The months slipped by, and although never truly coming to terms with what happened, he learned to live with his regrets. He felt guilty for allowing the mishap with the boats to hover above all else; it often replaced the good ones of Sophia and him. His thoughts were like a film negative, the same image but all the wrong parts highlighted. He went through his days lackadaisically until he could function without thinking too much about the left step his life had taken.

EMMA

Emma was scheduled to clean at Greggory's the next afternoon. Her sleep the night before had been restless and the hours before her appointment were long, but the time finally arrived. She started near the oak tree in her yard, followed the stream up to the road, and made her way towards the mirages created by the heat.

When she arrived, the empty space in the carport reminded her of the inoperable truck down the road. After squinting into the distance to see if she could find the vehicle, her attention returned to the house. She peered into the windows, wondering if she could catch a glimpse and in some way determine how much of the evening Reid had shared with Greggory; Greggory certainly would have inquired where his truck had flown off to.

At the door Greggory greeted her with a short, amicable "Hello." No interrogation. In the kitchen, he returned to fiddling near the sink with what looked like a disassembled lock. She was presented the usual mug of tea. All right, then. No sign.

After drinking her tea she was left to the simple tasks of sweeping and mopping. She watched the back of Greggory's head for some time before starting on her work, during which Reid was nowhere to be found. The house was quiet until

119

Greggory moved on to the side framing and intermittent thumps of a hammer echoed inside.

Hours passed in this strange episode—a twilight zone—until Greggory entered again. His forehead was wet with perspiration as he made his way to the kitchen, then shortly reappeared with a pitcher of lemonade, two paper cups, and two wrapped sandwiches.

"Here." He tried handing over the items.

"I don't think I can drink all of this," she joked, but he only continued to stare.

"If you don't mind, would you bring these to Reid near the truck? There's a sandwich for you too."

She nodded, "I'm sorry about the truck. We were—"

"Things happen," he interrupted, presenting the pitcher and two sandwiches again, this time obviously agitated.

She accepted, awkwardly positioning the items in her arms, and led herself to the door. He followed outside with his own glass of lemonade before easing into the rocker on the porch.

Only after traveling most of the way down Forester could she make out the Ford, its hood propped open, resting under the shade of two tall oaks. As if committed to jumping from an airplane with a faulty parachute, she gulped back the lump in her throat and crossed the street.

Reid was under the truck, and at the shuffling of her feet he shimmied over to see who it was.

"Howdy stranger," she piped, not sure if this meeting would be a continuation or condemnation of last night. She stood stiffly in the sun, squinting with one eye, while he studied her. With the help of the bumper he rose, and then poured a cup of lemonade. Finally, he smiled. Emma's shoulders unwound as she placed the lemonade and sandwiches on the roof of the truck. She shook her head and let out a relieved sigh. He smiled again.

"What?" she asked after his eyes remained set on her.

Without an answer, he shrugged. They both laughed. To this day, she wondered whether the course of their relationship would have tilted the same way if they'd met elsewhere—say, Greggory's house instead of the truck. Would he have looked at her quite as tenderly, or would they have reverted back to their adversarial ways? There was no way to know, but as they stood on the side of the road, the singsong of birds in the oaks and the hot wind brushing against their bodies, something seemed to click just right.

She asked him about the truck, "How bad is it?" to which he gave a breakdown of possible problems and their solutions. Finishing up his analysis, he suggested she move to the shade. "You're making me hot standing there like that." She climbed into the truck, the draft flowing to soothe her. Reid devoured his sandwich, his muscles bulging, his hands and face speckled with dirt and oil. She shifted to hide the burn in her cheeks.

Once finished, he crawled back under the truck and they began talking freely into the air, effortless talk about nothing in particular. Every once in a while she'd hear the crank of the ratchet stop so he could properly ask his next question. The cranking would continue again once she began her reply. As time passed, their talk waned, and the sounds of the birds and the ratchet took its place.

Emma reached over to press the gray power dial of the radio. Static noise mixed with the sounds of clanking metal and chirping birds. Reid stopped what he was doing to look inside the hood.

"Should I not play the radio?" she called from inside.

"No, it's fine. The problem isn't electrical." His focus remained on the engine.

Through the narrow space between the hood and body, she found Reid had taken off his shirt. Lines cut around his torso defining his abs. Her nose scrunched while she studied him.

Focusing back on the radio (trying to), she rolled through the static stations, exhausting the circuit twice until she accepted one of the clearer ones. Now and again the signal was impeded by another and the two mixed to create a weird combination of noise, but she leaned against the seat and closed her eyes anyways. Reid submerged from view. Occasionally she opened her eyes to see if his body had reappeared, but as her breathing deepened the warm air made her limbs heavy. Then, a song she knew broke through the fuzz, and she began lipping the words.

...the strands in your hair, the color... stop me, steal my breath... emeralds from mountains thrust towards the sky...I'll be, the biggest fan of your life.

The song was ending when Reid came to check on her, "Emma? Hey, are you doing okay?"

Sweat was dripping down his face and arms. He tossed his shirt back over his bare chest, but the image was already branded onto her memory. She realized she was sweating a little bit too.

"I'm fine, why?"

"Just wondering. I wanted to come over and tell you you're beautiful. I'm going to kiss you now."

"Wha—" Before she could voice the question, Reid's lips pushed against hers. He was relentless the way he held her, kissed her; she surrendered to his impulsiveness. She pulled him closer, held on to the fingers caressing her neck. But suddenly he stopped and stared. She almost pulled him back in, but instead watched his brown eyes. His hand smoothed her cheek as he spoke.

"I'm going to be the biggest fan of your life."

Before the words had entirely finished, they faded and were replaced by a set of very new ones.

"Emma. Hey, Emma. Are you going to eat your sandwich?"

It took her a second to make meaning, but eventually she came to. The sun in the sky had shifted noticeably. She'd fallen asleep. *Fallen asleep?* How long was she out for?

Her eyes widened. *He must never know.*

"*My* sandwich? No way," she retorted in hopes of appearing relaxed, to mask the tingle she felt.

She curled into a defensive ball with the plastic-wrapped sandwich clutched in her arms: a ploy for him to wrestle her. With one eyebrow lifted, he proceeded to throw himself atop her. Although she used her strong legs and athletic physique to her advantage, his body nonetheless pressed her supine against the cushion. She could smell the oil and sweat. The aromas and physical constraint caused the tingle to intensify. He really was quite strong, and his eyes really were deep brown. The two remained entangled for a few long seconds. Emma held his arms and felt his breath. Then, he snatched his winnings and rolled over to sit next to her.

Half-winded, she began to compose herself, "So, how long did you say you're staying here and how come I haven't seen you before?"

He gave a thoughtful pause. "Well, I'm staying until the end of summer. And this is the first time I've been to my grandpa's house. I remember asking about it when I really little, back when I was considerably shorter and a lot heavier, and—What?—Don't give me that look. It was a long time ago is what I mean."

"Aww how cute, chunky Reid," she cooed.

They both laughed.

"But really, why do you have to go back home?"

"Well, college first off. I can't just turn that down."

"Well, there are colleges out here. And…what's second off?"

"I didn't apply out here. And *second off*, I don't know if my grandpa can handle me living here that long. And *third*, it'd be difficult. I'd miss my old life. All my friends and family are back home."

"Well, I still think you should stay out here and keep me company."

"Just for you, huh?"

"Yep," she gloated, and they both smiled.

"Come on, let's head back. I'm done for today."

She knew better than to pry deeper. It was barely a day since they'd even become cordial to each other, but his presence the past few weeks made their intimacy feel longer.

They walked down Forester slowly, unconcerned with the growing shadows or beaming yellow rays striking the fields on the horizon. At the time Emma hadn't really considered the austere moment, but in looking back months later it was exactly moments like these that would paint her nostalgia for summer.

"You're always falling asleep on me," Reid taunted as their walk carried them.

She felt blood surge upward. "Not always," she retorted, still embarrassed at the conclusion of her eudemonic reverie.

"We've hung out twice, and both times you're over there snoring away," he made a gesture with his hands.

"I don't snore."

"Yes, you do. I heard it."

"I don't snore!" She punched Reid's shoulder.

"Come on, let's get back before you fall asleep again and snore my head off."

Their playfulness continued on the way home, and intermittently Emma would throw innocuous punches as though they were valid counter-arguments. Reid always chuckled.

Although she could recall nearly every moment they'd shared since, most were too mingled with hopefulness and conjecture to relay any objective truth. In the swashing of her memory, she placed meaning to the most trivial events, her feelings forged and layered like smeared paints on a canvas. The small talk, the way they would slow their saunters to catch just a few more moments, the sun hitting his body just right in the afternoon, their arms brushing together, sometimes bumping into each other, how his eyes would slide onto her as he carefully listened to her energetic commentary—her thoughts drifting upward and dissipating into high wisps—all culminated to intimate memories. Emma kept her artistic renderings of what happened locked safely away in her memory, while the actual events were left forgotten.

What she could relay accurately was the schedule of her routines. They always began with her walking to Greggory's and completing his tasks. Even though she was certain he knew more than he let on—she even suspected he purposefully matched them together—she restrained from speaking to him about it. When she was finished with her work, whether pushed out or acting on her own, she walked over to the truck where she and Reid met daily.

By late June, when the heat had settled and Independence Day was quickly approaching, their friendship had seasoned. Although it was undeniable there was something more in the works, she was nonetheless contented with where they stood. She did her best to keep the idea of friendship at the forefront of her intentions, to avoid those rusted pipes of deeper affection from bursting at their weakest point and ruining everything, but in truth the pressure was beginning to build. Her thoughts and behavior were nimbly and uncontrollably moving in a certain direction.

At the beginning of July, while they were together and talking about something or another, he asked an unexpected question: "Should we do something together for the Fourth?"

A spot where they could see fireworks, alone, came to mind.

"Well, I made plans with my friends," she lied. She didn't know why she deployed the selfish tactic, but nonetheless it came out as it did.

"Oh, it's all right then."

Then she brushed it off. "But I feel like you should see the area a little more. I'll be your guide this year. I'll take the dive from my friends for you."

"My guide?" Reid laughed at the thought. "Okay. I better not be disappointed."

"You won't."

GREGGORY

Although it didn't start out his finest, the next period in Greggory's life was his best. Many nights it was difficult to gain any ground against his wakefulness. He often lay thinking of the idleness of his life, or the tedium of adulthood: full-time work, drab routines, debts he began to accrue. Once in a while he'd consider the relationships he'd lost, and Sophia. At some point, life had become gray.

He was uncertain when he finally fell asleep on this particular night. It was late, or rather early, before his eyes relaxed and he was able to fall into a rare, dreamless slumber. When he awoke, the victory came. He stammered out the line without thinking.

With the lucidity that comes in only those first few waking moments, he said it again, clearly and surely: *18610 Spyglass Rd., Niece, California.* There it was, the ribbon of information had finally recycled to consciousness. Why the clarity hadn't come years earlier he would never know, but he was grateful that it came nonetheless. Jerking from his bed as quickly as his body would allow, cursing that he no longer had the same spryness he had only ten years ago, he found a pen and jotted down the address on an errant piece of paper.

His eyes, still unable to knock away his morning weariness, studied the slip in disbelief. *Could it be real?* Yes it could, but as the morning developed Greggory realized it would take some tenacity to act upon the gift. Doubts immediately crept into his mind. It had been *years*, and he wasn't quite sure what they shared in common any longer. So much time had been spent fixated on the past that he'd hardly accomplished a thing since. He had so much to say, his mind drew a blank.

That fear, however, was placated once he finally put ink to paper in the afternoon. He tapped his pen on the blank sheet while he considered, and then began scribbling. The words came pouring. Even after an ache filled the lower lobe of his palm and his writing degraded to sloppy, he cranked out another five pages—front and back—of frenzied commentary. The first draft was quickly replaced with another, neater one that left only the most important sentences. He scratched out many of his impassioned ideas, and in the end held four solid pages of neighborly material.

He carefully folded the pages into three parts—giving such acute attention to the act it almost spawned a headache—and placed the parcel on his nightstand.

The larger fear, and the one he rationalized only after completing the letter, was how little he could predict her reaction. He couldn't know whether she were resentful for his lack of correspondence, or worse that she had completely forgotten him. And then, even if she did remember him and hadn't indulged in anger, what's to say they wouldn't come to realize that they never shared anything in common in the first place, that his perspective on the past was largely fictive? That was a real possibility. If she had a boyfriend or husband, or even if she'd moved to a new address, his letter would be pointless. The dangers that could demolish his efforts were endless.

The odds were stacked against him and he knew it, so when he placed the envelope in his mailbox in the morning and it was still sitting there when he returned from work, he removed it and set it back on his nightstand. It took him three days to summon the nerve to venture to one of those blue boxes and toss the three ounces into the irretrievable cavity of blackness.

Like an anxious child scheduled for a school meeting, he counted the days it would take to receive a response and then proceeded to wait. For the first two days he did his best to press away the possibility of anything arriving. Instead, he would come home and track the mailman's schedule in an offhand manner. From the third day forward, not relenting to mathematics suggesting it would take five days for the letter to even arrive in California, he began waiting by his box five minutes before the mailman's determined arrival time. With a polite smile Greggory greeted the innocent courier and stretched a hand for whatever contents the man offered. From the shuffle in his step it appeared the deliverer was reluctant to meet Greggory on their daily encounters, but being a professional the man remained steady to perform his task.

After a week, stress noticeably slumped and contorted Greggory's frame. Someone must have called the police about suspicious activity because a patrol cruiser began parking across the street. Given his appearance, it couldn't come as much surprise, and in all honesty he hardly noticed until the day he was confronted. The officer stepped from his cruiser and crossed the street, interrupting the meeting with the mailman before Greggory could comb through the stack. There was no way to clarify with any sort of dignity that this daily interaction was based on servitude to hope, to love, so instead he told the man he was waiting for a fat, set-for-life broker's check. Failing to find any sort of incriminating evidence, the officer nodded politely and left them to their business. The mailman, however, had delivered enough notes in his career to see immediately through the fallible tale and to the true nature of Greggory's distress. From that point forward his sympathy materialized in a disappointed frown each time Greggory's shoulders slumped. He once asked, "Any luck?"

Shaking his head "No," Greggory's hopes had just begun to wane and falter when it happened. He looked down to the stack of mail again. Hidden between two bills, the envelope stuck out like a polished diamond in a coal mine. His smile grew so wide, so apparent, that the mailman congratulated him with a pat on the back. In return, Greggory mauled the poor man with an excited embrace. It was as if he'd hunted for buried treasure for years—Lord knows he looked the part—only to finally strike a chest full of bullion.

He marched to his house with a delighted clip in his step. Loose, flowing penmanship held her name in the left corner above the address *18610 Spyglass Rd., Niece, California.* His name was written impeccably in the center. After throwing the remaining mail onto the counter like sickly trash, he hugged the letter to his chest and made his way to his room.

He placed the prize on the nightstand and tapped his knee, thinking how and when and where to tear into it. Like the final hours before a wedding, his movements were dreamy and gilded. He expected he would relish the moment for the rest of his life, so he steadied himself and tried to embellish his surroundings for memory's sake. When he finally caved in, his heart dropped at how parsimonious the one page proved to be. It was his own fault, really—he built his expectations more mightily than the goddamn Great Wall of China. It was unfeasible to receive a tome imbued with the reckless details he desperately longed for, and after the second read-through he realized the correspondence was more than he deserved. She had answered all his questions in a simple straightforward manner, and even signed at the bottom *Miss you dearly, Sophia.*

He pored over the letter to decipher any secret meaning he may have missed, and after each successive time he was more inspired by delight. Once he could recite the poetic phrases by heart, he tucked the page back into its envelope and began writing his reply. The sentences spilled onto the blank sheets more easily than the previous time, and within an hour he had a third draft of five pages, asking new questions and holding new possibilities.

During their back-and-forth correspondence, Greggory never called Sophia, although he often considered it. He felt that his voice would betray him—awkward pauses, heavy breaths into the line, forced conversation. He presumed she felt similarly because she never asked either, so they kept to writing each other for two months until the idea of meeting sprouted on paper. The idea was hinted by him in one letter, but came to fruition as a direct question from her in another. Before confirming that he would, in fact, fly to California, he went to the nearest ticket office to schedule and purchase the round-trip fare. Departing August 9th from Logan International Airport in Boston and landing at San Francisco International Airport that same night, his departure was settled.

The minor details were quickly hammered out in the following letters. They decided to meet that first night at a restaurant in Sausalito overlooking the bay—the kind with fine linen and an optional wine pairing menu—and for the rest of the week he would sightsee while she was at work. Sophia offered her couch as a bed at night. Not that she was writing love letters by any means, but her words did begin to take on a warm traction once the pieces fell into place.

He used Sophia's cheerfulness as motivation to advance with his preparations. He hadn't traveled since his South American adventure, and from packing to the many mental notes he was reminded of the energy it required. When everything was finalized, he took a towering breath. He was ready for a new beginning, even if it began as a week-long stay behind the façade of visiting an old friend. On departure day he embraced his parents and bid them farewell. With contented tears rolling down her cheeks, his mother told him she was happy to see the excitement return to his eyes. He laughed and reminded her he'd be back in a week, then grabbed his tattered mesh suitcase and dashed to the taxi waiting outside.

While rushing to his terminal, passing food and trinket stands, a small green pendant in the shape of an elephant caught his eye. Hung limply behind a glass case, it reminded him of Sophia's. Although pressed for time, he refused to take the token as coincidence and quickly tossed his loose bills at the vendor. Shoving the velvet jewelry box into his pocket, he boarded the plane.

His time in the air crawled: dated movies, deep tones coming through the intercom, overpriced cocktails that he nonetheless purchased. But eventually he landed, just as the sun was beginning to set. He exited the plane, found his luggage, and made his way outside where a crisp, foggy night greeted him.

After driving north for a short time, he reached the heart of the city. The hustle of the traffic and the city's outlandish design spiked his anxiety. Unlike on the East Coast where drivers would honk and cuss profusely before going about their business, San Franciscans merely cut him off, nearly forcing him off the road to his death while they zipped by in expensive luxury sedans.

He poked past Lombard and made his way over the iconic suspension bridge, painted deep amber by the lamps hanging overhead. As his car rolled along, his glances alternated between his directions and the road until the name of the exit he was to take became comprehensible.

His shoulders unbuckled when the giant green sign with his exit appeared, and after he veered from the freeway the traffic subsided enough to allow him to reread the directions more thoroughly. He took a right, traveled four blocks, and then another right until he finally pulled into the lot. He'd made it: boarded the plane, spent hours in the air, landed safely, found his luggage, and drove through the tumult of exotic traffic to reach her, all with some time to spare. His shoulders buckled into tight balls again when he realized he would face her after all.

Stepping from his car so he could shake away the jitters, smoothing the creases of his pants—running his fingers through his hair—his gaze wandered until it happened: his eyes accidently landed on her. She stood patiently, a silhouette leaning against the top rails of the stairs. Her pale skin was ornamented by the dim glow of light. It was the only attribute that matched his memory, but somehow he knew it could be no one else. The pinpoint shimmer between her collar bones could only be the pendant she never did without.

She stood there magnificently in a sleeveless, black lace dress. It was sultry, cutting deep down the middle of her chest, the fabric resting delicately like flower petals on her long thighs. Although still thin, she'd nonetheless gained some of the weight lost during the long stay in the jungle. The plain image of her as a friend and confidante was scrubbed suddenly and irrevocably away.

Could he have turned around and left, had it been simple enough, he would have considered it. Even as she was in that moment, standing there simply with her arms crossed from the cold, demonstrated more than he deserved. His heart thumped, pulsed near his throat to restrict his breathing, but her forgiving eyes and aloof smile enlisted his sloppy gait nonetheless. When he closed the distance between them, he could make out the white-blonde hair falling below her shoulders, a loose locket resting on the indent of her clavicle. Then the vanilla hit his nostrils, a scent ingrained so deeply into his memory of her that he'd repeatedly searched for the fragrance during his time in Boston. Sadly, none he discovered compared to the real thing; the closest was a shoddy papier-mâché ragdoll imitating a masterpiece. The scent melted him.

With another step, he could see the blue striations of her irises and the small indent of her lower lip. Her round nose with its thick nostrils and broad smile were the same, and instantly her familiar face showered him with memories he'd almost forgotten.

He was close enough for her simple words, "Hello, Greg," to carom through his skull and settle the layers of unjustified doubt. Standing there, Sophia was a completely different person from the one he remembered, as if a clean face and fresh set of clothes allowed another angelic form to enter her body.

They exchanged giddy hugs, complimented each other on how well the other looked, and walked inside the restaurant. All it took was that initial exchange to realize their relationship had shifted, and was now held by an intimate vise. He followed her steps; her long legs strode elegantly along to make it appear she was floating. He had an urge to place his palm on the back of her neck—pull her in, confess his love, kiss her—but he didn't act. They were led to a table outside. It was cold, but they remained because of the view. The horizon was a lit-up bar graph of buildings. Waves could be heard crashing against the craggy boulders near the ocean.

While looking over the menu, Greggory peeked at her, which caused her to peek at him, which led to an old, familiar bout of laughter. It didn't take long before they were reminiscing about their days together and citing the incredulous moments they experienced—"I honestly could not believe Clarua was drinking it. I nearly lost my shit. Crazy wild." The subject transitioned freely from their time together to more intimate thoughts they'd never shared with anyone. He was thankful for the diaphanous fuzz—a well-chosen bottle of pinot noir—facilitating their conversation. Their talk became so unmonitored he began to feel as though they were two people who never separated, old friends or high-school sweethearts joining for their usual Sunday meal. When dessert finally arrived, they'd delved into subjects much deeper than he ever planned. A hard romance pecked and threatened to crack through their friendship right there at the table. A long pause ensued where they just stared at one another. Her eyes twinkled.

It was only then he remembered the pendant in his pocket. It grew weighty. He hadn't thought much when he bought it, but the more they shared the more its meaning snowballed into something more, as if the stone's value ran parallel to the intimate moments they modestly disclosed to each other. Just before the burden of the gift became too heavy for him, he clawed in his pocket and thrust it before her. His hands did their best to remain steady. Sophia broke their contact to analyze what he held, before accepting the token. Upon further inspection, a smile cut deep into her face. She put it on, and presented a self-conscious pose to ask how it looked.

When he kept staring, she stroked the thing and asked "What?"

In just an evening, sitting there during the meal and afterward when they ventured as far as they could to the shore (the rock barricade blocked any further advancement), Greggory began to see signs of the monumental storm Sophia had seeded in him. Once it culminated, there would be only one opportunity to escape it—if he left immediately. But instead he simply stood there, knowing he was about to dive into a devastating, indelible love from which he would never recover.

When time permitted them to return to Sophia's apartment, Greggory insisted on sleeping on the couch, even though Sophia politely relinquished her bed.

During the days Sophia was gone, and at night they would stay up late, in simple conversation or occupying themselves with activities near where she lived. On the second night, they decided to watch a movie and wound up on the couch. When Sophia repositioned onto her other hip halfway through the film, she found Greggory's wandering eyes and broke into a hilarious fit of giggles. On the third night she boldly took his hand and led him to her bed, citing the discomfort of the couch. They remained separated by pillows and a wall of folded blankets. On the fourth night the wall came down. On the fifth, without speaking they climbed into bed and fit together to form a solid mold. Sophia periodically giggled and nuzzled his chest with her nose.

Towards the end of the week, without ever pressing their lips together or acting on their physical impulses, the two had become reacquainted enough for their past to dissolve into a foggy delusion.

Seriousness about their future together silently mounted, until the morning of his scheduled departure when they were forced to address the issue or risk ruin. He didn't need Sophia to say anything for him to know she couldn't bear him leaving, but he also felt he couldn't impose on her life without her request.

To his fortune, all it took was, "You know…" on her part for his eyes to find their way upward from his coffee mug and seize the invitation in her tone. He nodded in affirmation, but to ensure there was undeniable understanding she finished her proposition, "… you could stay here longer if you'd like."

Greggory rose from the wooden chair and walked the four feet separating them. As he hovered over her, his fingers speared her light strands of hair—he had the overwhelming sensation he was watching down on himself, not quite certain what his body was doing—before they moved to caress her cheek. His lips led the advance, and with all the intensity he'd foregone since his return from South America, he met the soft indentation of her lower lip. She pointed her chin upward to catch him. They moved to the bedroom to join bodies, as their souls already had. It was the first time of two—the second leading to the birth of their son—they would become drunk with passion and draw out the ardor running deep within their bones.

He had aggrandized the idea of lust since he was young, giving himself completely to the chivalrous hope of being driven mad by it. When he was little, he remembered make-believing that he was navigating on a ship to the end of the Earth after being inspired by the quality, and from that moment forward Greggory would indulge his charitable fantasy that the week together contained an infinite amount of lust as he'd never experienced in his past. But however much she might have drawn out the quality, truth be told, it had always been her balletic grace and ability to subdue his fervor that made him stay. He needed that more than anything.

The levelness they experienced with each other deepened their love without pause during the following months. Although never expressing themselves through the revelry of passion as that determining Sunday morning, they became dependent on one another. In discovering each other, they began to discover a side of themselves they never knew existed. The only lamentation they ever had, even when the poverty line was a mere step away, was that they could not go back in time to meet sooner.

While living near the city, they became rich in love despite their lack of many possessions. It was their lack of possessions, in fact, that allowed them to pick up and move to the middle of nowhere, to a place where the stars shone as brightly as they recalled in their memories. It was the last piece of the puzzle to their happiness. After a month of negotiation for the small one-bedroom the size of a guesthouse, they spent all their savings to purchase the plot of land with the structure from a sympathetic farmer. Greggory found a job one town over, and Sophia accepted a part-time position from home. When everything was finalized, they moved into their new home where nobody could disrupt their eager solitude.

After buying groceries for the week, Greggory and Sophia managed twenty dollars to their names. They celebrated with red wine and baguette slices topped with cheap salami and cheese. As they watched the marvelous red and purple sun sink behind the hills, with a clinking of their glasses they cheered to a new life together on Forester Road.

EMMA

When she arrived on the Fourth, Reid and Greggory were lounging outside talking about a subject whose beginning she'd missed. Having not seen them immersed in conversation often, she considered whether it was impolite to intrude on their time together. Greggory saw her first, and in response to her questioning glance he offered a smile.

The wrinkles canvassing his cheeks and forehead seemed more shallow, his posture more welcoming since the beginning of summer. She sat, and they included her. Together they enjoyed playful banter, spirits set high by the holiday, well into the afternoon. Even among many memories of the three of them together, that afternoon stood out in her mind for a long time to come. Greggory even laughed at some of the small jokes they shared.

When morning ceded to afternoon, after Greggory kept his stare on her for too long, she asked, "Hmm?" and he clarified, "I was just saying that you two better be off soon. If you've decided to watch those things, you may as well get there at a decent hour. Off, off." He waved his hands.

Not that she'd completely forgotten her plans with Reid, but time had admittedly passed much more quickly than she anticipated. She looked down at her phone: three thirty.

Heeding Greggory's advice, she and Reid made their way to the working pickup parked under the carport. Anxiousness to be left alone with him sparked deep in her body.

"Please don't break this one," Greggory's requested before waving them off.

With a sharp *clnk clnk* the engine woke and a cloud of gray smoke blew from the tailpipe. Both took a long look at Greggory's property receding in the side mirrors as they turned onto Forester and headed towards their destination.

Reid asked for detailed directions more than once—he was trying to figure where they were heading—but Emma replied with only simple answers.

"If we miss our turn though... Yes it's on you, don't give me that look... Well I *am* following the directions, just—Hey! Don't do that! I'm driving over here, you little freak."

When she was younger, she'd taken this route with her parents for some reason or other—her doctor was down this way? Whatever the reason, it always took exactly an hour and ten minutes to get to the distant town. The drive started at the familiar country roads then moved into a forest some distance away, before finally climbing the mountain and descending to the old mining strip of 1850's buildings—a western version of some antiquated European town tucked along the Swiss Alps. The drive felt longer in her youth. She remembered playing that puerile game where she'd jump over the landscape with her fingers while distractedly asking if they were there yet.

The truck slowly advanced from the rolling hills into a closet of pines, oaks, and coastal lives. Outside, the various shades of green and brown passed like a camouflaged tarp being pulled away in some illusory trick. The smell of pine and dried foliage suffused the thin mountain air while rays of light flittered through the trees and splayed onto the road. As she rolled down the window, the draft whipped thin strands of hair into her face. A buoyant feeling coursed through her body, causing her to laugh lightly.

Except for the simple directions, little else was spoken between them. Reid tinkered with the knob controlling the radio. Broken songs occupied most of the frequencies, so they settled again on the station Emma discovered a few weeks prior. When she peeked over, Reid was bobbing his head. She turned back to the window and laughed, and in turn he looked over and smirked at her hair blowing wildly. Every so often they'd steal a glance, and wonder how they'd become so comfortable.

The ascent through the mountains eventually leveled off, and after another ten minutes the tunnel of trees opened to a grand painting of the valley below. If they looked closely— which they did—they could make out the microscopic dots marking various towns and structures.

Before they descended, before the trees some hundred yards ahead engulfed them again, Emma abruptly hollered "Here!" and pointed to a narrow alcove of dirt near the road.

With a jerk of the wheel, he redirected the truck and firmly pressed the brakes. He shot her a devious, tight-lipped expression to which she merely shrugged. "Sorry." There were two other vehicles tucked in the small recess.

"Here?" Reid confirmed.

She'd never visited the place herself, but there were whispers amongst her friends suggesting this was it. They grabbed the quilt blanket and sweaters and headed to the trailhead.

She knew it as "Bill's Place" or more loosely as "Bill's," but they walked past a wooden post with an officiously mounted placard designating the region in maps and GPS devices after Samuel Penfield Taylor who made his fortune during the Gold Rush (the same Samuel Penfield Taylor who was previously thought to be the late grandson of the Declaration of Independence George Taylor) as "Taylor Regional Park."

Most of what she'd heard surrounded the spectacular view waiting for them at the top of the trail, but one tale set out as a caution: locals were apparently quite unpleasant to outsiders. Those privy to the details of the location were reprimanded—one time severely she was told, beat to a pulp—if they disclosed specifics. She wasn't quite sure if the threats elicited from the stories were idle (she guessed they were considering the park was technically regional) or if she was even considered a local, but she remained aware of the warning as they carried along.

She knew they were in the right place when she saw the second brown placard at the trailhead, a landmark that had become almost more famous than the place itself. There were pen marks and some apparent dents, but it stood erect nonetheless. The sign withstood the many misdirected outbursts and beatings from those—angry teens—loyal to the name "Bill's." There was an infamous story in which a kid tried burning the post with a lighter only to be defeated by the flame-retardant wood sealer. When he came back the next day with a bottle of lighter fluid, a park ranger happened to stumble by to stop him. Similar attempts were made, and botched in similar fashions, until the sign was thought to be cursed and became resentfully accepted as a permanent intruder.

The sign glinted in its battered copper dullness as they walked by. Emma was uncertain if it was a good or bad omen of the journey ahead, until her worst fear materialized. Two men were headed down the trail in their direction. One was fitted with a mountain beard hanging like a dead rodent to his chest, and the (somewhat) more attractive one carried a long shaven face. When she saw them, her step stuttered as she considered the warnings she was given but failed to disclose to Reid.

As they drew closer, she could make out their studied manner. The bearded one held out his hand in distracted argument. They were completely absorbed in conversation, the commentary emboldened in part by a half-empty string of plastic that once contained a six-pack. Just before passing she could hear the clean-shaven one crack a joke and cause an outburst of laughter.

Then, without any warning, like a donation to the homeless, the bearded one handed Emma the plastic ribbon with three cans of beer still dangling on. The only words he offered were more of a side-note: "You two have fun." She fumbled to catch them, and when she looked back she was offered no explanation. Their backs remained turned, and they continued their sprightly conversation—arms still elaborately flailing.

She turned to Reid for his advice only to receive an earnest shrug: "Might as well keep them." Not daring to litter but considering the tokens more a burden than a blessing, she carried the cans with the rest of their items and proceeded onward.

The trail was chalked with loose dirt, and the shallow air began to heat as they ascended. Even the shade became uncomfortable at some point deep into their walk. The heat felt as if it were ready to break through the soft shadows given the opportunity, and the trees took refuge within their impenetrable bark.

After snaking through the forest and climbing up several cutbacks, they were high enough where the trees began to surrender to more hardy shrubs and grasses. Their walk continued upward as the land to the right of the trail eroded and became a vertical drop with a view of the valley. The sea of trees below extended to a yellow shore of hills in the far distance. Not that Emma was afraid of heights, but nonetheless she ran her hand along the mountainside to her left. She wasn't certain if her heart skipped along from the fear of death or the glory of the view.

When the trail opened to a rock landing the size of a baseball diamond, Emma announced that they were *here*.

There was still was an hour or so of daylight, and the temperature's daily plummet was just beginning, so lethargy settled their movements. They walked towards the side of the landing and took to a mild descent through long grass and craggy rocks. Emma smiled at the private clearing they discovered tucked into the mountainside. The sweeping wind pushed into their bodies as they fanned out the blanket, and before long they were sprawled out and talking freely. Their conversation drifted until Reid remarked, "So, should we try these?"

The cans sat patiently to the side of the blanket, nestled in the dirt. It was a dangerous affair, something they were told they shouldn't meddle with, yet lying there so innocuously (and even more enticing as a symbol of rebellion), the cans were tempting.

They watched the stationary aluminum pods for a minute until Emma decisively grabbed one and pulled the tab. The can opened with a pop, and light foam boiled over the lid before quickly receding to a pale yellow ring. Reid followed suit by removing the second. Before tasting, Emma took a whiff of the liquid—a habit she acquired early in life—in an attempt to discern its taste. Wide-eyed and raising an eyebrow, she shifted her head to Reid. They cheered with a muted clink of the cans, and she proceeded to swallow down two large gulps of the lukewarm beverage.

Her gulps were large enough to postpone the content's taste for several seconds, but once recognition travelled up her tongue and hit her brain, her face immediately puckered. She shivered in disgust, clicking her tongue outward, then grinding it against her teeth to rid herself of the lingering flavor.

"Tastes like piss, huh?" Reid chimed, enjoying her pain.

She nodded. It truly did taste like piss, but that being said it never stopped her from continuing to sip from the can as if somehow expecting to acquire the taste—all the way until it was empty.

The experience was far from appealing, and she couldn't understand why her peers worshipped alcohol. The effects didn't hit until later, and even then they were minor, but at the same time the conversation between her and Reid admittedly became looser.

Her body found itself spread out on the quilt, unguarded. She propped her head on one of her elbows. The humming breeze carried the scents of the forest and something sweet she couldn't quite name. The sun began setting. The evening became watery as they spoke between comfortable silences, talking about grand ideas with little merit to their accuracy. At some point, she opened her eyes to the wind whipping the nearby grass into a flurry of motion. Her gaze drifted to Reid, who was facing her. He spoke to her in a lowered voice. *What did he say?* She nodded nonetheless.

She later couldn't recall exactly what they spoke about, but she remembered his euphonic tone—the same as when he first picked her up—and how he watched her lips. She realized she'd been chewing the corner of her mouth. Although his expression showed no sign of change, he must have realized what she was thinking, the way she was watching him, because something was different in how he returned her gaze, as if he discovered some hidden truth about her thoughts and how the world operated.

From that realization, or from the red glow of dusk, or perhaps even from the beer, a tinge of color crowned her cheeks. She grabbed at the excess folds of the quilt blanket and submerged her head as best she could. Managing to cover her mouth fully, not trusting her body from acting on impulse, her eyes wandered to his lips again.

He smiled in return but remained gentlemanlike in his approach. More time passed, and darkness overtook day. Each time she looked up he was repositioned a few inches closer, never formally moving towards her but rather making small adjustments to his posture. Like a magician's trick the gap was suddenly halved, and then halved again. She could smell the fresh linen on his clothes as it mixed with the peppery scent of his skin. She could feel his steady breath. Everything felt amplified, yet all she could see was his face looking at hers. She could count the pores on his nose. She summoned whatever innate haughtiness she could muster to suppress the urge to leap up onto him. Her fingers were sweaty as they gripped the folds of the quilt. Betraying her, her lips rose above the ridged blanket. They were face-to-face, and in that rarefied moment when time stops, just before the plunge to your fate, Reid hesitated only briefly.

And in that brief hesitation an unexpected *boom* interrupted the moment. Two more explosions rang like a bell off the mountain before hitting their ears with a clatter. Their attention was forced over the valley to three patterned balls of red and blue and white expanding and then disappearing into the night.

Then another show began, farther in the distance, initiating a barrage of fireworks that soon included four shows at once. The explosions reverberated throughout the valley, stifled only slightly by the atmosphere between them, until the noise reached a steady stream of thumps like the clapping of a drum. Ten minutes in, they could smell the gunpowder nesting contently in the basin of the valley. The saturated air, the clamor, the dazzling colors all made for an impressive spectacle.

What must have been forty-five minutes passed until each celebration ended in the order it began. The sky returned to a void of blackness as the final explosion flickered like a candle on the horizon until it too was snuffed.

Emma exhaled a quiet "Wow," and nearby claps and hollers of excitement reminded her that she wasn't the only one who knew about this spot. She thought about shouting to return the camaraderie, but in the end she couldn't move herself to speak. She peered out into the distance, waiting, suspecting that the pause was merely a ruse to draw the audience back to the performance.

REID

They sat like statues on the quilt blanket. For a moment, everything was quiet. Even the trees stopped rustling, taking deep gulps of carbon dioxide in the relief that the world remained intact. But nearby creatures tentatively began to skitter and stir, steadily returning the balance of noise to the vacuum of space like osmosis. Most importantly, his thumping heart finally returned to the imperceptible normalcy he was accustomed to.

Daring to look over at Emma, he desperately wanted to again become the object of her gaze, to feel the invincible weight he felt when she looked at him. But as he sat watching her body—seeing the distraction in her eyes—he knew the moment had passed.

He let out a drawn exhale. Before this evening he'd felt such an intense connection with her only once: that first night in his grandpa's truck. Her haughtiness—the way her eyes could burn into your skull and stop you in your tracks—drew him to her. Since then, he'd repeatedly vied to coax that hidden dragon out from its obscurity, but Emma was clever in how she would avoid eye contact, the way she deflected glances and re-positioned herself. He had begun to think the experience was in his imagination, an illusion of her superior inner quality.

That was until just a half-an-hour ago when she looked him over with earnest interest, as if the second half of her personality had switched on. She watched him like a curious scientist as he gingerly pushed towards her. He wasn't expecting it, but he also wasn't certain he'd have another opportunity. The need to act or risk losing everything bore into him.

They walked away from the saw-like horizon of pines and into the moonlit forest. Although the same route, the trail became completely new with nightfall. The temperature dropped. The hoots of owls and click of insects replaced the gregarious chatter of birds, and the fragmented moonlight reflected objects into pools of shadow.

Their walk was unhurried, but his mind raced. Every five or six steps he'd detect the fringes of their sweaters brushing together. About halfway to the car, the brushing advanced to small bumps at the elbow, and finally their bodies flowed against one another—gently, like leaves falling onto a lake. Emma's arousing scent of privet caught him and in the long stretch leading to the truck the rough texture of her pinky glazed against his, sending a shot through his body.

He was about to make a move for her hand, but just as earlier the timing proved unfavorable: the stretch of gravel ran out, and they reached the bulky shadow of the truck. He'd unknowingly parked too close.

Except for the clanking of metal on metal and the engine humming in its fatigue, the cabin remained quiet on the ride home. The brush along the side of the road whirred past like dark, dense clouds. He looked over at her, wondering if she was considering the same things. Her posture was an ambiguous title to a closed book, refusing any insight into its content.

Then a frown spread across her face, and her eyes dropped in thought before she spoke. "Reid? Do you ever get sad after a happy moment?"

He wasn't sure what to say, and tried deflecting with silence. She continued, "Sometimes I get sad because moments end. It's weird that things just end." She held her hands in front of her as if the words were a riddle she was far from of solving.

In a soft voice, he tried consoling, "True, but sometimes endings are beginnings to something better."

He waited for her response, but it never came. The silence between them ate the time, and in a quick passing they were rolling down Forester at a somber fifteen miles per hour. The truck's rubber tires rolled to a stop on the side of road across from Emma's long driveway. He'd hoped to talk longer, sit longer, but Emma hopped out of the vehicle.

The night had grown frigid, and they could just begin to see the condensation on their breath. He followed her across the street and was relieved when she turned to face him. Her pale face was flush with moonlight. The moment on the mountain, her comments in the truck, made him uncertain how to proceed.

She was about to give him a hug goodbye when he finally chose to act. His words unfortunately came out forced: "Hey Emma, I've been thinking, and I've made up my mind that I really like you."

Her eyes became serious like warning signs, and this time she was the one to deflect. "I like you too." Her reaction surprised him.

She went to turn, but he grabbed her wrist with his cold hand, "No, wait."

He made to slide his own hand against her beautiful, clammy one, but she peeled away.

"I want to take you on a date." Try as he might to push past what was happening, the quick unexpected decline, he was unable to. His words were strained.

"Reid, we spend a lot of time together as it is."

Her posture warned she might flee at any second. Her gaze cut away.

He had already lost completely and had no idea why he continued, but he couldn't help himself at this point, "You make time slow down and speed up all at once when I'm with you."

He looked down at the ground embarrassed. He hated that he had practiced the lines before tonight. They were genuine, but given the new outcome they didn't have the same effect. A gust blew into them; the silence between them was diaphanous.

When he finally looked up to her, her head was cocked away. He'd said too much. The pipe burst and scalded him.

"*Please* Emma—Emma, please—go on another date with me."

"I can't." She barely formed the words, choked by her own reasons, but the truth was clear and hit like internecine warfare.

Emma turned and started walking down the trail to her house. The crunch in the gravel grew fainter until it disappeared with her silhouette.

The taut air loosened, but nonetheless anguish spilled thickly over him like molasses sliding off a spoon. He stood quietly, wondering what on Earth just happened. Nearby a toad croaked, as if it had been politely waiting for the awkward moment to end. He wanted to chase her and plead his case. He wanted to kiss her lips and forehead. He wanted to yell in rage. But instead he simply acquiesced to her rejection in silence.

He sat down right in the middle of the potholed street as another chilling gust penetrated his sweater. He didn't remember how long he was there, but eventually he clambered back into the truck and rattled his way home. He parked, and a rally of cricket chirps sounded as he made his way past the wicker rockers to the front door. Remembering how his grandfather had questioned him last time—the deadly question, "How'd it go?"—he stopped with his hand on the knob. The door swayed open with its notorious creak, but instead of entering he slid down the jamb, knees bent to embrace his body, and sat there. The moon illuminated half of his face, half of his body, while the other half disappeared into the darkness of the house. He pressed his face into his hands and muttered the single word, "Why?"

EMMA

She didn't dare look back until she was sure his features were out of sight. When a wall of oleanders and a veil of white fog blocked her view, she turned to see if she could make out his dark figure. Nothing. She returned to the trail and began kicking a fist-sized rock along the path in front of her. Her father always told her to toss those kinds into the nearby stream since it could be bad to run them over, but she continued kicking it regardless. Making a zigzagged route, she followed her errant punts until the house arose from the fog.

A part of her begged to relent to him—sport an ear-to-ear grin (the silly shitfaced one she knew was deep inside)—but once his words came out, her rigidity wouldn't allow her the pleasure. Perhaps the reason, so she told herself, was that he was here only for the summer. It was certainly more accommodating than the other she discovered while staring at him in the mountains: that he could ruin her with his love. She would fall too far and her senses would be too far gone if she caved. In a single effortless swoop, he would be able to devastate her. Then, he would leave. Fortunately, the fireworks started before anything happened. Fortunately, she came to her senses before he tried anything else.

She lifted her chin with the responsibility of her decision and gave the rock one more solid kick, sending it skirting underneath the oleanders and out of site. Confident in her rigidity, she made her way to the front door. A primal moment which never started could never unravel her.

III

GREGGORY

Shortly after their move to Forester, Greggory had established a routine. It began with waking just before the sun rose, when the house was beginning to accept dawn's flagrant rays through the window above the bedpost. They never installed curtains on the windows (only the one in the front room afforded any sort of barricade against the light in the form a jalousie), so the dresser across the room always lit a blazing orange at first light. It caused Greggory to stir from his sleep, until eventually his internal clock made the habit of waking even after the dresser was relocated.

He would then take exactly five minutes to watch Sophia sleep. Often she appeared so saintly that he would place his palm to her chest to ensure it was still rising and falling. Once satisfied, he would walk amongst the murky shadows to the kitchen and begin boiling enough water for two mugs of tea. After determining that everything was in its proper place, he made his way to the porch, swept the seat of the weathered rocker from the dust it had accumulated through the night, and sat waiting for the flooding light to shatter the stillness of the world.

The climate on Forester had always fascinated him. As in a desert, the day could begin at forty degrees and climb to over a hundred by noon. He enjoyed watching the dew on the grass evaporate and the birds cantillate with renewed faith every morning.

The whistle signaling the water was ready always brought another satisfied smile. A little game had sprouted between him and Sophia where they would wager how quickly she could remove the kettle. The chime always disappeared within a few seconds, adding another tick to her long winning streak. In the next few moments Sophia would come out bearing a smile and two mugs. He did his best to refrain from looking back to her, in fear he'd spoil what followed.

After placing the mugs on the stand between their chairs, she would wrap her arms around him from behind. Her hair fell into his face, and the two elephant pendants dangled on his shoulder. Her vanilla scent enveloped him. Without fail she would rest on him, kiss his cheek, and ever-so-faintly tickle his ear with a whisper: "Hey, you... I love you." He'd scoff playfully before turning to study her eyes, and then he'd tap her lips with a tender kiss. Only after that small moment would she sit in her own chair. Together they would sip their tea.

They became so precise in the timing of their routine that years later each could disinter the moods and health of the other from only a few seconds delay or quickening in each of their parts. If Greggory heard the whistle chime too long, he returned to the house to fetch ibuprofen tablets for her headache. Likewise, if Sophia waited too long for the kettle, she'd reach into the kitchen drawer for the thermometer.

It was the thermometer in fact that rooted the only argument to seriously jeopardize the foundation of their relationship. Their habit of grabbing it in times of uncertainty led to a unique dependency on the item. The irony was that he almost didn't keep the thing when they were unpacking. He remembered sorting out the important essentials from the junk when they first moved in. At that moment the thermometer was almost tossed away, but as it happened Greggory picked it from the pile intended for the garbage and—reasoning it was small and easy to keep—placed it in the non-garbage pile. The thermometer eventually made its way to a drawer in the kitchen where it sat without a thought for quite some years. It was a mishap stemming from a romantic gesture that finally allowed the tiny device to see daylight and acquire its important role in their lives.

Two days after their three-year anniversary—which they marked from the date Greggory initiated his exorbitant act of passion—there was a rare summer storm. The puffy grey thunderheads threatened ominously until one tiny rain droplet birthed streams in a matter of minutes. The rain pounded the roof of the small home, and as the tapping compounded Greggory became worried it would flood the house. Sophia on the other hand gleamed with a mad excitement.

The words she cried—"Isn't it marvelous?"—and that crazy look in her eyes would project in his mind like a film scene looping endlessly. The storm picked up until Greggory moved past the concern of a flood and instead worried about the torrential wind threatening to tear apart the unstable little box they lived in completely. Howling gusts shook the foundation, and roiling thunder and lightning stormed seemingly right above their rooftop.

His concern only evoked another shriek of excitement from her. But what's more, she wasn't content to be merely a witness;

she wanted to be part of the spectacle. She pranced to the back room and left Greggory alone to watch the falling sheets press against their kitchen window, creating miniature cascading waves that streamed into the yard. While patiently waiting for the moment their house was plowed, he heard bare footsteps, and then felt a tapping on his shoulder.

She wore a sheer nightdress and a confident smile. He'd become so accustomed to their slow-moving romance—given more to words and safety than sexuality—that when she climbed on him, embraced him with her intoxicating scent, it proved to be too much for him to protest. Straddling him, she let her body fall into his as she whispered indistinguishable words into his ear.

"Babe?" she finally inquired, in the sweetest of voices.

The little house began to tremble with another round of thunder.

"Can we please go outside and kiss like they do in the movies?"

She sat on him in that dark house in the middle of nowhere without wearing any undergarments. Every tiny movement of her hips was multiplied a thousandfold into his body. He realized she had caught him, played him like a sucker.

With his formless caresses on her collarbone he tried to prolong their inevitable venture outside. Although he was successful in stalling briefly, it wasn't long before he was swiftly (and reluctantly) pulled by the tips of his fingers. The weather *had* become slightly milder, he tried reasoning. Sophia cracked open the door, and—as if trying to persuade them to stay inside—a sweep of rushing wind pushed them a step back. Nonetheless, she led him headfirst into the splintering rain. Like the beautiful warrior she was, Sophia proceeded one step at a time even while dragging him behind her. They stepped into a frigid pocket of air underneath their awning where the odors of wet earth, sweet sap, rotted leaves, melted wood, and boggy hay culminated into the unique smell belonging to winter. Thick droplets plunked in a symphony of natural tones on the metal eaves and growing puddles. Still barefoot, she led him deeper into the storm. With their yard looking more like a lake, she guided him onto a shoal before turning to face him.

Her nightgown had become completely translucent, and her body underneath was naked and sharp. With the tuck of his hand on her arching back, he surrendered to her fierce act of love and pulled her to him. Truth be told, he could barely see due to needles of water soaring stridently into his eyes, but nonetheless he jumped to her wet lips. They clung to each other as only those who forget the world around them can. Without concern for who was watching (not that anyone would be insane enough to remain outside in conditions like these), his hand chased the ripples of her protected, spiritual body. His fingers smoothed over her breast as he kissed her neck. Her fingers moved fluidly through his hair, and after tugging—satisfied and with a giggle—she determined they'd been outside long enough. She wrapped her palm around his finger and led him to the warmth of their home.

Although slopping wet, she refused to allow the passion between them to dissipate. They kissed greedily and became lost in one another. She stripped off the soaking nightgown fastened to her body and threw it into a corner of the foyer. Hurriedly, as if there were only moments left, she worked the shirt over his head and tossed that into oblivion as well. She couldn't quite unclasp the buckle of his belt as she pushed him toward the sanctuary of their room, but Lord knows she tried. They rocked and clashed into the hallway in their pursuit, and when they finally entered the dark bedroom she climbed on top of him. She shook with unbridled excitement as he grabbed onto her vulnerable hipbones.

In the half-moment before they began, her head tipped near his ear and she tickled him with the familiar words, "Hey, you... I love you." When the room around him stopped spinning wildly, a bout of energy surged through him.

Months later, they found that their second grand moment of passion had resulted in a baby boy they named Paul. In the more immediate aftermath, however, Greggory's cheeks and forehead radiated with the heat of a fever. *That* was when the thermometer would first be removed from the drawer.

After three days of hoping the fever would lift, he traveled the long distance to the doctor's office to discover he had pneumonia. After the diagnosis, Sophia refused to let Greggory out of her sight. As his body trembled violently, he wondered why he ever agreed to such a ludicrous venture. She repeatedly apologized for the impromptu demon occupying her soul with, "Sorry, honey. I don't know what came over me."

But he could never stay mad at her for long—how could he? Eventually his sickly fever lifted, and the memory was stored as a relic. The thermometer, however, retained its important place in their lives. When their son was born, they relied on it to guide their uncertainty. The routine of grabbing the thermometer became so habituated that Sophia began picking it up during many other erroneous instances as well, such as when Greggory moaned more than usual about chores or when their newborn son refused to eat breakfast.

So, when the instrument that had quelled so many of her apprehensions was misplaced, it caused the single largest threat to their relationship. At first she simply approached Greggory to ask if he knew its whereabouts. He sat outside distracted by large blue pages that—when deciphered, at least—would allow him to continue building the second bedroom and storage closet of their house. With a wave of his hand, naïve to the gravity of the situation, he dismissed her question. Sophia was a patient woman, admittedly more patient than he, so she returned to searching. Becoming more agitated with each consecutive failed attempt at discovery, she eventually asked him again.

"Hun, you must have some idea where you could have put it?"

"Where *I* put it?" he scoffed without lifting his eyes from the pages. He was never truly aware nor intending to be critical, but when he fell back to memory, he could understand how he must have sounded. "I haven't seen the thing since you cleaned it off last week."

A ticking bomb, she continued tersely, "You're always rearranging things. Can you just think for a moment where it might have gone?"

Refusing to be distracted by such a petty subject, he once again answered without lifting his eyes. Greggory had always swept dilemmas he was indifferent to aside with sociable humor, but when he continued in his jocose manner—"I'm not sure where it could have gone Honey, because *I* didn't have it last."—Sophia exploded.

With scorn tucked neatly in her words, she rebutted, "Well you must not care about our son if you're not even going to give a second thought to where *you* put it. He's sick in there you know."

He finally looked up at her, "I care about our son."

With the deranged satisfaction at being able to dominate his emotions, she watched in silence. A gloating smile spread over her face.

"I care about our goddamn son, Sophia, and I don't know where the goddamn thermometer is. Okay?" his voice rose as he rifled through the words.

"Mhm," was all she cooed with a mocking nod before floating back inside.

For the next hour Greggory sat muttering some form of, "I didn't touch no goddamn fuckin' thermometer. I didn't."

The argument remained ablaze until the end of the day, when Greggory decided it was best to take refuge on the couch for the night. One night turned into another as the sight of the other drove each a step further than they had intended to let it go. Soon the nights turned to weeks, and their seasonal struggle bloomed into a longer affair. They remained cohesive around their son's needs and the maintenance of the household, but that consistency almost became a hindrance to their reunification. They used their respective contributions to the household, the parts that are necessary but nobody truly enjoys doing, as logical ammunition about being in the right.

In their spare time alone, they rediscovered guilty pleasures once enjoyed as individuals. Greggory could think and act and do as he wished—even taking up the puerile avocation of carving, which resulted in a birdhouse that hung in the adjacent field. Their refusal to give in eventually led to the continuation of their quarrel more out of convenience than conviction. He left his clothes in the living room cabinet and would make it home just before the leftovers turned cold. In his absence Sophia quarantined the bathtub most mornings, and the pictures, clothes, and womanly objects left in her bedroom experienced a spaciousness in ways they'd never had before. Perhaps with the baby and their aging bodies, each felt some lingering need to be seen as a separate person one last time before fully committing to the other, but at the climax of their vital disunion they alarmingly succeeded in that goal.

Their routine of waking in the morning and venturing outside for tea was what ultimately saved the relationship. During the days of their trial separation neither drafted the courage to terminate the process of traveling to the front yard and listening to the noisy clamor of the waking world. Sophia for obvious reasons omitted any whisper into Greggory's ear, but together they sat and sipped on their mugs. And although neither would admit it, they often communicated through their sips.

From seeing each other every morning, the appreciation for his individual freedom began to wither away. He found himself tossing and turning during the cold winter nights on the couch, and the thought of waking up to the din of morning silence became unbearable. During one fitful night Greggory crept into

Sophia's room in an attempt to overcome the angst, to seek evidence that he wasn't the only one who couldn't sleep. To his disappointment, she slept soundly with her arms placidly wrapped around her big, down-feathered pillow. He checked on Paul, in his crib also contently sleeping. Greggory had the malicious thought of "bumping" the crib so he could indulge in his son's cry, but he suppressed the urge. He returned to his disjointed nest on the couch, where he tossed and turned the rest of the night.

Then there was the night he woke screaming. The cause of his shrieks came—with an acute clarity he'd experienced only once before—from the awareness he was, in fact, the one who misplaced the thermometer. He didn't remember why, but he distinctly recalled laying the instrument of his grief deep in the cabinet above the fridge rather than in the drawer it had made into its home. To be certain, he rose from the couch and tiptoed to the kitchen. As expected, it was lying there indifferently, smiling at him, in the dark confines of the cupboard.

The next morning while Sophia was still sleeping, he abandoned their matutinal process and instead began his long commute to work early, leaving the thermometer lying on the kitchen counter for her to discover. When Greggory returned, just a bit later than normal, Sophia was already off to bed. The thermometer, however, was no longer on the kitchen table: a good sign.

He awoke the next day as usual, just prior to sunrise, and immediately put the kettle on. Outside, he counted the minutes while he sat, awaiting his fate. The world delayed its waking as the sun peeked over the hill a minute late, just long enough for him to let out a deep sigh, and then finally for the kettle to toot. Not long afterwards the creak of the front door sounded, and Sophia placed the mugs on the table. She made her way silently to her chair and stared out to the yellow hills before them. In her best attempt she gazed straight ahead without turning her neck. She relished the anticipation. He did his best to stare ahead also.

Then, as she was magically known to do, she giggled. The giggles evolved into raucous howls as the spate revealed the ridiculousness of their woes.

The largest fissure in their relationship ended with Greggory placing his hand atop hers. They almost immediately began talking about the strange details of being apart.

The next day he called to have the couch removed. He cited to Sophia that it was ratty and worn. The day after that he took her by the hand and led her to the end of their property, across the street, and finally up the hill. The trail was cluttered with coquettish foxtails and needlegrass. When she inquired where they were heading, all he would reply was, "Somewhere special."

While tossing and turning on that lumpy couch, he fantasized about what he would do when they made peace. His vision began small, imagining himself telling her how much he loved her, but as the lonely nights continued it fabricated into a grand sailing vessel. He could see a more courageous version of himself taking her confidently by the hand and leading her on some romantic expedition. He could see a more elegant version talking in whispers over a candlelit dinner near the ocean, or a more suave version seducing her by bold intervention. His passion was immense, his movements sexy. The language he would use was ineffable, but it would certainly come to mind when the timing was right.

Unfortunately, given the rapidity with which they made up, the timing never proved just right. But Greggory *did* plan on following through with at least one of his night's vows. Their bodies made it to the top of the knoll, and they rested under the shade of the only oak in the area while they caught their breaths. Once he began to breathe normally, he dabbed his sweat with the ends of his shirt and proceeded.

"I wanted to bring you up here because it has the best view, but also…" he scratched his eyebrow as he pondered his next words, "we've lived out here just shy of five years now." He got down on his knee and held her hand, "And in that five years of living together we never got married. I know we've had talks about it but never did it. So, I was wondering if you would marry me, Sophia."

The words spurted out more quickly than he would have liked, like a rock skipping along water, but nonetheless they were out. Although they had been living as a married couple since they moved, any discussions about a formal marriage had diffused and decayed once they calculated the costs of a proper wedding. The idea was consequently stored in the dusty, unused attics of their minds.

So, when he slipped the band around her finger and she put her hands over her mouth and watched him, he knew she was surprised. He continued on in his self-consciousness, "I wish I could have gotten you a bigger ring, but I also brought this so we can carve our names in the tree." Greggory fished for his tiny Swiss pocketknife and flipped the blade from its red casing.

Although he was embarrassed, she nonetheless jumped onto him—"Woah! Knife! Sophia! Babe!"—making everything instantly better as only she could.

She nestled into his chest as they rolled around on the ground. By that point she was crying and wiping her pink nose in attempts to appear respectable, which only caused another round of laughter.

"You're beautiful, babe," He encouraged.

"Sure we are. Me crying, snot shooting from my nose, and you soaked with sweat and dirt. What a couple."

He corrected, "A beautiful couple." They smiled and kissed again.

After lying in the red dirt, convinced they were the luckiest pair of united souls ever to exist, they made their way to the oak. The knife hadn't been sharpened from its last use, but he managed to lodge it into the bark and chisel away the letters of their names. He ran the blade over the grooves until he was satisfied and then stepped back. He nodded, kissed Sophia on the forehead, then nodded again, certain that the lettering was entrenched for a long time to come.

They sat beneath the oak and watched the world pass by. The eye-level cumulus clouds floated and cast splotched shadows over the contoured valley, and the ground they sat on was damp from summer showers. Sunrays whisked through the clouds, highlighting the edges into silver linings. They could visibly see their little house, and would have stayed overlooking the secluded valley and savoring their simple, deep love for the rest of the day, had Paul not been left at home. They were really gone only briefly while he slept in his crib, but Sophia's protective motherly panic would build quickly if they lingered. They raced down the hill almost as quickly as they charged up. When they reached his room, Paul was sound asleep—not even remotely aware, let alone concerned, with the titanic happenings of his parents. Sophia placed her hand on the wooden edge of the cradle. Greggory placed his hand on hers.

EMMA

Looking at her phone, she opened her bedroom door, almost exactly as her father opened his—so close that it almost appeared calculated—and the two stood face to face.

"Hey, Peeks."

"Hey."

"You're going to Greggory's?"

"Yeah, I'm running a little late."

His head tilted as he smiled, but his brows furrowed. Her thoughts were still stuck on Reid, on facing him.

"Oh, I won't keep you then. But, I have some time off work coming up." He sounded almost relieved telling her.

He often said he had free time coming up, but almost as often other things would come up before it actually happened.

"That's nice, Dad."

"Yeah, and I was thinking, if you're up for it we could go fishing. We haven't done that in a long time." By now they were walking down the hallway together, towards the front door.

"Okay," she answered distractedly, but somehow the comment settled confidence inside her. He pushed out the door, leaving him behind in the house.

"Okay. We'll talk more about it later. Have a good day at Greggory's," he called before she shut the door.

Her walk was hurried, her mind filled with the optimistic hope that somehow Reid would be unaffected by her decision, that somehow they could remain friends. After arriving, she sighed in relief when Greggory answered the door. She followed him to the kitchen table, searching for Reid's blurred motion in her periphery. When he didn't appear within a few minutes, her anticipation grew, and soon she found her finger tapping on the table. After a few more minutes of distracted talk, her attention trailed off completely. She tried to refocus on Greggory's words, but her emerging concern didn't allow the luxury. Just before she explicitly asked about his whereabouts, Reid sauntered in from outside.

Her first reaction was reprieve. She sat upright in her chair like a meerkat and her nods to Greggory's banter became vigorous, her agreement exaggerated. When she finally took the chance to glance in Reid's direction, his indifferent and closed posture immediately shut down any possibility of a greeting. She slumped back into her seat.

He walked to the cupboard for a glass and filled it at the faucet. Greggory continued unraveling his thoughts without seeming to notice a thing out of the ordinary.

As Reid was heading back outside, she tried one last attempt to engage. "Hi."

Although his response was cordial, all it took was the aversion of his eyes, his apathy, the overall uninterest in his tone to tell her how it would be: "Hi." The door chimed open and he was gone. Her heart sank a foot in her chest.

Of course it was inevitable that he would snip the ties that bound them, but she still managed to be stricken by the sudden change. Of the possibilities spinning in her mind, she'd failed to fully unbury this outcome, as if it were a sapless, million-to-one worry not worth the trouble of thought.

She felt the tiny seed they shared and fostered turn black. With enough care it had shown the fertile promise—solid and rewarding—of a robust sapling, but in the topsy-turvy change of events caused by her rash decision, the roots had turned velvety, contaminated and black. She was foolish, an idiot, to have come over again.

Her visits to Greggory's became scattered and were mostly spent trying to steal glances at Reid in hopes he'd notice and decide to rectify the situation. She left early on two occasions, barely managing to escape the house before crying madly on the deserted streets. That was when she began making excuses to postpone her appointments, and after enough evasions Greggory understood her hints and stopped scheduling her. He even ceded a hue of disappointment in a final, resigned tone.

She began to spend the extra time around her home and in the surrounding hills. Every once in a while, she'd catch one of her parents coming or going. Her father had to postpone the fishing trip as his work asked him to take on another project. She almost broke down in front of him as he broke the news. She stayed strong until she could escape to her bedroom and cry into a pillow.

Often, she would return to the oak where she'd unearthed the splintered chest to watch and wait for something to happen. Reid could sometimes be seen as a tiny dot in the distance. She sat observing like a hawk, trying to discern movements out of his hazy figure. Back and forth around the house he would make his route. Sometimes his movement led him down Forester to the immobile truck. Her brain would storm with frustration when his pixel diminished and blended with the distant backdrop.

There on the hill, she gained the perverse satisfaction of watching him, being able to see him without confronting his maiming indifference. She began frequenting the hill so often— sitting amongst the red dirt and rocks and patches of grass like a deranged goblin—that she began needing supplies for her encampment.

She would have continued making the daily trek up to her perch had the aerial vantage not almost caused her death some short time after its discovery. It was midday—hot—and she was crouched in the suffocating red dust when she became aware that the sun's corona shimmered a bit more brightly in the sky than she was accustomed to. When she looked down, her hands were trembling uncontrollably. The realization she was overheating and needed water surfaced, but her canteen remained at home. *Shit.* By the time she made the descent to flat ground the shake in her hands had spread to her entire body, and she felt oddly cool as if she were standing in a refrigerator. When she reached the confines of her house, she grabbed her canteen weakly and crawled to the living room to collapse on the couch. A nauseating lump settled in her stomach, and the room spun around her. She remembered having the lucid image of the world actively conspiring against her—the couch and coffee table conversing in subversive whispers—as her crippled body prepared to die. She tried to lash out against the objects, but the words required too much energy. With the world dimming away she fell into a lumbering fog.

But she didn't die, although some weakness and a truly miserable, sharp headache remained with her for the better part of a week. Even after her full recovery the affliction was linked in her memory with the rocks and grasses atop the hill. Her desire to see him tricked her into returning those last few times, but upon reaching the top she immediately learned it would be impossible to endure a consistent return.

As chance would have it, she didn't need the hill to keep him in her life. She found another avenue one particular Sunday afternoon when the sun was at its zenith and a reckless heat, hotter than the day she'd became sick, blanketed the asphalt. The morning began with her lounging on the couch—no lights on— trying to avoid having to venture outside. She had just turned off the AC; her parents were religiously against the unit, referencing the utility bill and their misbelief that air flow was the best method to dissipate heat. In turning off the machine after exactly thirty-five minutes, she'd been able to cool the house and have the bump in utility costs remain undetectable.

Emma was thereafter reasonably contented inside her home watching TV when she saw the same iced tea commercial she'd also seen two days before. She hadn't paid much attention to the silly ad the first time through, but that afternoon—perhaps withdrawals from the tea she was accustomed to receiving at Greggory's were affecting her—it triggered a craving.

Because she had no viable means of obtaining a can unless she walked to the store three miles away, she waited in the empty house for her cravings to subside. And they *had* subsided… until she saw the same damned commercial an hour later. Her legs revolted at the idea, but somehow her body pulled outside. Heat smacked her immediately after stepping through the door. The entire length of her driveway she cursed the temperature. Even so, her feet continued to carry along.

Before reaching Greggory's house, she crossed to the other side of the road, arching around the entrance as if it held some invisible barrier. When she passed the yard, she surveyed the house for some sign of activity. There was none.

Trying to convince herself that she hadn't intentionally snaked around his house—it was just how her feet carried her— she continued to the end of Forester and then right onto Stinson. It was at that moment she noticed a figure walking in the same direction but farther ahead. Her jaw clenched. Around these parts, there were only so many people it could be, especially in the open on a scorching day. The sun was blaring in her eyes, but, yes, it was him. She did her best to appear indifferent as she followed his lead from paltry shadow to paltry shadow. Try as she might, however, her eyes found themselves fixed to his back, and her body pulled her along as if by an invisible string.

She wondered if he knew, if he had the clairvoyance to know, that their encounter would take place, but she never closed the distance between them to find out. At one point she dared to reduce the gap, but after getting too close she shuffled back in fear of rejection. Perspiration began to weigh on Emma's clothes when they finally arrived at the grocery store.

The store was the same one they'd entered the night at the movie theater: black and white tiles, old-fashioned wooden racks, new cash registers (the only new things in the place). She made her way inside and was almost immediately lost amongst the clutter. The elderly staff mindlessly went about their business.

(It had been the generous idea of the Mormon owner, a graying prophet himself, to hire the elders he once held debts to in his youth. In his generosity, however, he failed to understand that their hiring would negatively affect the modernization and advancement of the withering establishment. The settled bones of the employees refused to wade through the gravitational currents of the world any more quickly than absolutely necessary. To rectify the situation—and it was always surprising to see how he carried out his strategies—the owner bought shiny new cash registers and hired Tim and one other young clerk as a way to add a touch of color to the sea of gray. Unfortunately his attempts never garnered the desired results of a legitimate supermarket, and the store failed to expand from the antiquated one-stop-shop it was—as much from the equity of employees as to the decaying shelves. The two new hires were perceived as circus oddities and the store a quacky, eclectic, but necessary clusterfuck of products.)

In her moment of distraction Tim waved at her from the register. She returned the gesture before reverting back to her stalking. As if she had magical radar, she tracked Reid's movements around the store, without looking, without anybody ever knowing her intentions. His path circled around, and in following him she found herself in front of the cold drinks. The many reds, yellows, and greens jumped out from under the buzz of the fluorescent bulbs, but the tall can of iced tea immediately caught her attention. She plucked it from the shelf, never taking a moment to stop in her primary effort, and continued down the aisle. When she reached the end, she turned her head to catch him, but he was nowhere to be seen. She swiveled her head down each aisle thereafter but found that he'd cleverly slipped away.

Defeated, she took herself to the check-out counter and waited in Tim's line, even though it had an extra two people. Like sleight of hand, Reid popped up in the furthest line. She watched intently for some sign of observation on his part—to satisfy her least possible sense of hope, validation—but it never came.

Just before his vacuous silence could damage her any further, Tim retrained her focus with his greeting. Noise washed over her: the ringing of the scanner, the rustle of bags, his words. "Hey, Emma. How've you been?"

The opportunity to redress their relations was nothing more than a sickly hoax, coming tauntingly close but never merging with reality. He walked out of the store with the same indifference he'd grudgingly offered at Greggory's.

She nodded again at Tim's blurred words until she received a blank stare. *What?*

"Oh, yes, mhm, just the tea."

After she handed over her cash they said their farewells, and Emma exited the store to make the journey home.

The next afternoon at exactly the same time she permitted the venture once again. She wondered, considered, and finally hoped for a déjà vu experience with a parallel universe twist of luck to allow the one detail keeping them apart to collapse on itself. She closed the door behind her and headed down the path towards Forester. The heat was milder than yesterday, and Emma took it as a bad sign.

As she weaved around the potholes, she scanned the horizon of her vision, tried to discern movement in the stillness. But when she didn't see him she tilted her head down, refused to look in the direction of Greggory's home, refused to search Reid out, until finally she arched around Greggory's property to the end of Forester, and tried again. Although some part of her expected to see Reid dragging along ahead of her, he was still nowhere to be found. Suddenly, the road felt long, and the pavement stretched lengthily. The silence hummed around her. Her head drooped as she took a right onto Stinson.

Her feet plodded along and her attention drifted to the slight rises and falls of the road while she passed each stationary shrub or tree. She counted each as she poked along. A mile into the walk, her pace picked up. She wished she'd be there already, wished she'd never started. After another five minutes of walking, she passed the tree that hung clumsily to the road, a marker indicating that the store wasn't much farther. Then her eyes reverted from the tree, and her vision wandered. Far down was a figure wavering in the heat, at the edge of the road. Her heart flipped in her chest, and she slowed her pace to keep from disturbing the universe at play. She hoped, while trying desperately not to hope. She didn't have the courage to rush forward and make out his clear features, but after following him a minute her strides picked up. Then, each step ticked away, not seeming to gain any ground. By the time the old building popped into view, she was still trailing a hundred yards behind. Afraid she'd lose him, her eyes fixed onto his back and she doubled her pace. Of course the roads were deserted, and nobody else would dare venture to the store by foot, but Emma finally closed the distance and confirmed it was Reid. Relief rinsed over her doubt. He would make the habit with her.

Emma followed him into the store, but backed off in her pursuit after she entered. He headed to the far side, somewhere away from the drink section. She went to retrieve her can of iced tea. Resting her palm on the can, she tried to figure how she could relay her feelings of regret, how she could confront him. Simply telling him couldn't work; she hadn't the courage nor he the forgiveness. Just as the previous day, Emma headed to the checkout counter and saw him exit the store in front of her. Her heart torqued. She made her purchase soon after and left, not daring to try and catch him, allowing him to disappear in the flagging heat.

That was how she established her routine walking to the store. It wasn't pretty in the hot summer weather. Most walks she would be sweating, and her sweat would mix with the dust and dirt in the air and cake on her cheeks and temples. But she kept to the routine—as long as Reid kept to his pilgrimage, so would she. They became precise in their timing, Reid learning to exit Greggory's property exactly a hundred yards in front of her. Like a loony spinster she'd weave her fibers of hope before shredding them when another day concluded with the same result.

But there were also the days when she failed to see Reid at all. Horrible. She remembered convincing herself that, as a sort of perdition, she deserved the one-hundred-and-three-degree heat and the sweat and the tedious road with its long cracks that people drove on indifferently and the weeds wilting nearby. The short leap to hell was within viewing distance when summer reached its crowning form. Not even her shadow accompanied her on these days. The veil of optimism began to rip away, and she could feel herself crashing into a pit of sorrow. Torture was waiting just at the edge, laughably able to wane over her at any time.

Adding to the hardship were her traitorous thoughts. She reprimanded herself for continuing the idiotic pursuit. She argued with herself continually, and only the side that most viciously attacked won. Those were the worst days of her entire summer (and even further back than that, really). The only thing keeping her going was the unwavering answer, "yes," when she asked herself if she would choose to meet him over again, given the outcome.

It was her weakest moment, but—surprisingly—things began to improve. Not all at once, but in time there arose hints. The gap between cost and income was diminishing the longer they held to their walks. Reid sported his eyes on her and even made eye contact from time to time, almost mocking their childish game, to see how far each could stretch the other's patience.

Along with the slow shift of their customs, Emma also noticed her disposition improve on the days Reid never appeared. When she rounded the bend to see the sun-scrubbed grocery store, it gave her relief that things were somehow *okay* rather than *hell*.

She'd approach the store and walk in with the *bing* from the overhead sensor. It would trigger the thought that she'd just entered the confines of air conditioning. Along with the temperature relief, the bleats from the scanners grew to soothe her. The old wooden shelves greeted her like wise relatives, and the aisle carrying her green tea held the comfort of a familiar and safe bedroom.

The only thing lacking was privacy. As she reached the drink aisle, she could feel the eyes of the employees lock onto her. One set of eyes in particular stood out from the rest. She was one of the ladies who, Emma assumed, held responsibility over the beverage section. She would always approach from behind, ineffectually pushing a broom, and in a tone barely audible sound a phrase that would become iconic: "Green tea is good for you, Dear. It'll make you live a long time, yep."

This lady—whose name she would later discover was Edna—was maybe sixty-five, maybe one hundred and sixty-five. She had fat saggy jowls, greasy hair, and a blank stare that rested just above everybody's heads. Emma had a difficult time taking Edna seriously as the woman walked away with that limping gait, but somehow her words found a place in Emma's skull. "Green tea is good for you, Dear. It'll make you live a long time, yep." Emma found herself repeating the words long after Edna would slink around the corner, and one time she had to silently repeat them in Edna's beaky voice for fear she had the day off. To Emma's startled appeasement Edna appeared in the nick of time, like a firefly from God-knows-where, to intone the phrase.

The adage became so exalted that Emma wondered if she also announced it to her family. Emma could picture Edna's husband and their adult children (perhaps indeterminably elderly themselves), all with similar saggy jowls and limping gaits, disseminating the knowledge of green tea making you live indefinitely. Emma was certain that Edna's family wasn't drinking green tea packed with sugar and artificial flavors, but rather the extract of earthly green leaves that had been hand grown, picked, and brewed. She could see each one in the family repeating the line like a little prayer before drinking their product at the dinner table. What if she lived one hundred and sixty five years like Edna? Is that something she really wanted? If it meant becoming senile and walking around with a limp, probably not.

During her trips to the store, she not only became accustomed to Edna as a companion but also began to rehash her friendship with Tim. His dazzling white smile honed in on her, just for her. He was able to sense in that tight cavern of her soul the feelings of torment and helplessness, and with an overly-simplistic joke or contagious laugh somehow made daft the lodged demons within.

After leaving the oasis of the store with a cold can of tea to combat the heat, she felt a step quicker. Her distress attenuated to manageable.

GREGGORY

Paul went through phases as he grew older. There was the phase when he crawled, peed, and shat everywhere. An episode when he smeared feces all along the hallway walls, burst into a hysterical fit when Greggory and Sophia found him. Eventually, he learned to walk, beginning by hobbling his way to and fro between each parent. Along that time, Sophia began calling him "Polly." Greggory knew "Polly" was short for "Mary," and was very much against the idea. But eventually Polly stuck for Greggory as well, at least when Sophia wasn't around.

When Paul grew even a little bit older, he learned to pronounce his own name. His lips curled into a cute "O" as he repeated his name with a long, childish drawl. Shortly after, he began kindergarten. Sophia crouched down beside him on his first day, almost came to tears, as she whispered into his ear, "Now Polly, Mommy's only going to be a short ways away. Have fun and make lots of friends."

In learning to raise Paul, Sophia and Greggory reopened to the outside world as a pair. Couple's activities were eventually replaced with parent-teacher conferences and coordinating playtimes. On a few occasions they even hosted birthday parties.

When all was said and done, though, Greggory and Sophia still couldn't help but feel like outsiders to the rest of the world. Although integrated, they discovered that they never really fit in. Their input on parenting was always greeted as tender (but unconventional) propositions, and their modest living habits often left their son uninvited by his peers. As late-blooming parents who chose happiness over material comforts, taking vacations by camping in the backyard, they did things a little bit differently than the other parents.

In the years to follow they maintained their morning ritual, and their relationship deepened. They never stopped focusing on each other, but merely transitioned from world travelers to microcosmic beings. Eventually they were so close Greggory knew the words Sophia was thinking before she spoke them. He discovered the ability one morning when Sophia had just set down the phone with one of their son's teachers.

"He's doing well, but—"

"Yes, but he needs to read more," he finished, the words coming out of his mouth without true recognition of what he was saying. They were in many ways the same person, now.

At night he held Sophia more tightly, and over the years she curled into a mold of his body. It was during these moments they could feel each other's forearms becoming rough with age, their hands weaker. When they smiled into each other's softening faces they could see the plains of wrinkles on the verge of deepening, and when they dressed in the morning each noticed without announcing that the other was shedding what little burdensome flesh remained. Even their strong, sexual scents noticeably eroded to a rounder form. Her vanilla was always *there*, but in time the odor lightened and developed as it took on other aromas, as wine would when aged in a barrel.

They weren't old by any means, but they were no longer young. Still, where hints suggested their maturity, every morning's whisper of "Hey, you... I love you" revitalized their souls.

Their lovely ignorance of age, that blissful disregard, led to shock when they were inevitably reminded that their bodies had become less cooperative. During one of the first hot afternoons of summer, it happened: Sophia was clenching her arm in agony when he arrived home from work. She described stretching up to grab a vase in the cupboard above the fridge—one of the last sections of her spring-cleaning rally—when the mishap occurred. Her arm extended just far enough into the cupboard to brush the vase with her fingertips, causing it to wobble on its edge and threaten to crash. Sophia sidestepped to catch it and in doing so lost her balance, as if the chaos in the vase transferred right into her bones. Her slowing reflexes were defeated by gravity's pull and she landed on her side. Almost instantly a sharp pain filled her underarm and hip. Paul came running to see what had caused the rumble.

Greggory immediately tried to negotiate a doctor's visit but she refused, assuring him it wasn't as severe as he perceived, and reminding him of the weekend camping trip they'd promised their son. It would be inconvenient to make the journey to the doctor's office, two towns over. The next morning two bruises rose on the plush surface of her skin. Once again she assured, "They're not as bad as they look." It took a lot to hold his tongue and wait, but Greggory did just that. It wasn't until Friday night arrived that the bruises subsided and he allowed himself to believe Sophia's words. A mild cough replaced her injury, but she was well enough to camp.

In the morning Greggory woke earlier than usual to pack the truck: small stove, propane, pan, utensils, thermos, wrinkled forest-green tent, food, coffee. It was still dark while he fumbled with the gear, but the black-felt sky eventually lightened to a murky gray. His head was wet with perspiration, but he was still drowsy. The last of the morning's weariness still nestled in his body as he went to the kitchen and prepared tea.

He went through his routine, until finally he made his way back outside into his rocker. The leaden sky began to take on a stroke of color above the horizon. When the chirp of the kettle sounded, his body jerked and cut through the last of his mental fog. Soon Sophia and Paul appeared outside, one hand tugging on their son's hand and the other balancing two mugs. Her frown turned to a long, grateful smile.

The steam from his tea globed in the mug, then lifted and faded as they sat drinking. As a family, they watched the world wake before walking to the truck.

On the road Sophia curled against the passenger door to regain some of the sleep she'd foregone. Paul curled against her. Greggory glanced periodically in their direction with a smile, until the morning wore and they both woke.

They drove away from the potholed asphalt and disheveled valleys of their neighborhood to long stretches, the road shedding its few turnoffs in the process. The truck ran along the straightaways, lilted into easy bends. The sun rose. Yellow hills streamed alongside them.

Paul sat up between them, his legs bobbing as the suspension of the truck absorbed the unevenness of the road. He asked simple questions that were also profoundly complex: who, what, where, where, how, why? Sophia and Greggory glanced at each other before taking turns to answer.

Finally Greggory slowed the vehicle, searching for a road they'd followed only once before. His eyes narrowed as he studied the blurs passing along the shoulder. Then he saw it, and eased the truck in a new direction. Fine, dry dust spat from the rear tires and formed a cloud behind them. The sound of crunching overtook the radio. They rode along an unmarked trail deeper into thickets of yellow weeds.

The truck reached the end of the path, and Greggory turned onto an even less maintained track. They exchanged glances, grins, while their son did his best to peek over the dash. The truck inched forward over ruts and grooves, perhaps no more than five miles per hour, and once they exhausted what little trail remaining, they stopped.

Greggory wasn't exactly certain where they were. It was a nook of sorts, though no boundaries contained the area. Tall grass, shrubs, and bald spots blended into the nearby hills. The air was dry. Somebody might well have owned the land, but it could hardly be considered "private" property. There were no houses, or dwellings. There were no structures at all except a wooden bench at the edge, and what appeared to be the fire pit they constructed when they were last here.

They'd discovered the campsite out of plain curiosity, trying different roads just for the sport of it. Now, it was familiar. The three filed out of the vehicle, and Greggory began unloading immediately, looking for the lunchmeat and bread he'd packed away.

They ate their turkey sandwiches at the bench, then snacked on trail mix. Greggory wasn't quite certain what drew them out here again. Everything around them languished by at a slower-than-normal pace: the wind, the sun, the shrubs and trees. Everything felt wide-open, and simple.

Throughout the day they told stories and walked the footpaths (or animal trails, perhaps?). Their son played with sticks, whapping them against the overgrown weeds and the ground. Greggory and Sophia sneaked intimate words, their eyebrows perking up: "Hey, you... I love you."

Before light escaped the valley completely, Greggory and Paul collected twigs and small logs for the fire. The pair squatted as Greggory held a lighter to the kindling. Once the embers grew, all three of them huddled around the fire, Paul finding his way between them again. Sophia pulled a bag of marshmallows from her daypack, and Greggory smiled when Paul's eyes lit up. The flames of the fire wavered in his pupils.

An hour passed. Night haltered the sky, and pinpoints of white shone through the dark canvas. Hand-in-hand, they climbed into the tent. They hadn't any sleeping bags, but they laid heavy blankets all about. Pillows bunched in a cluster at one end. They repositioned themselves and bunched up similarly.

Through the netting above, they continued to watch the galaxy pinwheel in the sky. The crescent moon lolled. The night lingered. The starlight bathed Sophia's smooth features, their son's round ones. Paul had long ago dozed off when Greggory kissed Sophia on the forehead goodnight.

When he woke, the smell of damp ground wafted in the tent. The cold stung his lungs, but somehow it was also refreshing— as if humans were supposed to suffer with a morning chill. His body ached on the side where he'd slept. When Sophia stirred, her ripe cough sounded the thickness in her chest. All three climbed out from the tent and stretched before packing the truck and returning to the lives that awaited them.

In the few days after their return Sophia's cough developed. Because they'd already neglected her symptoms, it was easy to continue to do so. They were just beginning to get ahead with their finances, their savings account growing nicely, and Sophia didn't want him to stay behind to babysit her. She didn't need to see the doctor...truly. It would pass. It took nearly a week, but with an ample amount of over-the-counter medication—and rest—her fever finally lifted.

EMMA

When she wasn't following the back of Reid's head, she was selfishly relying on Tim's playful banter at the store. Eventually, he became a normal part of her routine.

Perhaps it was a reliance on this routine that gave her a sense of comfort, and when it was disrupted the chaos in her life surfaced and became palpable. It was during one of her walks to the store that Tim seized an opportunity to ask her something unexpected, if she wanted to go to the "End of the World" with him the next day. He must have noticed her surprise, a small trace of the chaos, or her smile confuting some part of her facial expression because he added, "If you'd like, of course. You can even bring your tea." He smiled weakly in hope of lifting the tension.

She tried to hide the wide panic in her eyes and agreed with meek conviction. "The End of the World" was a term they coined back in middle school for the place at the very edge of Forester, just past where all the houses faded. She hadn't returned since they last spent time together, which was now more than five years ago. After agreeing, she fled the store and made her way home alone.

When the buzz of her phone came, she still half-expected Reid's number to appear. A rush of agitation washed over her as she looked down to see it was Tim's. He could have asked in a less direct manner to allow her to escape the commitment, but he pressured her into continuing their... whatever it was. At the store she swore she could feel his eyes burn into her as he waited for an answer. She had no way to decline.

Reluctantly she confirmed and then headed to the bulbous end of Forester. The sun was kissing the tips of the mountains, signaling that the temperature was just beginning its daily plummet. The coarse wind spilled from the valley, making the walk admittedly enjoyable.

Tim's house stood just visible through the veiny tree branches at the end of the cul de sac. Except for a straggle of black and coastal live oaks, it was the farthest man-made object before a great expanse of openness that marked the "End of the World."

Emma reached the door. Anticipating her arrival, he opened it before she could knock. His smile was radiant, his clothes new. It fed her irritability as they greeted with cordial hugs.

All her other duties swirled in her head—cleaning the kitchen, writing that summer essay for school, finishing the book she vowed to complete a week ago—but her attention remained.

Tim occasionally secured a glance at her while they plodded along the path leading to the back of the house. As they passed the siding, her head hung low. Her grave mood became so boorish that Tim summoned the courage to ask, "You know, we don't have to go if you have something else you need to do."

Emma perceived it as another trap.

"No, this is all I have planned for today." She smiled weakly.

Upon looking back with any sort of objectivity, she granted that her demeanor appeared nothing less than a total bitch, but at the same time she was in such a horrible spot emotionally (and lacking any sort of support with the whole coping thing) that she acted the only way she knew.

As it was, they made their way to the back of the property and continued to the lining of trees ringing around a large, open expanse. The ground was desiccated and cracked into shallow hexagons as if it were once a lakebed. Large rocks and driftwood were strewn about. As with the previous times they'd come here, her imagination led to listening for a coyote's howl and watching for tumbleweeds bumbling across the plain. The land before them was so remote for this part of the valley that the terrain was a wonder unto itself.

"Remember that?" he said bashfully pointing to one of the tall, plinth-like rocks in the near distance.

Emma nodded and her haughty entitlement dissolved into a smile.

With that memory she strung together another one. There was the time they heard hooting from the invisible owl. They searched their surroundings for hours trying to find the source but eventually gave up, and only then, when they headed back to his house, did they encounter the bird complacently perched on the back deck. It ruffled its feathers as they approached, as much surprised to see them as they it. They roared with laughter as it twitched its neck towards them and then darted off in flight. They named him Fred.

Then, there was the time Emma swore she heard the shrieking yips of a coyote, perhaps even a mountain lion. Immediately she was overcome with fright. Tim claimed he never heard the yips, but admittedly his hearing wasn't the best. They listened in silence for another indication of such ferocious creatures, and of Emma's sanity, to no avail. Emma gripped Tim's scrawny arm well into the night.

This was the first spot they truly spent time alone, and the first spot either experienced the novelty of kissing.

GREGGORY

After their camping trip, something unnamable shifted in how Sophia and Greggory perceived their lives. They felt they were aging, and began to preoccupy—ingrain—themselves into routines that could distract them, as if throwing themselves into the next adventure would somehow stop time, would satiate some instinctual need. Their love, their son, work, camping, family meals. It was a race to do them all. Autumn arrived. Their son received good grades in English. He'd benefitted from the hour they scheduled for reading every night.

Then, she got sick again. This time it was worse. Greggory never considered the recent illness to be associated with the one from the camping trip, but perhaps the first never truly went away. With their lives so prominently in the forefront of their thoughts, they'd glossed over her fatigue.

This time, however, there were clear signs: dizziness, joint pain, muscle aches, fever. Even the roof appeared to be bearing down over her when he returned to their bedroom. Darkness. Greggory finally addressed the issue formally: he took time off work to look after her, and suggested that they make the hour-and-a-half drive to the doctor. "A severe case of pneumonia is nothing to play around with," he said, agitated. "Tea and ibuprofen won't knock this one out." She reluctantly agreed.

The doctor was booked until the next afternoon, but when the time came Sophia removed her veil of strength and revealed just how much her ailments had taken a toll. The bags under her eyes sagged, her shoulders slumped. She stood to go to the bathroom and nearly collapsed.

They arrived and sat in the sullen waiting room, filled like most with the heavy air of rumination, until their names were finally called. With a start they jumped up from the couch and followed the nurse to a private room. Greggory sat in the empty chair and stared at the Manet print hanging above the exam table. Sophia climbed onto the table, paper crinkling, and proceeded to look at him with feeble eyes. The wall clock ticked.

Just when they were regretting having driven all that way, the doctor clambered in with superficial pleasantries. He wore a white lab coat, his expression analytical and his grin inviting. After presenting a few sensible questions while listening to her chest with a stethoscope—"How long have you had it?—Have you felt any pain?"—he asked if they had time for an x-ray, "just to be safe." They obliged, though Greggory could see the stress mount on his wife's face in the form of furled lines on her forehead and a distant gaze. He remained, left to stare at the Manet and listen to the clock.

She wasn't gone long, but upon her return she could offer only an uncertain shrug. Her poor health had overstayed its welcome, so when the doctor reappeared without concrete answers Greggory's foot began tapping impatiently. The doctor relayed to them that Sophia needed blood work, "to secure more comprehensive understandings of what is happening in her body." They reluctantly agreed to make an appointment at the lab for first thing in the morning.

They woke to their usual routine, giving priority to their soothing habits over the weighty, dubitable appointment. They did their best to ignore the unease hanging above their heads. It wasn't until deep in the morning that Greggory presented lightly that they should get ready.

After washing and dressing, they made the long drive to the lab. They entered a clean waiting room with white walls and simple furniture. A faint smell of anesthetic pushed through the doors, causing Greggory's stomach to churn. Once they were called, a young lab tech led them to a room where he carefully instructed Sophia—eyes locked onto hers to ensure she was paying attention—on the procedures.

He didn't remember much in terms of the test itself or the following days while they awaited the results, but he did recall entering the doctor's office and cracking the joke, "So, it's a pretty bad flu then, huh?"

He remembered the young doctor wearing the same analytical expression on his face while looking downward at his clipboard with resolute and precise attention. The clock ticked loudly.

Then the doctor spoke an unfamiliar sentence. Greggory saw his lips move, but he hadn't heard anything.

What? "What?"

"Yes, I'm sorry, but let's consider our options."

"No, what did you say?"

"It looks like Mrs. O'Sullivan has acute myeloid leukemia. It also appears the bone marrow is making abnormal red blood cells and platelets. We still have more testing to do in order to determine which subtype it is. Right now, though, let's consider our options." His voice was distant, but the word "leukemia" throbbed in Greggory's head. The doctor's grin was less inviting. Greggory shook his head uncontrollably, disbelief. His heart began palpitating strangely.

They sat with wide stares. Neither fully comprehended what the doctor's utterance meant. His words were a mirage, a hazy fake that couldn't possibly be real.

"She caught a cold while camping," he tried admonishing politely. "How does that equate to leukemia?"

As if expecting the question, the doctor's words sliced precisely through Greggory's hope of inaccuracy: it had been developing for some time, and the symptoms she was experiencing were common signs. An image of their son flashed in Greggory's head.

Sophia permitted her first words by asking how far along it was. The doctor danced around the topic and refused to commit without more tests. They left the office under a cloud of fear and vague, unarticulated numbness. The next few days were spent moving from one waiting room to another until they received the news that the disease was in its advanced stages.

Burgeoning tragedies are ubiquitous, so often heard and reported on, but they feel like worlds and loves apart. Just three months ago they had been perfectly content. Three months. Now, they were another statistical tick of analysis, hearing those inaudible words, living with an impossible cataclysm. Greggory couldn't stop imagining doctors all over the world delivering the same news, two or three simple sentences every minute of every day, words that would introduce sorrow and multiply infinitely until complete devastation.

∞   ∞   ∞

Leukemia seemed like a foreign land, something theoretically reachable but never really possible to arrive at. It felt mundane, advertised and commonplace but never actually relatable to them. They couldn't quite comprehend the humor of the sordid joke they were sold.

When they arrived home, they sat outside in their chairs waiting for (but not wanting) the sun to set. Their son could just barely be heard playing inside. Perhaps deep down they sat waiting for the words to translate into meaning. Each sat silently. He reflected on all the little signs he had neglected to observe—the bruises that never went away, her fatigue—wondering how much time he would have needed to catch the sickness at its beginning stages. He thought about the night he held her under the stars.

The ultimate realization didn't hit that night, nor the next, and over the following days they avoided the topic for fear of it materializing. Instead they stuck viciously to each other—sitting closer, lingering longer at their favorite spots, holding each other a bit closer at night.

Time slipped by. Sophia's mornings began later and later, until Greggory was left sitting in his rocker alone. He'd tiptoe to their bedroom after reheating the tea kettle and find her in a cold sweat, grimacing from pain she faced even in her sleep. He would nudge her carefully and present a weak smile as he offered her favorite mug. She would decline the tea cordially—she always did in those later days—so Greggory would set the mug on the stand and climb into bed next to her for a few moments longer. She'd place her frail hand on his chest before drifting off with haggard breaths, back to her painful sleep. He'd then go about his duties—child to school, off to work, the world around him somehow not slowing, not aware.

They could both see the inevitable. It refused to wait for anybody to say what needed to be said, refused to let them grow old together, refused to allow their son to have a mother. The safe solitude wrapped around their country lives unraveled, becoming penetrable to an unimaginable truth.

It was on a day in winter when he woke up to his empty new routine, went outside, and sat hoping she'd come out at her usual hour—usual smile and giggle—and somehow everything would be okay. Thirty seconds passed as the tea kettle chirped, and then thirty more. After a long minute, he went to the kitchen and turned the unforgiving kettle off himself. He crept to their room to find Sophia awake.

Her depleted body beckoned him to her, but she couldn't quite pronounce the words. As he sat on the bed, he took her hand to help steady the tremors uncontrollably rippling through her corpse. A gray film glossed over her eyes, but he was beholden to the jet blueness he knew was beneath.

Without any force at all, her trembling hand tried to pull him to her. She let out a choked giggle at her weak attempt. He forged his lips into a grin. To hide the sadness in his eyes, he leaned in to whisper into her ear "Hey, don't hurt me now" and kissed her forehead. The silver in her hair and wrinkles on her face had developed considerably in the past few weeks.

He turned his ear to hear what she prepared all her energy to say. She pronounced it with more clarity than he'd ever heard in his entire life, "Hey, you... I love you."

She shut her eyes and released him. With that, she was gone. A brilliant golden droplet dispersing into an ocean of black. Her palm revealed the two elephant pendants she'd never taken from her neck since he presented the second, a long time ago.

His back rounded and quaked; his breath refused to return. He placed his hands over his face and whimpered, but his body refused the comfort of tears. His mind was fuzzy and blocked, as if stuffed with gauze. He waited forever on the bed next to her.

In the days to follow, his son often woke him at night, standing under the doorframe of his room, crying. But Greggory could offer no help. His movements and actions felt surreal. Everything else commenced so quickly, his mind was still stuck at the moment they camped under the stars. Only his body cut through the confusion, and fell directly into an abyss of physical, visceral sorrow. He didn't resist being stuck there; truthfully, he was confined in a dark hole one way or another.

Her clothes lying neatly in the dresser, her shirts dangling in the closet—the elephant pendants—the kitchen chairs, the thermometer in the drawer, coffee mugs, dressers, spoons, carpet stains, and even the light filtering through the transom, were all memories that became reminders she was gone. There were countless small accessories marking her eccentricities and her as a whole, but without her the relics were unanimated. Without her they stood out like empty totems, like blatant red flags in a sea of gray relentlessly probing his vision and causing him to suffer at every turn.

Greggory felt time itself grow old and die, leaving only insatiable stillness. His face became bony and developed deep wrinkles. Disintegrated threads of clothing hung with graceful anguish from his once-triumphant frame. Autumns and springs dripped past in a fugue, and as the seasons transitioned into longer stages his son—his neglected son—became his only real clarity.

Unfortunately, his relationship with his son fared no better than Greggory himself. Because Paul had the benefit of youth—a cloak of innocence—he was capable of moving on with his life in the years to come. A great divide formed in Paul's memories. The days before his mother left held affection and joy, when they would camp and explore and love as a family. Although he relished the early flashbacks, he owed these etches to the reverie of his childhood. Then there were the recollections after her passing. These latter memories were filled with his father dwelling in the darkness, with gloom, with neglect. The only time his father left their small home was when he went numbly to work or the grocery store. Between the limits of their rural community and his own growing convictions, it was no wonder Paul was driven to escape the bleak environment of his life when he grew older.

The catalyst for his son's ambitious plans came years later, when Greggory's father fell to sickness. Greggory's mother had already passed a few years prior, so the boy offered to look after his ailing grandfather. The initial visit was brief and Greggory's father determinedly recovered, but the event would later allow for the secondary endorsement, the argument of school *and* an eye on grandpa. The matter was settled when the acceptance letter from a liberal arts college back East arrived in the mailbox.

As a last-ditch effort to rebuild their crumbled relationship, to somehow retrieve the feelings they once shared, Greggory bought a rusty Ford pickup for them to rebuild together. Up until graduation day of high school, the Ford sat under the carport as an idle reminder of their unsalvageable relationship. On several occasions Greggory started to suggest that they work on the truck, but he stopped short each time in fear of the reply.

Paul didn't bother waiting until the end of summer. The day following graduation, Greggory patiently sat at the kitchen table; it was dusk when his son walked into the house. Greggory fumbled his words: "You know, you're always welcome to stay here whenever and for as long as you'd like."

His plea was returned coldly. "Thanks Dad, but it's probably best for the both of us."

The next day his son left.

Greggory received word of his father's passing eight months later, and a few years after of his son fleeing to Indonesia with a girl. Greggory was alone.

IV

TIM

After sixth-grade camp ended — what a nice feeling it was to return home — school commenced as usual. He and Emma met and continued as they left off: awkwardly. At first, he met her just to honor his commitment.

He'd had a difficult time looking into her eyes — at her at all, really — those first few days. It wasn't only that, though. His skeletal frame and pastel shirts, oversized and threadbare, made him seem almost like an obsequious servant when he stood next to her. His deficiency was so obvious that at one point he overheard a derisive comment aimed towards him in reference to Dolby, pre-sock, from Harry Potter.

To make matters worse, his speech often worked against him. He was soft-spoken, and phrased all his sentences as questions. He articulated carefully and spoke only when necessary. When he was younger, his teachers and parents thought he might be slow, but as time passed they found he simply acted with an overabundance of caution. Although he hated this quality about himself, at some point he permitted it to be true. Part of him wondered how Emma stuck around past the first day. Even more amazing was her commitment after she came to know his authentic self, which was completely different from the courage he exhibited at camp. Heck, if people knew the truth, that he saved Emma largely through a rush of panic, they'd probably laugh him to shame. Perhaps, he reasoned, it was because she was still considered the new girl at school. She had been attending only since the beginning of this year, when her family arrived seemingly out of nowhere. As such, she didn't have the luxury of fitting in, either.

But even if he and Emma looked more like mal-adjusted siblings than partners, they persisted and went on to form something resembling a relationship.

Their subdued connection remained for only the initial few weeks, Emma at first allowing their exchanges in hushed whispers before she became annoyed and grabbed his hand in a frustrated swoop to lead him where she wanted to go. From then on, she was chief; she made decisions for both, doing so as if it were natural to her, and he followed like an obedient dog. Even before Emma he'd hung his head and found it better to be invisible than included, so when she took control it was easy for him to acquiesce.

If she was especially bothered by any aspect of his reserved nature, it was his refusal to meet anybody's gaze. She tried standing in front of him, crowding his view as he spoke to her. She tried surprising him, coaxing a glance out of his pools of blue with a coquettish flutter of her eyes. She even tried to infuriate him in hopes a heightened discussion might extract what she was searching for. But all her attempts went awry. He had a keen sense of aversion when he moved his line of sight.

He'd slice away from others with such skill that she once noted how people would stop speaking to him midsentence, as if he suddenly became a ghost. Furthermore, when he *did* look at her, he was some place far off: considering, contriving, but not there. He was the Invisible Man. She'd get worked up about how he was "intentionally pushing himself away from the world."

Somewhat ironically, long after they stopped seeing each other and his sense of personal validity finally took root, he noticed from a distance that she herself adopted and learned to wield his power of aversion. He was like a sorcerer passing the trade to his apprentice.

After her many attempts to establish a human connection all ended in futility, she began to avoid him whenever there was an excuse to do so. He saw that it was happening, but couldn't stir himself to change. Their handful of weeks together softened his actions at camp into a memory, and then the memory fluttered into nothing more than a cloudy idea. He'd even forgotten his vow to protect her.

Then, one day after math class when he was staring off into nothing (mentally preparing himself for the inevitable speech about needing more space) while smiling weakly (after receiving his math test and finding a better grade than expected—blind luck) Emma came bustling over in a whirlwind of fury.

"Hey, Tim," she sneered, looking instead at the girl Jessica sitting next to him. "Are we still going to *your* house after school today?"

They hadn't planned to meet after school—they'd *never* met outside of school—but Tim was too surprised to decline. He nodded in agreement. It wasn't until well after the event that he realized she stormed his way because she thought he was offering his smile to the girl next to him.

After the bell chimed to end school there was never any confirmation that Emma was actually coming over, so he dismissed the idea as errant interpretation. That, and he couldn't imagine what he'd do if she really decided to come over. He took the bus to the grocery store on Stinson and walked to his house, closing the case until further evidence emerged.

He climbed the stairs to his bedroom, sat at the desk, and pulled *Elementary Algebra* from his pack. However, it didn't take long after he started on his math homework for the silence of the house to become distracting. The monotony of the equations, the still air, begged for the fanciful possibility that Emma would knock on his door.

The weeks around her had affected him. He liked it when she told him what to do; it made his life easier. Her confidence was pleasant, and he began to yearn for her sweaty palm to drag him along. He began to think of her canvas high-tops, her favorite pair of black jeans showing just a slit of skin around her waist, the time he caught her at school braless since her slim frame almost—almost—didn't warrant one.

His imagination assumed a dominance he never had. He pulled her close to him. He could feel her familiar wrist as he led her next to his bed and pulled her gently onto the covers. Her thickets of wavy hair would fall around his face like a willow tree, and her lively eyes would bear into him…

Just as his thoughts were climaxing, he heard a soft rapping on his door. It grounded him.

His mother called from the other side. "Tim, Honey, you have a friend here waiting for you. She says you two were scheduled to meet today?"

He frantically covered his exercises by snapping the book closed and obliging a reply. The tremor in his leg would have been noticeable only if someone had pointed it out. He opened the door to his mother's smile. She looked past him to the math book lying inoffensively on his desk.

At the bottom of the stairs he found Emma analyzing the awkward vacation portrait of him and his mother riding an enormous walrus at Waterworld. His mind briefly convulsed with the possibility she would be led to the kitchen's expansive bureau of embarrassing photos.

Fortunately, his movements down the staircase caught her gaze, and they smiled politely at each other. He tried to say something, anything, but his thoughts were blocked. When she returned to analyzing the house, he could sense her developing boredom. She looked around as if staring at one of his math problems. His mother smiled giddily at the rare occasion her son brought somebody (a girl, even!) to their home. She clasped her hands in excitement, as if somehow expecting him to snap out of his awkward introversion. With uncanny resolve, his eyes remained fixed on the floor.

A long pause stifled the air, and his mother was just about to offer Emma a drink or food or activity when the words spurted from his throat: "Want to go outside? I can show you this spot out back."

Even though it was approaching one hundred degrees, she agreed, contented to abide by his rare suggestion.

"You two wouldn't prefer to stay inside? It's hot out. You wouldn't want to worry your old mother, Tim. And Emma, Sweetie, do your parents know you're here? I feel like it would be best if I watched you if they don't." She reamed away, her disappointment at not seeing what they'd do abhorrently evident.

To his relief they both deflected her suggestions, opting for outside. It was probably the first time he and Emma shared a thought.

Tim quietly led her to the worn trail mapping his house.

"Sorry about my mom. She just gets excited when people are over."

"Oh, it's no problem."

"Are your parents like that too?"

"No." She closed the topic abruptly.

They passed the back porch and yard. Like most homes in the area, the property had no fence. Instead, ashen oaks and scraggy chaparral spanned to the distance. A little further ahead the trees and shrubs thinned to an open, barren landscape. The scene wasn't appealing, nothing like a movie or bucolic painting, but the plants fit into the environment as if there could be no other option.

Looking into the vastness, the brackish weeds and craggy boulders standing like sentries, she slipped a "Whoa," as if the scene knocked the wind out of her. "It's like the end of the world out here."

Tim nodded, inwardly elated to have done something valuable.

But, as with most of his efforts, intentions were altered by interpretation. He'd meant to show Emma the tire swing not too far away. It was on the edge from where they stood, just a few trees down.

In their, or rather Emma's mesmerization—as if it alluded to some childhood memory she couldn't unhinge—they remained stationed at the tree-line. When Tim realized they weren't going to get to the swing, he suggested a large flat rock to sit on. Perhaps due to the "it's like end of the world" comment, it wasn't long before Emma scanned the area and began a game. "That right there?" She looked down the shaft of her arm to where her finger was aiming. "See it? Looks like a giraffe." Tim let out a burst of laughter when he found the tree she was referencing.

He went on in turn. "See that cloud, though, over there? Mhm, yes—hippo."

This time Emma was caught crowing. In this fashion they began reeling off resemblances of anything and everything they could see in the scrubby wasteland. As the objects became more and more detailed—"See the right side of that tree?"—their laughter became more raucous. Soon, they were leaning into each other to be certain they were viewing the same object.

It clicked in Tim's brain that this was the closest they'd ever been. He could smell her spritzed perfume, a dainty scent of flowers and apricots. He'd caught whiffs before, but never at this proximity. Like a rifle to his head, her body enlisted his attention. The earlier thoughts in his room penetrated his mind, daring him to peek at her breasts, before his turn came around again.

On cue he'd point to another object before again submerging into his euphoric imagination. The game went on until the sky became too dark to see, and he suggested they return. He shifted his eyes onto her before they rose to walk back. It startled him to find she was blushing. For the first time, her dominance was replaced with timidity.

They spoke in hushed tones on their return, and somewhere along the way their hands tangled together. Just as they arrived at the large house Tim's mother called out for their return. It was in this way they found a common ground.

EMMA

That first time at his house, she was surprised how differently he acted—he was much more relaxed than at school. He even made her blush; never before had he revealed his eyes so readily, and it caught her off guard. After that first meeting, the pieces fell into place, even if Tim's demeanor remained reserved most of the time.

She would wait for the "okay" to visit. It was always after five o'clock, as Tim's mother insisted that "dinnertime" never be interrupted. When five rolled around, though, she would canter over to his house. She'd leave well before her parent's arrived home from work, before they could ask where she was going, and before she had to tell them she was going to the top the hill across the street, or someplace down the road, or just out and about.

His dirty sneakers and stained shirt led the way to the "End of the World" in search for new corners of the landscape they could form shapes from. Tim even took the opportunity one afternoon to show her a tire swing hanging from a battered tree. Although the rope was held together by crackling threads and it appeared dangerously unstable, she allowed him to push her. She remembered swinging through the air, hooting with excitement nearly the entire time. An image of Mrs. Decker looking outside in terror crossed her mind, but to Emma's great disappointment Tim's mother never came a-hollering.

They'd sit outside in the dark until precisely eight-thirty, when Mrs. Decker shouted for their return. Tim led the way as they carried themselves towards the orange glow of the porch, scouting for errant rocks until the dim lights sufficiently lit the terrain. Mrs. Decker's silhouetted figure emerged into view just beyond the billows of moths, mosquitoes, and gnats. Upon reaching the house, Tim's mom tousled his hair and offered a forced smile, and Tim smiled sincerely in return. At the gesture, Emma shuddered. Watching them together made her resent Mrs. Decker a little, maybe more than a little. The regular five o'clock dinners, her attention to his daily life, tousling his hair—the coddling—flashed in her head. This couldn't be real.

But it was clear by the end of the first week that Mrs. Decker would continue her habit of hollering at exactly eight-thirty. She would continue looking at her son with sublime endearment. She'd keep tousling his hair. A change occurred, however, when Mrs. Decker began to believe her imagination more than the truth about what Emma and Tim were doing at the edge of the property. Emma watched the woman's disposition degrade accordingly from anxiety, to annoyance, and finally to resentment. Her nightly calls took on a note of severity, and in their final form they became high-pitched screeches filled with fear and frustration.

It wasn't her tone that betrayed the mounting frustration. Up close, Mrs. Decker was as savvy at managing that same smile and mellifluous air as in their first meeting, always asking, "Did you two have fun?" Rather, it was the slump in her shoulders and the haggardness of her appearance. She began wearing bags under her eyes, and her attention was directed with quick whips of her head. Moreover, she always seemed to be waiting for slips in Emma's answers, by way of verbiage or tone. Her attitude gradually became so paranoid that Emma would fantasize about Mrs. Decker's eye twitching when Emma responded with the same answer she had the day before. Emma wasn't proud to admit it, but she took pleasure in taking Tim away from his mother.

Outside of their brief encounters at night, Tim's mother began attacking her with strange questions in their exchanges alone. If Emma was left with Mrs. Decker for any reason, the lady would ask: "So... what did you two do? Do you always wear white shirts? Sweetie, I wonder how proper it is for you two to stay out past dark." But however much Mrs. Decker probed and prodded, she never stopped Emma and Tim from spending time together, not until she could uncover some concrete evidence at least—that was her method.

At one point they caught his mother peeping out the back window, spying to catch them in some salacious act. It was obvious that Mrs. Decker was waiting to discover Emma's malintentions of sexual conduct, so Emma indulged in exacerbating the woman's absurd whims by offering the most ambiguous answers she could think of. Through it all, though, Mrs. Decker smiled and patted Tim's shoulder with infuriatingly genuine endearment, walking him back inside their lovely home.

Their roundabout warfare intensified until Tim's mother went as far as contacting Emma's parents to voice her concerns about the affairs of their children. To this day Emma couldn't believe that Mrs. Decker had the audacity to call her home's landline, and hints from her parents suggested they were as surprised as she.

Nonetheless, Emma received a stern but regulated inquiry as to who Mrs. Decker and Tim were, and why her parents hadn't been told about these visits until now. In the end, they took a diplomatic stance and granted that they had neither the reason nor the mindset to restrain their daughter from seeing him.

Emma wasn't familiar with her parents sticking up for her, but she had the impression they'd gone to bat for her this time.

From the look on her father's face—lit by the amiable light of the kitchen's fluorescents—when Mrs. Decker called a second time, Emma sensed that he thought the woman was as bat shit crazy as Emma did, even if he later refused to admit it. He politely declined her request for dinner Thursday by informing her of their obligations to a charity event hosted by his workplace. The next call he made was to his boss, apologizing for taking so long to respond but noting that he and his wife would be happy to attend the charity event. After hanging up the phone, he made a few inaudible (yet severe) comments to himself about attending work outside work and neighbors needing to mind their own fucking business. Emma's mother had learned long ago to hear those words; she patted him on the shoulder to soothe his frustration, then reminded him that their daughter was still in the room.

Afterwards, they finished their rare family meal together, but Emma's head remained fixed at her plate. Her father's jaw was balled in a knot for a long while before it finally relaxed and he sighed. Even so, Emma knew better than to speak, so she instead continued to poke at the hunk of chicken next to her vegetables. The clinking of silverware on plates felt very loud, and a blue veil seemed to grow over everything.

After the table was cleared, Emma made up her mind: she'd deal with the assault from Mrs. Decker in a different way. Although hesitant, Emma asked if she could meet Tim for a few hours. "It's not a school night. Please, just for a little bit?" Her parents considered (they hadn't spent time together in a long while), but she was old enough to make her own decisions. With a sigh from her father they granted the request with terse nods.

Before they had time to change their minds, she fled the house, counting her strides in sequences of tens. When she reached Tim's door, Mrs. Decker answered with her usual veneer of pleasantry. Emma returned a broad smile and commented about meeting Tim, hearing her father's voice ring in her head as she dealt with the woman. At his name she carefully watched Mrs. Decker's eye for signs of twitching. Nothing. Instead, Mrs. Decker went upstairs to fetch her son. Proof that Emma had somehow worked her way into that clam of a soul came in the hushed bickering she could barely make out upstairs. Nonetheless, the two returned seemingly unaffected. Mrs. Decker held the same dazzling smile. Without words, Tim grabbed her hand and they walked to their usual place.

The air was heavy when they stopped. They tried some of their typical things—the name game, even the swing—but they proved useless in combatting the silences, lingering overhead like an injury.

They sat and stared straight into the scrubland. Tim reached for Emma's hand. His palm was sweaty, but she allowed him to weave his fingers through.

After a time, his raggedy breaths found the confidence to speak: "So..." He paused, carefully considering his next words. "My mom gave me the sex talk." Another pause. Both their heads remained fixed forward, but he had to loosen his grip when he realized he was firmly clamping her palm.

Immediately, relief rinsed her worries. "And?" She remained collected.

Not expecting the question or having practiced anything further, he scrambled for an answer.

"—And, it's just kind of weird? You know? I mean... We never..." He didn't need to continue.

She turned to face him, discharging her confidence. He readjusted towards her, his face pallid. Mrs. Decker's high-pitched screeching echoed in her head.

He began to pull his hand back, turn away, but with her long fingers she kept hold of his and forced him to look at her. It wasn't with strength—she hadn't the physical strength over him, regardless—but rather with the dead force of her intention that she stopped him cold. She glanced down at his hand and then back to his face before gently, as if not to wake another person sleeping beside them, climbing onto her knees and crawling over him. He leaned back. Her slim chest hung in front of his face. Her expression was whimsical, and she crashed slowly forward. There was no mistaking the pause that allowed for any sort of objection, but at the same time there was no room for it. He was still as a cat confronting a rattlesnake.

She used her arrogance to hide the shaking until her lips landed onto his. The kiss lasted only seconds, then she retreated and smiled at him, still on all fours, eager to determine if she were any good. Tim sat, petrified. She pushed her bangs aside and went in for another, and then another, until her nervous body relaxed.

Her acts of bravery settled into exploration, and she slipped her tongue into his mouth. It squirmed around before she pulled back for air. Her body tingled, and as Tim settled himself he found the audacity to project his own cap of vigor.

Emma took his hand in hers and began caressing her face with its smooth texture. She kissed the tip of his palm before another round. They continued experimenting with kissing and gentle caressing well into the evening.

It wasn't until the piercing sound cut through the trees, right on cue, that they stopped. Mrs. Decker's calls came more quickly than either anticipated, but a look down at Tim's watch showed that it was indeed eight-thirty. They walked back to the house hand-in-hand, swinging their arms. The heat of the day had given way to a crisp night air that dried the sweat onto their faces.

When Mrs. Decker came into view, a wide grin circled to Emma's ears. She knew there was color to her cheeks and dirt smeared on her jeans. Tim was oblivious to the silent warfare that had developed between the two women in his life, and he greeted his mother with the runoff elation still remaining from their private moments. Emma's eyes gleamed as she offered a laconic, boasting spear: "Hey, Mrs. Decker."

She could see Mrs. Decker's jaw lock. With a dignity Emma found hard to believe, Tim's mother maintained her polished manner.

In a last attempt at the woman, she gave Tim a long hug, pressing her entire frame snuggly against his. Her exhale was exaggerated, almost a moan, before she released him to Mrs. Decker's custody. Another round of goodbyes ensued before Emma directed herself home.

On the long road back to the house Emma felt both victorious and guilty for her wicked treatment of Tim's mother. When she arrived home, she immediately went to bed and snuggled up in her heavy blankets, wishing someone would walk in and comfort her. When no one came, she closed her eyes and tried justifying that Mrs. Decker had it coming. She retold herself the line over and over until she looked at the clock and it was midnight. A slice of guilt leaked steadily; Emma could see Mrs. Decker standing with her hands on her hips trying to appear resolute.

Her apathy towards Tim hummed right along in her guilt. She tried to tune it out, but Tim's gullibility hadn't allowed him to see the pawn he'd become. He was sure to extract more meaning from the kissing than she. He was like a puppy, following her lead, loyal to her command. He had no idea that their earlier activities represented more of an end than a beginning.

In time, he'd catch on. He'd probably hate her when he realized, but that would be okay, she told herself; it's what he needed to move on.

The next day at school Tim acted like a dutiful husband. He brought her small snacks, carried her backpack between classes, ran to retrieve her belongings at the end of class. He'd reach for her hand and she'd give it to him limply. His efforts to appease her became painstaking. Good doggy.

In truth she longed to have the old Tim back, even if her gaze went unmet and he stood quiet like a post. The only normalcy came during their regular attendance at the End of the World in the evening, but even that was tainted with the residue of their past.

Soon after, his mother's horrendous battle shrieks turned into something worse: flaccid calls of defeat. Emma would have dismissed the notion, blaming it on her own conscience, had it not been for the glassy look canvassing Mrs. Decker's face, as if she'd been drinking in the hours they were away. Sometimes she would refuse to meet Emma's gaze. Mrs. Decker's tone melted into a soft, liquid torrent of agony. Emma dreaded seeing her this way, but couldn't help consider her actions a clever change in tactics, a ploy to oust her.

She kept her eyes open for microsigns that would prove Mrs. Decker's depravity. Emma reminded herself that Mrs. Decker was not only a well-respected figure in the community, but one year she was elected to city council; surely she knew how to get what she wanted. She was no fool.

In the end though, what caused the complete crash between her and Tim—the Fat Boy of incidents—didn't come from Mrs. Decker as Emma thought it might. Emma would have fought on, even so far as admitting a base enjoyment in the matter, but she was blindsided by an overwhelming clout from another source. The unknowing counterpart to Mrs. Decker and the poor devil to finalize Emma's decision came from Tim himself.

TIM

A few weeks had passed since their first kiss, and although everything looked healthy on the outside—they still participated in their normal activities—the grotesque struggle, the corpse of their relationship, could be felt rotting away from the inside. It was unmistakable.

Not grasping just how severe the situation truly was, Tim intended to show the effort he was willing to inject into healing their future. The form: an exotic, beaded bracelet he'd picked up the past weekend at the flea market. He found the item while attending the monthly trip—a bonding activity—with his mother. The two somehow began making the long drive two years ago after his father left them. From whatever provenance the trip was spurred, he and his mother held to the activity faithfully.

A single vendor, a broad and swarthy Middle-Eastern man, stood out from the rest when they arrived. Tim remembered the man's dark skin and white teeth. Confidence radiated from him, as if he wasn't a vendor but rather a Persian king standing amongst his subjects. Before Tim could walk in his direction, ask for a blessing, he was ripped away and led to the bog of the marketplace by his mother.

In a final glance Tim's eyes waxed over the dark-skinned man, who returned a clairvoyant smile. Then Tim was yanked away by his mother's invisible leash.

For the next half-hour Tim followed his mother's steps through a sea of heavyset pedestrians. They gasped on him with what seemed like heavy breath for a walk on flat ground. Each vendor's tent was set up to block the harsh three o'clock sun, uncountable foldout tables erected in neat rows between each aisle. They were furnished with embroidered tablecloths to properly present the merchants' goods.

If a vendor had done well for the day, he retreated to the shaded oasis under his tent and watched over his belongings, like a miser would his gold; those who had yet to meet their fictitious quotas stood up, beckoning customers with one-line hooks in their final attempts before the business day concluded.

The sounds of clattering objects, creaking carts, laughter, and light-noted jangles penetrated Tim's eardrums in a harsh rhythm. He and his mother passed tables displaying Indian spices, chili-peppered corn, ponchos, gossamer China sets, plastic utensils, oriental rugs, blankets with tiger prints, gilded Buddhas, African beads, and even baskets of Mexican tamarind pods. He imagined there was an item for every need a person could think of at one corner or another of the market. They swam through the waves of dark-skinned, light-skinned, skinny-faced, stout-faced, long-nosed, sweaty people looking at the many objects, while the cloud of red dust—kicked up from the trampling footsteps—mixed with the stench of perspiration and ardent spices to form a unique fragrance of population.

As they made their way down the tented corridors to peruse the variety of foreign contraptions, his mother kept a steady eye on him. After a long stretch of walking Tim realized that they'd looped around to where they first began, and after scanning the stalls his attention refocused on the enigmatic Middle-Eastern vendor. Tim's gaze ambled unmet in his direction, and he noticed that just beyond him was his island stand of handcrafted jewelry.

Quite quickly the man, in his twisted eye, noticed Tim. It caused a bout of fright and Tim deflected, but when his gaze was forced back out of curiosity the tall vendor was waiting patiently, with the instincts of a gypsy, to accept and relieve Tim's uncertainty.

Then, as if the mysterious man commanded a strange magic, the unthinkable happened: his mother incredibly and as if under a trance told him to stay put while she went to take care of some personal business. As far as he could remember, she had never left him alone when they were at the market. She pointed at where she was headed and trusted Tim's mental ball and chain to keep him where he was. The mysterious vendor was only a few short paces away.

As soon as his mother was far enough, Tim's gait automatically floated towards the booth. He approached close enough to make out the odor of cardamom and cloves seething from the vendor's clothes, and the details of his black eyelids, thick eyebrows, and glistening beard became visible. The man must have known that the awkward teen was standing right next to him, but Tim wasn't directed with any comment. No, instead he was allowed to look at the jewelry without obstruction. The man wanted him to marvel at how the symbols painted on each bead caught the eye, how the distinct cuts allowed light to refract brilliantly off the dark surfaces. Tim's imagination of the token's worth climbed steadily the longer he stood there.

He analyzed the bracelet before noting the price: twenty-five dollars. Still eyeing the object, he dug into his pocket and confirmed that he had only a little more than fifteen in crinkled bills and loose change. A frown spread over his face. He planned on buying lunch with the money on his way home. It wasn't very often they were down this way for his favorite sandwich shop, Mr. Hensen's Pickles.

As Tim was considering his misfortune, the swarthy vendor chimed in with his buried voice, "You like zis one, huh?"

Tim looked up. The man's face was saturated with sweat, his pores were large, and his skin was worn from the sun. The smells, the location, his accent all drew Tim to value, to *want*, the object even more.

Tim nodded at the vendor's words.

"You know," his eyes squinted to emphasize the bargain, "zis' one is only twenty-five dollars."

He made a two and a five with his hands.

Tim fumbled in his pocket so they could re-inspect the bills together. He pulled out the scant wad; a dime fell to the dirt.

The vendor's eyes dimmed with disappointment. He let out a drawn exhale while he scratched his beard, doing a personal math Tim could never understand. Tim looked up in his self-commiseration before the man replied superciliously with one finger, "Fine. Fifteen dollars zen."

As the vendor finished relaying his decision, Tim heard his mother articulate his name with her notorious screech. Tim looked back in surprise to see her approaching, searching wildly. Aware of the esoteric nature of their dealings, the tall man quickly traded the bracelet for the blot of cash in Tim's outstretched hand.

Tim stuffed the bracelet into his pocket just as his mother grabbed his shoulder. The bearded vendor continued to scan and holler at the crowd as if they had never spoken, without even a glance at Tim or his mother.

On the drive home his mother went on about how she shouldn't have left him alone and she wasn't sure what had gotten into her and it was dangerous and he could have got lost. Tim was too preoccupied to digest her words while the exuberant little bracelet burned in his pocket. His right hand burrowed into his jeans, and he neurotically stroked each individual bead with his thumb and forefinger. He liked how the scabrous points ran over the grooves of his fingertips. With each successive stroke he was constructing how he'd present the treasure to Emma.

When they stopped for lunch, his mother paid after Tim reported that he had forgotten his money.

In his mind he presented the tender gift in a grandiose gesture of courage. It would display the hidden flame within his timid body. It would absolve him of the problems he'd created. The bracelet would illustrate how much he cared, and consequently thrust them back to the warm and exciting start of their relationship.

He carried the artifact, the promise it represented, close to his body when they marched to the End of the World. As he followed, Emma's dark hair waved in the breeze, her slender shoulders were haloed by the sun's rays. Tim had the presentation planned already. He knew exactly where they should stand, sit, face each other.

They made it to the tree line. *Perfect.* Emma decided to sit on their usual rock as he knew she would. *Good.* Everything was going well, just as planned, until she repositioned herself to catch more shade. *Damn.* Her angle was just a pinch too far outward. It was slight—negligible to anybody else—but his senses became acutely aware of the detail. The afternoon heat quickly began to bathe him. Emma, on the other hand, seemed distantly unaffected. However, some ineffable quality was most certainly off in the strategy. Tim's brain instantly hit an overload, but he was already too deeply committed to abort, a warrior plunged into a losing battle.

He cleared his throat of its itch. She looked at him as if he were ill, making him especially aware that his wan complexion had likely grown even more pallid in the past thirty seconds. He cleared his throat again before concluding that it was best to simply dig for the bracelet in his pocket. He pulled the object— his valiant sword and scepter wrapped in the mystical presence of the swarthy vendor with his glistening beard and twisted eye, wrapped in covert dealings and a tenacity that allowed him to circumvent his mother's inquisition, wrapped amongst the many eyesome treasures at the marketplace—and showed it to her in the flat of his palm.

Her eyebrows wove together as she studied what it was he held: a simple bracelet.

"So," he announced in his raspy voice.

She studied his face and became even more puzzled.

"I've been thinking about how much time has passed since we first came out here."

She nodded but patiently waited for him to continue.

He cleared his throat a third time. He could feel apprehension inviting him to retreat from the nerve-wracking ordeal. As he tried to shake the feeling, it sunk its claws deeper.

"I just feel like we've been growing apart, so I bought you this."

He offered his palm. By the quizzical look on her face, she probably would have accepted anything he pushed onto her—a burning bag of cat shit, a tarantula—but nonetheless he felt lighter having relieved himself of the trinket. He tried his best to maintain eye contact, but his gaze fell to the ground.

While holding the object, Emma stammered out, "Oh, thanks. It's really, lovely... That was nice of you." And then she patted him on the shoulder.

For quite some time she held the bracelet awkwardly in her palm, as if it were a live animal that was climbing to her forearm, and then she returned to facing straight ahead not knowing what else to say.

They sat there for a long time until he asked, "Hey, Emma?" He peeked over at her, "If this really was the edge of the world, and we were the last two people on it, would you be okay with that?"

She never looked over at him; instead she scanned the field before them, the wind still playing with her thin strands, and said with a nudge of her shoulder, "Of course."

With her answer, she slipped the bracelet around her wrist. He smiled.

The next day, describing how she needed time by herself, Emma broke up with him.

Over the next few weeks she seemed to adjust well enough. He, however, was left to stand in dark corners unnoticed. With his unique ability to avoid eye contact he watched behind a mirror at the happy world passing before him.

After school when he was again alone, he reminded himself that such a thing was bound to happen. It was just a matter of time. Looking back, he wished he would've been bolder with his intentions, back before the bracelet or the End of the World became stale, so far back he hadn't even known her at the time. If he could have shown her how much he cared or how much she lifted him, the course of their relationship could have been different. He knew that much.

But, that was just a fantasy. As it played out, he learned to live without the feeling of connection. His concentration on the arts and sciences multiplied. He had no real hobbies, so his last chance to fill the gap was by getting somewhere in life. He started immediately.

He still couldn't suppress her from his mind—or heart— entirely, however; that would be impossible. When the night was still and his mind wandered, he would imagine Emma's happy laugh, sitting beside him without a care in the world, her beaming eyes and the brush of her fingers against his kneecap, the first time they kissed. *Damn.*

V

EMMA

They had, indeed, shared some intimate memories. Perhaps that's what drew her out here. The memories crashed onto her harder than she expected. The expanse before them hadn't changed; worse, the trail leading out here was more worn, as if somebody—he—had been coming regularly since she left.

She peered over the landscape, still waiting for a tumbleweed to bumble across her view. Was she using Tim as a stand-in for Reid? The thought had crossed her mind, but she didn't want to admit that such malice was in her nature. She couldn't be swindling him a second time at happiness.

He rolled off another comment that wisped into the air. "Hmm? Oh, yes, the rope swing."

When she looked over to it, only a bristled cord with dangling tendrils remained. If she'd walked closer she would find the other half of the rope attached to the smooth rubber tire of past days.

Her attention refocused, and they continued reminiscing. At some point her leg began shaking with a desire to flee. She never disliked Tim, but she regretted carrying their relationship any further than friendship.

They stared blankly ahead. She expected him to bring up Fred the owl, or the night of her silly fear, but he sat without a word. He didn't press her to speak so they sat silently reflecting, trying to find meaning in the objects they once named.

When the darkness drew in, Emma waited for his mother's shrieks. The ghostly wails were engrained in her memory. But this also never came.

"That's amazing," she said out of nowhere.

His head swiveled towards her, eyebrows furled in question, eyes still trying to find a courage they never had.

"We spent an entire evening out here not talking. I didn't know it was possible to do that with somebody."

He waited for her to extrapolate.

"I kind of liked it. I can't do that with many people."

Her shoulders relaxed. Admittedly, she would have vexed his words, any of them, so the silence between them was for the best.

When the light of day was lost completely, faking shivers he asked, "Ready to go back?"

She nodded and embraced the nostalgia of squinting in the dark as they found the path. Navigating the trail was easier than she remembered. It was cool outside, and the unhurried walk, Tim's easy breaths, the smell of sodden roots culminated into a memory she held well into old age. It popped up years later when she was outside hanging laundry. A breeze cast through her yard, dissipating the sunken heat, and something in the air pried into her memories. It was without rhyme or reason, really, but even decades later when a shaky twang developed in her writing and her eyes grew old enough to betray her, she could recall that single, random moment on the path with perfect clarity.

When the moment passed, they arrived at the back porch. The orange bulb canvassed half their faces and left shadows of their features. His mother had opened the back door and was waiting underneath the doorframe, preoccupied. She started in surprise when she saw them. The easiness of her and Tim being together, the soothing silence, led Emma to (almost) believe that Mrs. Decker was an illusion, a memory. When Emma saw Mrs. Decker, her foot caught the ground and she stumbled. The full-figured woman stood before her, alive and absolute.

As they drew closer, Emma found the change in Mrs. Decker's demeanor stranger than anything else that evening.

In a tranquil tone—not a note of resentment or frustration or revenge—Mrs. Decker called out, "Oh, hey you two. Did you have fun?" Even her smile was genial.

The length of time couldn't have left the woman completely amnestic to who Emma was, of their warring paths. *Impossible*.

Snuffing her bafflement, Emma replied with a nod, "Yes, it was nice to come out here. Hope you've been well, Mrs. Decker."

With an exaggerated nod, a gesture grand and refined, Mrs. Decker answered in return: "Most certainly."

Emma took a step closer to see if the crazy bitch was drunk. She appeared normal enough, and didn't smell of alcohol. Had it not been for one final comment—"Emma, my Dear, watch for cars on your way home. There are some crazy drivers on the roads these days"—she would have held to the agreeable idea that Mrs. Decker had just forgotten who she was. Instead, Emma thanked her and left, utterly confused.

She fled into the stony night, disoriented by the differences in everything she once knew. Her time with Tim had been so completely antipodal, like parallel universes. The handful of years felt like eons. Only the land remained unchanged. An eerie feeling knotted her stomach.

In the days to follow, Emma concluded that the event between her and Tim had been mostly pleasant, and she was even open to the idea returning, but when he asked she nonetheless found reasons to be unavailable.

When Tim persisted, her excuses became more exorbitant, not because she was stoutly against the idea but because she felt it necessary to push back. Given how she couldn't apply the argument that she was helping Greggory—she hadn't visited in well over three weeks—she went as far as to suggest that her parents were bringing home a new dog and she needed to be there when it arrived. It wasn't a total lie. Her parents had, in fact, brought up the subject one night, but it was far from the truth that *that* was the day they'd carry out the idea. Tim began asking so often the request became trite, and with every excuse she felt less inclined to make her daily walk and confront the tilt of his head. The heat, barely catching a sliver of Reid (if even that), spending the money she was supposed to be saving, all began to tax her.

Worse, there was no convenient alternative route that allowed her to avoid Greggory's house while sharing a path with Reid. Her stomach churned every time she reached the property. His house was erected so resolutely. It would be so easy for him to slip outside and confront her. What would she tell him if that happened? She had nothing. Her head hung low, knowing she was fully visible, day in and day out. Each time she passed she imagined him eyeing her with a disappointed sway of his head.

When her guilt intensified, she tried looping up the hill behind her house before cutting over to Stinson, but it proved too risky. There were too many dangers: unexpected rattler nestled in the grass, holes causing her to tumble, inhospitable bushes to get lost in. Plus, this path and Reid's would never intersect. She'd be beaten down by the wild flora, endangered by the fauna, miss Reid, and then meet Tim's questioning. Not the best solution.

She thought of navigating the huge field buffering her property from Greggory's, but that too proved futile. On the outskirts of her property, of everybody's property, was a network of rusty, barbed-wire fencing. Years ago it was erected to designate property lines—way back when physical boundaries were necessary. However, as time wore on the matrix was rendered obsolete. Shrubs and long grass had grown to block the visibility of the steel, and the detachment of the land allowed people to forget about the network altogether. The one exception: when a girl attempted to pass through the meadow. Cutting across the field was hopeless.

The lack of alternatives and the awkward feeling from passing Greggory's house entrenched much of her frustration, but what caused the most grief was her longing to return to his home, help him with oddball projects, listen to his restrained talk, sip fresh tea, gloss Reid over from an affectionate distance. But that could never be the case after everything that had happened, the way she left without word. Her pride was too constricting and her actions too severe. Emma continued to walk with a hurried step past Greggory's. She'd continue until the dilemma became too mountainous and she stopped altogether. That was coming soon enough.

GREGGORY

The dream always began with his vision blurred by a curtain of buoyant white blossoms. His head would turn until he noticed the nearby cottonwood tree from which they gently floated. Their parachutes twirled upward, and soon the wall of fuzz diluted to transparency. Only then did she come into view, standing directly beyond the stream of petals. She waited there, commanding him from an alcove amongst waist-high cheatgrass. He could faintly catch her vanilla. It rejuvenated him, made him feel whole again. Just before he became completely lost in the scent, she refocused his attention by spinning in a pirouette, her dress floating grandly in the air. At her playfulness she covered her mouth and laughed—giggled—as she so often had. Then, he took a step forward. Glowing angelically, she beckoned him, relaying her desire to have him reach and feel her again, to share another precious moment together. His focus was unyielding. He took another step. Her blue eyes became visible, and the vanilla began to mix with her natural odor and that of springtime. It was inevitable that he would reach her, but as soon as he tried to take one more stride, he awoke.

He'd be drenched in a cold sweat, and it was always dark outside. Sitting up on the edge of his bed, he desperately yearned to hear her voice tickle his ear, for her giggles and their arguments about thermometers to reign over his life. His fingertips remembered how it felt to run along the inside of her forearm and shallow valleys of spine. His nose still carried her smell. His ribs could still feel her elfin jabs to make sure he was awake with her in the middle of the night. He missed how their heartbeats would join ever-so-slowly when they held each other. Lying there alone, he clung to the pillow that he refused to wash—even though the remnants of her smuggled scent had already faded.

In the time since his son left, Greggory holed himself in the darkness of the house, barred away from the world. The years passed. He'd long ago been released from work, and adapted well to his small income from the government and the last of their savings. His body's daily routine was the only way to distract his mind: wake up, go to the sink, put tea on, drink the tea in the living room, and then take on the task of bookmaking. Yes, bookmaking.

The effort began after Greggory, in a sudden urge to pen the details of her life, scavenged for a writing material. During his initial attempt he found a scrap of paper on which to write his notes, but later he deemed the quality too poor. Neurotically he began cutting printer paper down to a size more worthy of intimate scrawl. In his first attempts he bound the homemade articles with Elmer's Glue.

This was how he came to cut, collate, construct, and assemble the materials. He never felt the paper cuts. And by the end of the day, after concluding that his new work was unworthy, he'd toss it in the wood-burning stove and begin anew in the morning. In his habit he cobbled together everything from small books to large ones, thick covers and thin covers, weighted paper, colored paper—even using cardboard from a cereal box in one desperate attempt, and going so far as ordering vellum and gold-dusted ink in another. But all of his efforts failed to pass final inspection.

He spent his days working continuously, stopping only for lunch, until night came and he made the long, lonely trek down the hall to his bed. As soon as he reached his room, his dream awaited him like a drug-addicted friend—initially appealing because of the warm companionship you once shared, but by the end only taking, darkly stealing, from your life.

The one activity to disrupt his anesthetic practice, in fact his only reason for leaving the house at all, was the grocery store.

He hardly felt the grumble in his stomach, but amidst the numb blur that became his life Greggory remained dimly aware that he needed food. Only when he was on the verge of paralysis from lack of calories would he make the trip.

This was his life. He might have continued this way forever had his dreams of Sophia, her phantom, not disturbed him so greatly. At the beginning, despite never reaching her he nonetheless cherished the opportunity to see and feel and smell her again. But then, waking one night screaming, he came to the realization that the illusory images were becoming more real to him than her memory. It led Greggory to his insomnia.

He began sitting awake at the kitchen table in the middle of the night, the window cracked, smell of damp hay wafting in with a drift of wind. He'd stare out in his fogged vision at the land flushed with moonlight, and try to pick the soft mysteries from the shadows. At one point he wondered when the once-triumphant melody of crickets and musical set from night birds realigned into an anguished nocturne. If sleep happened to overtake him on any given night, he would fall victim to it in fear rather than with grit.

Time slipped past. He hoped to fall to insanity as a way to escape, but there was no such luck. His exhausted listlessness granted senseless action. His indomitable concern of not being able to distinguish her from his dreams took on some validity during the course of those sleepless nights. He later remembered only fragments from his years of half-living: his hand shaking uncontrollably from exhaustion as he tried to bind his most recent book, sitting blankly behind the wheel of his truck, tearless sobs in the rickety kitchen chair. He had difficulty pulling any concrete action he performed to memory. Until the moment his life finally changed, again.

His mind was still blurry after such a long time living with the shadows. He was finally burnt out. After drinking his traditional cup of tea, but before working on the next book, Greggory took action: he flipped a coin. Heads he would continue on, tails he would end it all. He could see the dazzling little coin flutter in the air as he flipped it. He could see it hit the ground with a *clnk clnk* before spinning into a translucent sphere. For a long time it hung suspended, refusing to make a choice, until finally it began to slow and wobble. Greggory—black rings around his bloodshot eyes—stared at the linoleum floor transfixed, waiting.

Until the day he died, Greggory could clearly see the exact spot it landed, bravely shining heads.

With the decision made, he knew what came next. Slowly, thoughtfully, he entered his room and stood over the chestnut box on the nightstand.

Drawing back the lid, he lingered for a long moment over the elephant pendants, everything he had ever cared about in one little box. Then he closed it. With it tucked underneath his arm, he made his way out of the house. Grabbing a rusty shovel in the process, he walked slowly up the same hill where he'd once proposed. He only barely noticed how much he was sweating when he reached the top.

He wiped his forehead with a sleeve and looked up to the clouds. They floated in front of the sun, splintering rays of light in all directions. The warm wind picked up and blew into his haggard body. Greggory closed his eyes. The sweat began to dry in his wiry beard, and for the first time in a long while, he felt a sense of relief. He whispered his thanks for the brief moment, the gentle wind and sun's rays, before proceeding.

His hands shook from age more than fatigue. He struck the red Indian dirt several times before the sun-baked soil cracked and it became easier to spade away large clumps.

Only after he dug to clay did his dusty hands go back for the box sitting on a nearby rock. He smoothed his fingers over the velvet wood and said one last prayer.

The box was too clean as it sat in the harsh soil, but he nonetheless tossed the first large heap back onto it. One spadeful became ten, and quickly the hole filled. He packed the last of the loose soil before giving the mound a light tap.

Greggory stood quietly for what seemed like days before a speck of earth turned dark, and then another. The clouds were broken in the sky, but the large cumulus above began dispersing droplets. Without looking back, Greggory hurried home. He made it just in time to take refuge from an attacking downpour.

His clothes were damp as he walked back to his bedroom. There was a shiny rectangle rimmed by thick dust on the nightstand. With a round swipe, he smeared it, feeling as hollow as he expected he would.

The storm raged for days, the spray of droplets growing thicker until they resembled their mighty winter form. The puddles built into ponds, and then into streams. The wind howled down the valley and combed the grass, coaxing loose strands to fly off into oblivion. Greggory's tearless sobs went unheard by the world.

After days of torrential downpour, as swiftly as it began, the clouds drifted and sunshine flitted through the puffing masses. The single cloud that started everything floated away languidly. The darkness of Greggory's room was roiled by blinding sunshine. He tried clinging to his miserable state but was forced outside to assess the damages.

Everything but their morning rockers was either destroyed or swept away. The rain-plowed yard held just enough resemblance to what it once was for Greggory to recognize it as his own. With the resignation of a monk, he stepped out and carefully picked up a scrap of metal once belonging to the porch table.

In the weeks to follow he went on to mend the broken home. He began by placing the things left behind into metal garbage cans. As days passed he became dissatisfied with the progress he was making, so he revamped his efforts by filling the bed of his pickup and hauling the loads to the dump. He came across everything from broken lawn chairs to plied siding from houses, to fragments of wood and metal, to unrecognizable objects from whoknowswhere. He inspected each like a fossil before tossing it in the mound of junk.

When the larger debris was accounted for, he moved to brambles and mulched leaves—and at one point he was shoveling bare land—until he stopped to laugh at his pedantries. The yard was now almost bare.

The fixation he once held with bookbinding was replaced with simplifying and reinforcing the yard. When he found less work outside he moved inside the home, and after ridding himself of nearly all his material possessions he began to rebuild. His first project was replacing the dislocated shingles atop the house. It was shoddy carpentry work, but toward the end he discovered he had a knack for it. Stepping back to marvel the finished product, he was disturbed by the crooked brown slats he placed down at the beginning, so he went back over them a second time. Next was the truck for his son that was left to rot. After that, the battered porch railing. In a flurried motion he soon spread his efforts to the rest of the property.

At the crowning of his rebuilding, when he would tear down and refurbish different parts of his home on a whim, for whatever reason he left the window in the living room that no longer slid open, the dilapidated fence, and the patchy grass in their injured states. (The patchy grass, however, learned to grow on its own, and spread to the rest of the yard as the years pushed forward.)

The more specialized his jobs became, the more Greggory found himself in the hardware section of the grocery store. It was the most tormented part of his new practice: in such a small town, word traveled. People he'd never even met watched him from a distance with the knowledge of his sad story. He'd only just gotten use to these people no longer stopping unexpectedly by his house to relay their condolences. He slunk around the store like an exotic animal on display. It made him resentful of his work, but as quickly as the feeling came he would return home, revisit the imaginary coin lying heads-up on the floor, and continue his efforts with renewed faith.

∞   ∞   ∞

Disrupting events are bound to occur. They always do; it's just a matter of time. He tried to live a stable life, but somebody or some thing always came when he was just beginning to find a balance. Two major events disrupted his new life. It was early springtime and Greggory was at the beginning phases of installing a new kitchen window.

He was sitting at the table, staring blankly and thinking of the finished product. *The most effective way to rip the thing out would be a crowbar*, he concluded. Then, a UPS truck came bumping along. As it creaked to a stop in front of his yard, Greggory caught the face of the disgruntled driver in his brown uniform. After a few inconclusive moments, the driver jumped from the truck's perch. Greggory became agitated almost immediately. He was sick and tired of others intruding on his peace. But the skinny driver scanned over the address, disregarded the unwelcoming stare, and jogged lightly towards the house. After glancing at Greggory through the window, the driver knocked. Both waited in silence for a long moment before Greggory slid the kitchen window up, just a fraction, just enough to be heard.

"What do you want?"

Not knowing how he should proceed, the fellow addressed the window. "I have a letter for Greggory O'Sullivan. Is that you?"

Greggory paused to consider his response.

"Yes. That's me."

"Well, do you want your letter?"

Greggory mulled over his answer.

"Yes."

Not understanding customers like Greggory, the driver approached the window shaking his head.

"I need you to sign, *sir*."

The crack in the window grew two inches, and the driver slipped through a black brick of electronic hardware. After Greggory sketched his name with the plastic stick, he pushed the block back outside to trade for the letter. The man could be heard mumbling under his breath as he marched back to the truck. He climbed in and drove off to the next isolated address in the middle of nowhere.

Greggory's attention shifted from the window to the mystery in his hands. The familiar handwriting had developed a careless flow that comes only with practice and age, but it was still recognizable as his son's. Greggory studied the return address, *Baltimore, MD 21205*, before his eyes glided to his name. It was certainly intended for him, so he tore at one of the corners, careful not to damage the contents inside.

There was only a single sheet, folded in thirds, written in a neater hand than the markings on the front.

> *Hey Dad,*
> *I know it's been a long time*
> *since we've talked and first off I*

want to say sorry for running off. I was young and dumb. I'm not sure how you feel about it, but I hope you know that I miss you. Anyways, I tried calling but the phone is disconnected? You don't have the same number?

Greggory had long-since removed the phone from the house, as he expected exactly zero calls.

What I'm about to say might be a lot to take in, so I hope you're sitting at that old kitchen table you love. That girl I went to Indonesia with, I married her not long after, and we've been together ever since. Even more, I hope you're sitting! we have a son. You're a grandfather. His name is Reid. I wanted to tell you, but I wasn't sure how you'd take it. He's a good kid. A few years back he started asking about you, and although I wanted to tell you, I was afraid of how you'd react because of all that's happened between us.

He'd really like to see you this summer if you're up for it. It's his last one before college. Time flies. Call or write me and we'll talk about it. There's a lot more to catch

> *up on but I'll leave it to that for*
> *now.*
>> *Love always,*
>> *Paul.*

The letter took up the front page exactly, and was finalized with an odd, pin-sized dot of ink that revealed the courage it took to write. After reading it a second time, Greggory leaned into the wooden chair. He smoothed the paper at its folded ridges and began twirling his fingers on the tiniest corner.

For hours he sat and considered how to respond. The revelations contained in the letter swirled in his head. He sat long enough for the sun to set and the familiar song of cricket chirps and toad croaks to flutter through the five inches of window space. Night dew began to collect on the table. He read the note one more time, with supreme concentration at the pinpoint inklet. *Fine.*

As dejected as he felt when his son left, as much as he wanted to feel upset and angry, he wanted his son and grandson even more. While sitting he let the rubber knot within his chest unwind, mulled over how he could possibly tell his son how badly he wanted to see his grandson.

For the next few days, he labored over writing a response—still resolving to keep his phone disconnected—and ended with a two-paragraph reply. The message revealed just enough to show he was interested, without revealing his desperation to reconnect with his only family. He signed the bottom with his earmark, a long flowing "G" and sharp, quick "y" before tucking his fate—in an all-too familiar fashion—into an envelope.

While dropping the first of what would be many letters off at the one-room post office in town, he remembered that he needed a rubber mallet to complete his new project, so he stopped by the grocery store on his return.

He'd become quite skilled at weaving through the aisles without notice, but the optimism expressed in his quickened step must have given him away because a young, ambitious fellow interrupted his rare moment of contentment to exchange words. Greggory allowed the exchange for a moment while he sat daydreaming about his house, the window, his son, his grandson. *His grandson!* The formless words flushed like liquid through Greggory's ears until the man paused and caused Greggory to fall back to reality.

He was *still* gabbling away. *My God.* Out of the jumble of meaningless words, Greggory picked out the few red flags: "daughter" and "help you."

"…with chores or things around the house, you know. I always see you working outside and fixing things—I really like what you're doing to the yard, by the way…"

At the mention, Greggory tried concealing the mallet he'd just picked up. He waved away the man's suggestion, but the imbecile father wouldn't let up, to the point where Greggory's position collapsed against his will.

She'd start in early June, the man concluded—the same time he just committed to, wrote for, his grandson to visit. Once again he tried telling the bloke it was a bad time, to *please* fuck off, but it was too late. The gent walked away in utter merriment for having just ruined Greggory's small moment of joy. *People.*

He consoled himself with the thought that the man was merely blowing smoke as a kind neighbor, but nestled in his gut was an unsettling feeling. To avoid any further molestation he fled to the safety of his house as quickly as he could, and after returning immediately began plying apart the upper planks of the window. With each successive nail that gave way, his mind slowed until calmness gradually returned. The old rancher who sold him the home must have been a carpenter, because the nails would have easily remained burrowed in the wood for a hundred years.

He placed each one in a small Ziploc bag. His trials in carpentry were forgiving: his tasks could always be adjusted or redone until the outcome proved favorable. People, on the other hand, were not. They were foreign objects to him. They were mercurial and relentless and unforgiving.

This was the first time he would open his life to the outside world since Sophia passed, and as if one person wasn't enough he'd gone and allowed two people to stampede in with full force.

Greggory sat at his kitchen table. A single floodlight illuminated the window frame. He'd pried loose only the first board. Greggory worked through the night.

VI

EMMA

On her fifth birthday, Emma wanted a *horsey* more than anything else in the world. And she most definitely made her parents aware of that wish. At the time, she had five pristine horses in her collection of animal friends. One was black, one white, one a fawn Arabian, one a stout pony, and one named Henry (her favorite, because her father offered the name). Rather than receiving a live horse as requested, her father bought her a sixth—a beautiful brown and white—and took her to visit the local corral. Emma remembered crying wildly upon seeing the huge animals from a distance, baying and swaying their heads with majestic grace. With her father watching over her, they approached the gate and she fed them apple slices from her palm, her father repeating softly into her ear, "Hold your hand out flat." It was a cool day for the 20th of July, even cooler from the stony metal gate she stood on, but it was a magnificent memory. "Peeks, be careful getting down," her father reminded her before she jumped from the gate and into his arms. That's how it was when she was little; her father protected her, always.

Later (or perhaps it was even before her fifth birthday), another moment stood out from the rest: her mother sitting on the couch and her father on the recliner, both watching her from their seats in the cozy little living room. There was no reason that they ought to be staring so intently—Emma was just playing with toys on the ground—but she felt an overwhelming warmth and happiness when she looked up to her parents' eyes. Each tilted their head and smiled at her, looking on with curious enjoyment. Everything felt frozen in time except for her and their small movements. Then time returned and her parents looked at each other, smiling as if they'd just gotten married again.

Moments like these shaped the person Emma would become, and wrecked her a little when she grew older. When Emma was young she always had her parents' support, and although she was only five, or six, or seven, they often asked for her opinion and considered her wishes, in both matters of the house and her life.

When she was four: "Peeks, do you want to brush your teeth or your face first?"

Four and a half: "What do you think Emma, should we get the brown chair or the black one?"

On the day of her fifth birthday, after she and her father went to feed the horses: "Start school this year, or next?" Emma was on the edge of the age when it came to beginning school, her parents explained, and they wondered what she thought about starting the following year instead of this one.

Of course, Emma was too young to really understand what the hell she was, or was not, committing to—all she knew was that she loved her mother and father—but the idea of waiting didn't seem like a bad one. Emma opted to stay with her parents.

When her first day of school finally arrived, Emma remembered her mother hugging her tightly, tears streaming down her cheeks, as Emma was released to the custody of the teacher.

In time Emma learned that school was a way of life, and as she grew she saw which of her parents better understood the daily struggles of a six-year-old. It's a given that we love both of our parents, but there's always one who seems to understand better. For Emma, that was her father. Whether by real or fictive means, Emma and he held onto something profound. Together they fostered a bond comparable to the deepness of the Mariana Trench, something barely understood and ever-expansive. Deep. In part, it came from the fishing trips and the easiness she felt in being around him, his ability to understand. In part, it came from his firm embrace, like he was squeezing away any doubt that he loved you. He was a concrete wall, a superhero. He was there, and always would be, she was certain.

Still, at age nine Emma detected the slightest of shifts. If you'd looked at her family for the first time, you'd never suspect anything was off. They still ate nightly meals together, her father still told her that he loved her, her mother still helped pick out dresses in the morning. But things were off. Her father stopped asking about her day, or what she'd learned, and he didn't offer that grizzly hug. Instead he stared blankly ahead at the dinner table, his thoughts far away. For the first time, Emma remained quiet rather than reeling off her small complaints and victories. In the morning her father left earlier, and at night he'd return later. Emma's mother still spent the time to help her study, but she wasn't her father, and he was a hard person to replace.

During that time, two years before they even moved to Forester, Emma began generating her own opinions. The ways of doing things moved away from "Peeks, would you like this, or *this*? A or B? Yes or *no*?" Instead, she was left to think for herself, left creating the A's and B's, Yes's and No's. That's when she realized she wasn't a child any longer.

And then came the move, after her father was offered a new job in the neighboring county. Any hope that things might return to what they once were withered over the next few years. On her fifteenth birthday it was decided on her behalf that she could have her own key to the house, and take the bus home from school. Her mother began a business selling landscape photographs and paintings in the same city where her father worked, and they would leave together early in the morning. On the weekends, her father often had "one small thing to do at the office," and her mother took the opportunity to maintain her studio or meet with clients. Every now and again Emma would join her during these weekend trips, but that soon became tiresome. Her mother in her sharp pantsuit and jacket always appeared busy with clients. She'd offer winks to Emma from a distance as she led these strangers around the building or to the show room.

Emma began staying home on the weekends and taking the bus home after school. She'd arrive to an empty house. The years passed.

On her fifth birthday, it was a trip to the corral. Her eighth was to Yellowstone National Park. Tenth was the aquarium in Monterey Bay. No matter what was going on in her life, what sadness or awkwardness, Emma counted on the surprise birthday trips with her father to bring her back to the warm and secure part of her childhood, the part where she was innocent again. But on her sixteenth birthday, a trip didn't happen. Her parents—father—decided she wanted clothes and a phone and a bicycle rather than a new memory. Instead, she spent the day remembering the old ones. A tiny ball of sadness settled in her throat

On her eighteenth birthday, she was still taken aback that the trips had stopped. A fifty-dollar bill, a new pair of shoes, another new phone, and a family dinner replaced any surprise. In the morning her mother asked what she wanted to eat, and at night set out to make it.

Around the dinner table they sat silently until her father attempted conversation: "Hey Peeks, are you excited about being eighteen? Finally an adult, heh? I guess that means you can buy cigarettes now?" He winked, trying to spark a laugh. Her mother gave him a look.

"It feels nice, I guess." She tried smiling.

Silence fell over the table again. Her father continued, awkwardly: "Well, what have you been up to lately? I've been so busy with work these days that I haven't kept track." He laughed to himself. "Do you like helping Mr. O'Sullivan?"

A thought of Reid came to mind. "Yeah. He's nice." — Except, of course, she stopped visiting him almost three weeks ago, and had instead been following his grandson to the grocery store in the hundred-degree heat. She thought it was best to refrain from sharing this detail, now that she considered it. Helping, helped, it's all the same thing. — "I've just been, you know, hanging around. Going on walks."

"Sounds like you're busy, but the exercise is good. I know you're older now," there was a strain of shyness in his words, "but if you *wanted*, we could still go on a trip somewhere. I don't know if girls your age are into those sorts of things."

Bitterness at the idea rooted within. Perhaps she felt mocked, or perhaps she felt hurt. Either way she felt defensive.

"Thanks Dad, but you don't have to. I really like my gifts. Thanks for them."

Sometimes people act polite, even though it's obvious something is wrong. This was one of those times. But her father didn't know how to react to it.

"Are you sure? I could maybe take some time off in the next couple weeks."

"It's okay."

"Okay..." He became quiet again.

They shared more words before dinner ended, her mother included, but Emma didn't particularly remember them. She listened to her heart beating in her chest, did her best to train her thoughts on Reid.

∞   ∞   ∞

One week into August, she finally concluded that this would be her last walk—for tea, for Reid, for Tim, for anything. She held onto the image of Reid, but it wasn't worth the dehydration, sunburns, or exhaustion. And quite frankly, over the past few weeks she'd relearned and restarted to appreciate the freedom of autonomy. She had finally concluded that she didn't need Reid, and she didn't need Tim. The secret pleasures that come from trekking around the land, from reading without concern to time, from running around her house like a feral animal for the hell of it, and of course independence from the social chains of dating, were quite invigorating.

The only obstacle left was how to reasonably explain to her parents why she was no longer helping Greggory. Not that she'd gone in quite some time anyways, nor would they really care, but her parents would nonetheless confront and reprimand her based on principle.

Those were her thoughts when Reid appeared in front of her, as he so often did at this point in her walk. He was still at least fifty yards away, but her focus nonetheless shifted to him.

REID

This was going to be his last walk, he decided. Waiting for her figure to appear in the distance so he could jump ahead of her, squinting to be sure it wasn't just a mirage from the heat, was like a prison sentence. The relentless sun, having to always work outside at that time of day, his mind fixed on one thing and one thing only, and the questions he asked himself—Would she show at her usual hour? What if she stopped? How long would she continue?—were excruciating. The ridiculous little game had gone on long enough.

He never expected to make it all the way to the store the first time. Fortunately the latest project he and Greggory were working on needed a better wrench than what they had. He'd thought about approaching her at the store, but in the end he couldn't decide if she'd smile or snarl in response. He slipped away after concluding the latter. She'd already rejected his efforts once, turning him away as coldly and crushingly as a stranger. He could predict easily enough what would happen if he tried again. It needed to be on her terms.

Following the first trip there were others, always requiring him to think about another tool or grocery item before he set out, and on the road the whispers to confront her quieted, routine taking their place. Now, three outcomes remained: she would approach him in an effort to reconcile, she would approach him to tell him off, or she would stop showing up altogether. He'd originally presumed she would give in quickly, but that had turned out to be very wrong: it had been weeks. So there they were, stuck in limbo.

And then there was his grandfather. When Reid kept finding reasons to go to the store, Greggory must certainly have suspected an ulterior motive—why he was fleeing to Lord-knows-where in the middle of the day—but sponsored his pursuit by graciously allowing Reid to work outside. Greggory went as far as to explicitly suggest that he approach Emma to see if she'd return. Without her presence around the house, the mood had lost its easiness and an air of uncertainty loomed, like a village with no awareness of when the sun would rise again. It needed to end.

Reid craned his neck to see if she was still following him. She was.

EMMA

After passing Greggory's house with her head down, she quickly reached the end of Forester and made a right onto Stinson. A half-mile later, she realized she'd closed the distance to Reid by twenty yards and stutter-stepped, startled. There was still a good space between them, but things weren't happening as she was accustomed. He'd never turned his head so candidly to look at her. He'd never slowed so much. Usually, she would be quickening *her* strides to catch *him*. Emma slowed her pace to allow the charade between them to continue.

REID

After looking back, his attention returned to the road ahead of him, scanning for the occasional rattlesnake stretched across the pavement. He'd once almost stepped on one. It wasn't just Emma — the heat, the long walk, his own thoughts, and a careless rattlesnake had all contributed.

A simple, brazen plan came to mind; he just needed to get a little farther ahead to execute it. After slowing, he noticed Emma slow also. His strides tightened even further, causing his gait to inch along, forcing the gap to fold.

He could hear his breathing through the dry and dusty passages of his nose, and he became aware of his arms swinging. The aroma of sun-baked grass and horse manure lingered from somewhere far away. The wind rattled against nearby leaves. Sweat was just beginning to bead on his forehead. It took longer this time, a full mile, but the gap reduced by another twenty yards. Only ten remained.

EMMA

It felt like falling; she couldn't stop herself from moving forward. The distance between them was a thin sheet of air. She tried to pull herself away, to turn around, but her feet rambled on.

They were about halfway to the store now. Rather than turn back, her strategy moved to how to circumvent him. Emma's gaze moved just above his head to the pale August sky. Streaks of vapor sat above the horizon where clouds tried unsuccessfully to form. The sun's warmth spooled onto her skin. The few cars that ever occupied the road, heading some place far away from this forgotten neighborhood, were nowhere to be found.

In a few more steps, he veered to the middle of the road beside the worn double-yellow divider. A lump knotted in her throat, and a sort of queasiness settled in her stomach. She could almost feel what was coming. And then it came: he bent down to tie his shoe. Her breath derailed.

There was never a backup plan, abort mission, cop-out, for such a situation. Even trying to circle around him felt impossible. Her pulse thumped wildly on her temple, and her mind went blank. All she could do was pray for the impossible fortune of an aneurism in the next few steps. Although she slowed her pace even further, she knew it was inevitable that she'd reach him. She kept a steady eye on his body as she hugged the side of the road. The dirt stains on his shirt, the stubble peppering his cheeks, and the veins running along his arms all became visible.

Just before she could get around unscathed, he stood, shot a fraudulent smile in her direction, and continued onward. She refused to look to the left where his arms swung. She refused to inhale for fear she'd catch his scent. Instead she told her legs to move, but in an instant they forgot the distance and rate each was supposed to carry her.

Beside her, he slid his hands into his pockets. His gait remained indolent, and he made two noticeable turns of his head to evaluate her resolve. The third time, she tilted her head in his direction and glared at him, squinting in frustration at his idiotic smile and coquettish demeanor. Then, he turned to her completely, causing her heart to dance with renewed vigor. Instinctively she stopped, and returned a disapproving shake of her head for breaking the rules.

Shattering the silence without concern, without respect for social amenities, he shrugged. "What?"

She feigned as best she could and offered a reply: "*What* are you doing, Reid? Every time I go to the store. Why do you keep following me?"

He looked down the empty road at his back before returning with a fit of laughter. It had come to an end, shown how ridiculous they had been with just one facial expression.

"By the looks of it, *you* were following *me*." He stretched out his hands and remained steady. "Almost every day, Emma. What are we doing?" Sincerity entered his tone.

He took a step towards her, and a thread of fear wove into her body. She took a half-step back.

She tried to reiterate her comforting fiction: "I go to the store a lot. I don't have a car."

"C'mon Emma, seriously. I do these little walks to see you." He stepped closer, now face-to-face.

Her sweating was only made worse by the silence around her. The world held its breath, and all the little creatures avoided the heat in some shaded hole as they watched the two from a distance. A breeze swept into them, a few birds chimed their opinions, but otherwise the land was quiet. She tried her best to conceal the emotions running through her.

"Reid, I don't know what to tell you."

"Yeah, but—"

"But nothing."

Focusing on one of the larger stains on his shirt stifled her tears.

"Emma..." he tried again.

Her eyes whipped upward for just a second—an instant—before returning to their focal point.

"I love every second we spend together, Emma, even the weird ones where you're following me or I'm following you."

From either his words or her gaze's stray, a tear escaped and rolled down her cheek. With her fists clenched, she began wiping the sockets of her eyes, as if she could cauterize the wound. Reid stepped in and placed his fingers on the back of her hand, but she yanked away.

"*Emma.*"

She stood frozen. He moved in to touch her shoulder. The worn barrier began to collapse. When she didn't jerk away, he stepped closer and placed his palm on her back. Crumble. Her body remained still, so he wrapped his arms around her. She caved to his embrace, but refused to rest her head against his chest. Her thoughts fell back to the resolve she felt just half-an-hour earlier. It had changed so quickly. Her firmest intentions to go about life alone wasted away in a second.

Between the quakes of her back while she caught her breath, he spoke softly into her ear, "I couldn't help it. I needed to see you."

"I'm sorry about that night," she allowed, mumbled, surprised herself.

He went for her knuckles, and began tracing the grooves of her strained bones. She squeezed her hands tighter until they were white. Then, inexplicably, they loosened and took his fingers. She paused for a deep, deep breath and allowed him closer.

"Every time I saw you, you drove me crazy," he said, as she began to breathe more normally. "But..." he smirked, "why couldn't you have chosen a time later in the day so we weren't walking in the heat?"

A smile cracked her lips as she wiped at the moisture around her eyes.

Their shirts became sticky from clinging to each other, but for the longest time they couldn't pull away. They tugged on each other, and inhaled their fused scent. Their clothes rumpled. She'd wasted so much time stubbornly resisting his embrace that their remaining days together were already sliding into sharp focus, like a camera lens slowly shifting to a distant object.

So, when she let go of him and allowed his fingers through hers, the heaviness never went away. Although they could talk, message, and text when he left, Emma already began to think about, began to understand, that they never would. What was happening between them was an early morning shadow before noon, destined for failure since the beginning. But they needed to play it out, wait and see how the final act would conclude. Because, try as they might to separate and stay away, they nonetheless felt a pull, a need for each other. For Emma, it was evident by how her body relaxed and the words slipped from her mouth. She began bumping into him every few strides, forcing his glance to hover over her as they continued down the road.

After reaching the store and sauntering back to Forester, they stood in front of Greggory's house. Reid invited her in, but she declined. Instead she gave him one more hug, and forced herself in the direction of home. By now she knew she'd have to confront Greggory, but she hadn't the courage today.

As she strode towards her house, she felt a need to tell her parents about what had happened, starting right at the end of the story and letting her emotions fill in the details. But when she stepped through the door the rooms were empty, as they so often had been that summer.

VII

EMMA

Although still reaching a hundred and five in the sun, the temperature in the second week of August had at least tapered to a *steady* hundred-five, like an oven reaching its set temperature. There were still rare days here and there when it reached one-hundred-ten, one day even one-twelve, but mostly the heat was predictable and summer was winding down. Further, anyone with reason to venture outside either acclimated to the diabolical rays or established a routine to avoid them altogether. Like husky dogs shedding a winter layer, the few who befriended—or more accurately, acquainted themselves with—the heat had bodies that adapted. They bore thick skin and thin blood as evidenced by the rusty suntans they'd grown into.

For Emma, it was no different. As she walked down Forester, the sun bothered her less than the anxiety she felt in seeing Greggory. Two days had passed since she and Reid reconciled. Since that time, she knew she'd have to speak with the old man. Although he wasn't the most understanding of people, it had to happen. She prepared the excuses — she was busy with school approaching, her parents indebted her to another cause — but after she arrived at his yard and passed the second beat-up truck and tattered rockers outside, she wasn't sure what words to use.

The calmness she'd felt repeating the lines in the comfort of her house became foreign. She heard the echo of her rapping on the knocker. The notorious hinge from the door sounded, and the dark crack of shadow cloaked Greggory behind it. The smell of spices wafted out, and anxiety overtook her.

She tapped her index finger against her pocket, expecting anger when she said "Hello," but when he came into view, Greggory grinned. He returned her greeting and offered iced tea outside. The warmth in his voice caused her cheeks to burn.

After she situated herself on one of the rockers, he went back in to retrieve their drinks. Her hands continued to fidget. When he returned he maintained his grin, and before sitting he handed her a glass and patted her knee as if knowing her guilt.

"So, Greggory," she began, promptly and with a severe expression.

"Hold on," he interrupted, "Let's just try the tea first. I may have seeped it too long."

Focusing on the glass in his hand, he took the smallest of sips, analyzing the combination as if wine-tasting. She waited for him, anxiously swishing a gulp around in her mouth.

"It's just right," he confirmed before continuing earnestly. "It's nice to see you again, Emma."

She nodded. "Yeah, I've been meaning to come by and talk to you." Her head remained locked downward, "It's just…"

She stopped to think how to continue as all her practiced lines became white blanks.

"Emma, it's all right."

"No, it's not. It's just that I started really liking Reid."

She couldn't believe she'd said it out loud. That certainly wasn't the plan. But, there it was. Nowhere to go but forward.

She continued: "You probably didn't know this, but when I was working inside I could see you two through the window. He was really sweet. And you remember that night at the movie theater when the truck broke down? We walked home and I thought he was going to grab my hand. Then we started hanging out after that, and that's when I couldn't stop thinking about him."

Her focus remained still. Then, she surprised herself and shared how she and Reid spent time together, about the Fourth, how she left him on the road alone. "I didn't look back when I was walking, but I felt so sad. I just didn't want to fall for him, you know? He's *leaving*." Like the widening crack in a dam, her words began with a shadow of detail and then exploded to release the river behind it.

"I stepped outside and cried because Reid wouldn't look at me. It was my fault but I felt like I was suffocating."

She went on about the long, hot walks to the grocery store. It all came pouring. At one point she even considered telling him about Tim, but decided against it.

He listened quietly, and sat without showing what he was thinking. Until she'd exhausted herself of everything she could say, he simply sipped the tea and nodded.

Her face was a warm scarlet, and she was astonished by every new sentence she allowed herself to speak. It was the first time she'd spoken to anybody about her summer. Finally, exhausted, she sunk into her chair and tried to recall any last details she might have forgotten. After blurting a few more random additions she stopped altogether, and silence occupied the line between them. She hesitated in order to ask a question, but then didn't know what it would be.

Holding her firmly in his sight, he interrupted: "Well."

Her eyelids tightened as she waited to be castigated, certain she'd been mistaken in divulging so much. When the air remained idle, she looked up to face him. He took another sip before replying.

"I can't say I know exactly what you've been through, or what you're going through." He sounded old, wise with experience, blistered with pain. "But when it comes to love," he sat back in his chair, "I do know a little bit."

He paused again, took another sip.

"It involves those pendants I've seen you wear once in a while." He pointed to the one around her neck before tilting his head upward and continuing in a slow, deep tone. "Imagine my surprise to see you'd stumbled across them. But the more I think about it, the more I don't mind at all." He paused and took a deep breath, and when he was ready, he told her. Almost everything.

He shared how he'd lived back east, and how his father spoke of the determined look in his son's eyes before Greggory joined the military. Sounding a little surprised to hear himself say it, he told Emma about his journey to the Amazon looking for some grand, life-changing adventure only to find a life-changing woman who wore an elephant pendant. He explained how he eventually chased Sophia back to California—picking up another elephant pendant on the way—and moved out here when the house was little more than a shack. He married her on the hill just over there, he pointed, and they raised a child.

Emma clung to his words, grasping without realizing it was the elephant pendants she now wore. He stopped to take another sip from his glass. A disappointed look crossed his face when he realized it was tea and not something more potent. She waited for the liquid to trickle down his throat. By his distant stare, his words had been locked away in a vault similar to hers.

When the pause drew on too long, she blurted, "And what happened?" It came out a bit brash, but she was relieved when the question spurred him to continue.

His words trailed from his throat, from deep within, where they'd been stored a very long time. Like heat they rose upward, before crashing to her ears with inexplicable weight. When he finished sharing about Sophia's passing and his spiral downward, how he lost his son, Emma's throat tightened.

Towards the end he spoke to the air, eyes fixed. Lines of condensation trailed down the glass of tea and left a damp circle on the table. Both their rockers remained steady. She ran her fingers down the pendant around her neck and waited for him to finish.

"Sorry. It was a long story."

She shook her head but had no words.

"But what I'm really trying to tell you," again he paused, "is that if you know you love somebody, try not to dwell on the past or the future so much."

He tapped her kneecap with his answer.

"Do your best to love right now, or you might regret when you lose them. I know if I had to choose to love and lose or not love at all—You've heard that saying, right?—Yes—I'd say love and lose. I'd make the same choice if the opportunity came around again."

He paused. Then slowly, "I'd spend another lifetime suffering if it meant one more day with her."

She hid her face behind the glass in her hand and blinked back tears.

"There, there," he consoled. "We all have things that happen to us."

Wiping away the stream from her cheek, she let loose a choked exhale. He gave a defeated chuckle.

"Thanks," she peeped.

"Of course, Emma. You're always welcome here."

She rose from her chair to embrace him, and he batted her away unsuccessfully before accepting, patting her on the back with his feeble hands. After the moment passed, he mentioned gruffly that Reid was still trying to fix the damned truck. At his mention she perked up and excused herself with renewed vitality. She trotted down the driveway, leaving Greggory to rock gently and sip his tea.

∞   ∞   ∞

When she arrived Reid was in the passenger seat, hunched over and reading one of the manuals. She tapped on the metal hood. His steady expression turned to an impish grin, and she clambered in to kiss him.

"How'd it go?"

"Well."

"Your eyes are puffy. Were you crying?"

She nodded and he stifled a laugh, for which she punched him in the arm.

"I'm sorry. But if it helps, I have something to make you feel better."

"What is it?"

"Correction, *where* is it. I've been meaning to show you this place since we made up. Let me just finish here." He worked under the hood a few more moments before reaching for a towel to wipe his hands. "You know, I think my Grandpa enjoys having me working on this old thing. He could've towed it but never did. I've probably done more harm than good." He laughed at the thought. "You ready to go?"

She nodded and Reid grabbed her hand, leading her back down the road where she came. Along the way, she bumped gingerly into him, feeling at ease with everything in the world. Her nose poked into his shoulder and his arm wrapped around her. It was one of those summer days when everything around them could be heard, when the warmth shortened the distance between noises.

Reid broke her train of thought after they'd passed Forester. "Emma?" His looked at her.

"Hmm?" She looked over him with a sheepish grin.

"I'm glad I got to know you this summer."

Emma smiled. Their walk carried them farther down Stinson, where the road bent away and cast Forester out of view. A few strides later Reid exclaimed they were *here*. They stopped where the houses of their neighbors were no longer in view, in a spot right in the middle of the street.

Emma looked around with long twists of her neck. "This is the surprise? The middle of the road?"

Reid pointed to the opening in the wall of chaparral lining the road. It was a trail, almost.

"You want me to follow you in *there*? You sure you're not angry with me about earlier?" she chided.

Without answering he took the lead into the untamed bushes. She followed. The tunnel of brush reached and ripped at their clothes like fishhooks. There was presumably poison oak lurking nearby—easily missed if one wasn't paying attention—but Emma focused on her step regardless (a habit stemming from an incident when she fell into a stream). As they advanced deeper into the maze, the trail became littered with shiny coastal live oak leaves and scabrous acorns marked with a small "X" on their caps. The ground was colored gold. She felt like a hound rifling through the bushes in chase of a rabbit.

By the time the tunnel narrowed again it was too late for protest, but in truth Emma was thrilled by the adventure. Every now and again she would look up to the afternoon sun flickering through the trees. Following behind Reid at their careful pace was like floating in slow motion, in a dreamy mode. She expected him to turn his head and smile at her. She waited for him take her hand. *Look back* she repeated, as if she could control his actions with her mind.

She was about to yank his arm to force the event, but became distracted when the thick brush opened abruptly to a canal of space. There she stopped and waited for the next set of instructions. A long aisle of barbed-wire fence bisected an alley of matted yellow grass. The fence was part of the network she'd discovered days earlier—*Shit was never-ending*—though it was evident that this portion was much older. The rusty strings slung low and were nearly innocuous, just about ready to wither and disintegrate.

The sun beat on them as Reid navigated down the fence. He counted the poles with a point of his finger, calculating what she knew was coming. She couldn't possibly conceive making her way over without getting snagged, but about fifty yards from where they sprouted Reid instructed her to do just so. He himself clambered over with athletic grace, and looked back at her proudly.

"Over here."

She looked at him with wide eyes.

Whatever she was thinking, however, she didn't act on it, because the next thing she knew she was climbing over herself. Had she been wearing a dress, it would have certainly caught on the knots, but as it was she made her way over carefully.

Before both feet landed on the other side, Reid beckoned her with his hand and blazed ahead. She shook her head in mock annoyance before racing him down a new, more defined trail.

The dry, compacted dirt became rich with moisture, and the air was noticeably cooler. Pale-green clumps of stringy moss shrouded the limbs of trees. Birds could be heard chirping more vibrantly. Somewhere in the distance was flowing water. Decomposition and growth, the perpetual churning of matter back into the ground, accounted for a woodsy smell.

Only swatches of Reid's white shirt were visible as he turned behind each consecutive bend. She was just about to lose him when he stopped, pivoting to catch her by the shoulders. He announced (again) that they were *here*.

Before she could peek over his shoulders, he commanded her to close her eyes.

With several large gulps of the fresh air, she complied.

She took his fingers, quite aware of their soft, damp feel.

"Don't let me trip," she requested before he tugged gently forward. They brushed past an errant limb; the leaves felt like paper confetti as it stroked her forearm. The spongy ground became iron. The rush of water grew louder. Reid stopped.

"Okay, open."

It took her a moment to orient herself, take in everything at once, but beyond Reid's broad smile was a sparkling grove. They stood on a rock shelf that pressed against a small dam, neatly cobbled together with large stones. A stream cascaded over its smooth edges into a pool below, and then carved around a bend out of sight. Across the way the depths were shallow. Water purled over thousands of multi-colored pebbles.

It wasn't so much the waterfall that ultimately stole her breath. The verdure, greenness, freshness of sedge lining the stream, and incandescent leaves hanging above like a million parasols, were equally stunning. The sun shone through the diaphanous leaves, creating a cordial and bright halo that radiated warmth onto her skin. Dragonflies and dots of insects hovered in a buzz above the water before darting out of sight. The stream presumably connected to the same currents that ran through her property—just as the wired fence—but this felt so completely different, so fantastical. It was difficult to believe it was here. The mixture of water, sun, current, greenness, and buzz of insects left Emma believing that if fairies—or any mythical creature for that matter—did exist, it would be here.

Although Emma later prized the thought that she and Reid discovered the wellspring—the dam having magically sprouted on its own—she later found that knowledge of its location wasn't exclusively theirs. It had been frequented enough throughout the years to earn the unofficial name "Davvy's Dam."

MR. RICHARDS – A SECOND SIDE-NOTE

Sometimes people die, Mr. Richards explained to himself after he moved. *It's just the way things turn out.* If he really considered it, he took the death more harshly not because it was the last of his three older brothers but because he knew he was next.

It gave him a sense of urgency to do what he'd meant to do while his brothers were alive. He would continue the unforgiving family business running the Richards Family Walnut Orchard, but would start fresh, an idea that was formally resisted by his brothers. There was no need to struggle against the hot, sweaty climate in Georgia; it was much better to live with the dry heat of California.

While searching for his new location, when he was merely passing through in his travels, he stumbled onto the valley. It just happened, after he took a moment to clear his mind in the woods, that he was suddenly aware how the area met all the conditions of a walnut orchard.

It wasn't long before he hauled everything he owned and began working relentlessly on the few acres he purchased. He wished he could say his hard work paid off those first few years, but the number of green bulbs that grew and turned into hard walnuts was more than disappointing. Nonetheless, it wasn't long until the crop began matching the regal foison romanced in his mind, and by the fifth year he'd struck gold in terms of production, perceived by many as pushing past the land's limit.

When the rewards arrived in those latter years, there were still two remaining issues that ultimately prevented Mr. Richards from ever becoming truly successful. The first was the rumor of his eccentricity. When the locals caught him dowsing madly on the land he would later purchase, they thought he was a lunatic. He could still picture their quizzical expressions as they congregated, spoke of the white-whiskered man working in his dirty denim overalls and grimy baseball cap in the blasphemous heat. And once rumor got out in the small community, it developed malignantly, spread like wildfire. Merchants were cautious when they dealt with him, and some outright refused to work with him on the grounds there was something strange, unsafe, about how much he was able to produce. As a result Mr. Richards haggled and scratched by.

The second pitfall—and the more taxing of the two—was the love for his old piebald stag Davvy. The decrepit, rangy horse had been at Mr. Richards' side since it was a foal prancing proudly in its youth. The early version of Davvy was how Mr. Richards liked to remember the animal, even if the horse could scarcely turn his head—hold himself up, really—any longer. Perhaps Mr. Richards didn't detect the languid way Davvy learned to chew, the unwelcomed mode only lending itself to the old, because he'd developed the habit himself, but there were plenty of other signs he chose to ignore in order to preserve his lovely ignorance. If he fostered the illusion for any reason, it was because Davvy was more than a companion to Mr. Richards: Davvy was his only friend.

Davvy listened without protest and without judgment. I mean, yes, the horse would stammer his right hoof or whinny in response now and again, but that was only when Mr. Richards admitted he had gone too far. Davvy accepted Mr. Richards' eccentricities, for the most part, unconditionally.

After a long day around the farm, in the ebbing afternoon sun, the two would plant themselves in front of the small shack they called home and permit their usual customs. Davvy carefully accepted carrots with his protruding teeth, while Mr. Richards sat in his plastic lawn chair sipping on canned beer. They'd converse for hours; every few minutes Mr. Richards would toss another carrot or pet Davvy's mane, until night grew over them.

At some point Mr. Richards observed that Davvy was having difficulty crossing the nearby stream, so he did the logical thing and built a dam. In truth he set out to build an underwater catwalk to connect the two sides, but as he built the wall to slow the force of the stream it turned out more a dam than anything else. It was the admirable thing to do in order to save face for the old horse; there was no telling how embarrassing it would be if Davvy realized that a wooden bridge had been erected just so he could cross the river. *No way, no how.* He refused to vandalize his friend's declining image, and dismissed the idea firmly with a wave of his hand.

While Davvy was corralled, Mr. Richards began working diligently to create the structure. He would return in the afternoon, look Davvy in the eyes, and offer a shrug as he answered, "What? I had some things to take care of around the farm. I didn't think you wanted to come."

It took months, but only when the dam slowed the currents upstream to a near halt did Mr. Richards consider it complete. With an excitement he thought fled with youth, he went to fetch Davvy and led him by his loose scrap of bridle to the completed structure. They approached the stream, and while Mr. Richards was secretly presenting his finished work—watching for Davvy's reaction—Davvy cautiously walked to the dam a short distance away and explored the adjacent rock shelf. Stamping the shelf with his hoof, Davvy left a long, lightning-bolt crack in the hard rock, an impression that would long outlive both of them.

Not long after, kids and sometimes families—the same ones whose parents refused business with him—came to lounge. They made the dam a hangout locale, polluting the water and leaving garbage everywhere. To combat the threats to his home, Mr. Richards erected a network of barbed-wire fence that perimetered his land. In reaction, many of the locals fenced off their own land if only to snobbishly prove a point.

Mr. Richards and Davvy, although never becoming wealthy in their farming endeavors, were content with the austere lifestyle they adopted. They ate carrots and drank beer—shared friendship—during the warm summer days and freezing winter nights, until Davvy died at the ripe age of thirty-six. Mr. Richards followed within the same month.

Soon enough the walnut orchard withered and relented to the unforgiving chaparral already abundant in the area. The stagnant water contained on one side of the dam began to stir and flow regularly downstream. The land was eventually left to and forgotten by the public. The only lasting vestige of Mr. Richards or his life remained in the name "Davvy's Dam" and in the dam itself—Davvy's mark. There it lay, an oasis to anyone who stumbled serendipitously along.

REID

The dam Reid stumbled upon held an unexplainable mysticism that the two never completely understood until its story was relayed to them by a stranger some time later.

When he reached the barbed fence, there was no telling why he decided to hop over other than a gravitational pull he felt to continue on with his Lewis-and-Clark-style expedition. The harsh shrubs ferociously trying to keep people out very quickly enticed him to stay. After finally reaching the welcoming oasis, all he could think about was showing Emma.

They hovered at the top of the spillway and watched the water cast long shadows and white heliocentric highlights as it rippled outward and downstream. The sun refracted prisms in the water, yellows and greens and blues just beneath the surface mixing with orange and gray near the bottom. A hint of pine lingered in the air. It was nothing less than beautiful, made even more so by the recognition that the fungi and decay would eventually take over and erase all traces of human impact.

Reid came from his reverie when he realized Emma was speaking to him.

"It's amazing."

He nodded before heading to the ledge to sit. She joined, and together they dangled their legs over the shelf. Emma's shirt had streaked with dirt from the woods; he looked down to see that his own clothes had received the same beating. From the heat or dehydration or just shock at seeing the mess, he burst into laughter.

"What? You weirdo." Puzzlement crossed her face as he riled. The birds quieted for a moment before resuming their chatter. There was just enough stillness to notice how low her shirt cut.

She spoke while he regained his composure. "It's so nice here."

She slid her hand against his, pinkies touching. He didn't dare move. His eyes drifted towards her. She remained locked ahead.

"So," she stated as if it had been a long-time discussion they were continuing.

"What?" he asked with a lift of his eyebrows.

"Let's jump in."

Without hesitation she got up and flung off her shoes.

"Seriously Emma? What about your shirt and shorts?"

She smiled.

She was wearing modest white shorts and a grey shirt. Her sleeves hung just below the round of her shoulders.

"I think they'll be fine, Reid," she mocked.

Before he could protest—calculate where and where *not* to leap—she hurled herself from the ledge and into the chilling current below. She reemerged and howled with excitement. With nothing left to do, he was forced into standing, taking off his shirt, and then jumping after her. The water knocked the wind out of him, but as with Emma he felt alive with excitement. The icy liquid ran over his nerves. He could feel the stale sweat wash away. His tired mind sharpened.

When he came up for air, they laughed and played— capitulated to summer. Emma splashed and jumped on him, and he wrestled in defense. Her slippery body wrapped around him. He fought her just enough, privately enjoying how her inner thigh brushed against his. He abruptly realized—the look in her eyes—that their play had taken a new meaning.

His mind fluttered, and he became aware of every touch from her body. Her hands pressed to submerge him. He came for air. Arms on his shoulder, breasts on his back. Underwater again. Smooth plane of her stomach sliding between the soft skin of his forearms. More air. Fingers slipping along his back, hair draping over his face. She climbed on him in victory, and managed a small bite to his neck.

He pulled back, and together they hovered over the water, looking into each other. Her breath floated on the surface like vital fog, mixing with his. He closed the space between them again, the points of his fingers sliding to the low of her back. She shot him a look. The gloss on her lips, her round nose, the way she pulled back when she smiled, the longing to be near her, touch her, explore how her skin pulled along her body, dictated his movements.

She took control by grabbing his wrist, and together they paddled to the shoal where they could wade freely. Without looking, Emma turned and backed into him, urging him to deepen the grasp on her hip. The curvature of her body fit snugly against his. She laid her hand atop his. His free hand meticulously grazed the surface of her skin, feeling her rib, the ripples of her abdomen, her hipbone. Not knowing if he should continue, his hand made a circle, barely touching her skin, along her pelvis.

Her breathing deepened, and soon she tilted her hips into his waist. She did it once more, causing his right leg to quaver. She reached for the back of his head and ran her fingers though the wet clumps. As if another, more tenacious soul occupied his body, he dared to rotate her until she twisted around to face him. Rivulets of water traced the soft indents of her face; she looked into him with wide, bright eyes. She wrapped her thighs around his waist, and his leg quavered again. He held her hips and pressed his body against her. She smiled. Her elbows led her arms past his neck where she cradled his head.

From her careless grin and giant exhalation, he wasn't certain if she had control of the thrusts of her hips, but she showed her dominance by lifting a finger to his lips. He remained motionless.

With the irrefutable evidence—that single motion of her finger—the chirps of the nearby birds faded. The undulations of the water faded, the smell of pine and earth teeming with life faded. The world faded, and before Emma could twister her body into another thrust, she removed her finger to allow his lips to crash into hers. Before he could fully grasp what was happening, he pulled back and then crashed again.

The rest of the world spun while he gazed into her emerald eyes. He felt her tongue slip around his. They breathed into each other.

He could have held her there in the stream endlessly, but after a long time kissing and feeling each other, hands probing freely, Emma pulled him away with a wry smile. "You're bleeding."

Only then did he notice the taste of copper in his mouth, and he almost didn't believe it until he padded his mouth with his fingers to confirm that, yes, he was bleeding. It was indeterminable whether she'd nicked him with her tooth or his tongue overextended in his efforts, but if the injury hadn't occurred, they might have continued until they became exhausted enough to sink and drown.

He gave her one more kiss before swimming across the stream and climbing the rock wall. She followed. The thin cotton shirt vacuumed to her body, encouraging his eyes to sneak back to her. He could see her black panties through the wet shorts. He gave her another kiss while she was wringing her hair.

When they left the dam, it was late afternoon, and the summer sun was beginning to dim. Shadows stretched longer, and the breeze cooled. Dust and slivers of grass floated in the air. The birds' chirps dissolved, and the sounds of crickets would soon pick up. The journey back remained slow and pensive. Uncertainty found its way into the cracks of their happiness, asking when and how they'd see each other when night came, when the week concluded, when he went away. But no matter how slowly their feet plodded along, they had no choice but to move forward.

Their hands clasped as they made their way through the clawing brambles to the paved road. His legs felt spongy, and the hardness of the road ricocheted through his body. The intimacy they shared, her bumps, carried him the rest of the way down Forester.

When they approached the white fence marking Greggory's property, the day felt surreal. Reid offered Emma a long sigh.

"I could walk you the rest of the way?"

She declined, and the distance in her eyes returned. They embraced, kissed. Without conviction, Reid presented the idea, "I love you."

When the words floated from his lips, they felt stiff. He knew it. They didn't come with authority. They came too soon. He wanted to retry *I love you. I love you.* But she kissed him and turned. When she made it ten yards away, she turned back to him.

"Reid?" she began, "How do you know you love me and not just the idea of me?"

Because I do.

He hesitated and fumbled in answer. "I just do."

She grinned, but the angle of her head provided a clue that his answer was lacking. She turned again, and he stood watching her figure blend with the horizon.

EMMA

It wasn't quite déjà vu, but walking down the road felt familiar, like their story had already been written and tucked away in the fine print of history. Without meaning to, she considered the small box she'd unearthed some time ago—Greggory's box. How many golden afternoons and twilit tragedies enameled the road they walked on? With every dusk that passed, something invisible and ancient, encompassing and immeasurably thin, layered the valley and hills of her neighborhood. It concentrated in the pockets of her home, and thickened enough throughout the years to become detectable. The land was shaped by laughter, walks, tears. The world around them could just briefly be felt catching, imprinting, and baking these moments.

But she was now alone again, and the road felt vast. The wind swept across the valley in wide strokes. Vultures swirled overhead. The distance between their houses felt enormous.

She padded her lips to be certain the copper taste wasn't coming from her mouth. *All clean.*

How he glanced over at her, thinking she didn't notice, like she was the most precious thing in the world, frightened her. She considered her previous efforts to block him out: the hapless wandering, traitorous thoughts. They knifed her nearly to death. She knifed herself nearly to death, draining herself from any other focus this summer. Could she do it differently this time? Probably, but she knew infatuation was too inviting. To relapse into the same unhealthy habits would be inevitable.

No, she would stick it out this time and find an alternative for the heartbreak she knew was coming. Nobody ever cared to tell her that even when romance was good, it hurt.

VIII

EMMA

Looking back, what happened next might have been inevitable. Everything had led up to it.

Emma started the day helping Greggory. He had generously allowed her to continue her regular chores, even though she would be relieved of her duties in September when school began. It was already early afternoon when she came over, so by the time she finished it felt as though the day was wasted. Greggory asked if she could go get Reid for dinner, and remind him that he *would* tow it this time (now confirmed as an idle threat Greggory employed in a game between him and Reid—it was evident by now that Greggory cared less about the old, broken-down hunk of metal than he did about his grandson wanting to work on it).

Emma agreed to relay the threat, and began down the road. It had been a nice day. The heat never climbed to its peak, and the breeze was comfortable.

The first thing she asked him after poking her head in the cabin was, "Is the truck done yet?"

"I think so. I was just looking over something." His concentration remained on the manual in his hands.

The same birds chirped as they always did. Reid's masculine scent caught her, and she went to kiss his neck. His concentration broken, he countered with a kiss of his own. A knot of seriousness crossed his face, "I've been thinking."

She climbed in and played with the knobs of the radio until a soft hum broke through the static, "Mhm?"

"Well you know you asked how I know I love you and not just the idea of you?"

She'd tried to put the moment behind her, but it kept coming back.

"I remember." She stopped what she was doing to look at him.

"Well, I've been giving it some thought, and what I've come up with is that I knew I loved you, Emma," the way he pronounced her name caused her pulse to flicker, "when I got home, just getting back from seeing you. I was sitting in my grandpa's rocker, the one outside, and just staring out to the distance. Even though we'd just spent time together, I missed you so much it hurt. But it's more than just that, too—really—I…"

He started awkwardly, but then warmed up as it came spilling out. He described how she covered her mouth when she laughed, and how she coyly tilted her head in response to his questions. How he knew she knew he'd been watching her when she reached up high, revealing that slit of skin. He described her soft lips.

Emma did her best to keep her focus on him, and not shy away embarrassed that he'd learned all these intimate things about her.

He went on, and she discovered things she didn't know about herself—crinkling her nose and laughing at her own jokes, holding her breath when she was nervous. Warmth expanded inside her the more details he gave.

Before he finished, Emma reached for his hand and pulled him close, watching his eyes. She ran her fingers over his palm. He stopped talking. She dared to smile up at him and pull his fingers to her lips, boldly slipping her tongue around his thumb, swirling it gently, re-experiencing the energy they felt at Davvy's. Her eyes remained on his until she saw his expression soften. With her incisors she held his thumb like a pencil on a clipboard until he laughed and pulled away.

There was an option to play it safe, keep it kosher, but she gripped the driver's door and yanked it shut. A current ran from the tip of her head down her spine, and the world around began to fade, just as before. She climbed onto him. Spurred at her boldness, his lips found their way to her collar bone. The air became charged, and soon their breaths began deepening. Every step further was curious, dangerous, like wading through muddy water. Perspiration crossed her face.

In the moments to follow the windows fogged, and their bodies became invisible to the outside world. Their sweat intermingled, and the heat—deeper kisses, bolder caresses—intensified. Emma sank into the cushion of Reid's arms. Her breaths became long and drawn-out. She clutched at his shirt and pulled it over his head, and with a beaming smile he reciprocated, exposing her black-lace bra. His eyes skittered across her half-naked body before he vigorously returned to kissing.

Matching his movements she slid her hand over his abs, his chest, shoulders, bicep, before toggling with his belt. A tingle formed on her neck, her collarbone, and the soft skin above her breasts. Another zip of electricity ran down her spine. She readjusted to allow his vying hands to unhook her bra, and blushed when she became aware just how fair-skinned her breasts were. Reid smiled before his tongue returned to her collar bone.

As he made his way along her sweaty body, the tingle centered at her hips. He repositioned her onto her back, taking control. While listening to his labored breaths, she felt him move to the tender parts of her stomach and then a little deeper. She couldn't help but moan when he ventured further. The sanctuary provided by the big metal button on her jeans all these years felt deceiving, a straw wall waiting for wind. The denim loop glided effortlessly around the button to unlock her body. Past the prickles of hair, his humid breaths finally reached her most tender secrets, causing her muscles to contract and her back to arch. She ran her fingers through his damp hair, stopping him once in hesitation, before relenting. She tried reaching for his belt again, but he was too far away.

Whether from the electricity or a nervous fear, her legs trembled. Her body felt awkward, and her cheeks burned. She tugged on his hair, causing him to come back up with an intoxicated smile.

"Hey, you," he whispered.

His hands returned to her body.

She slid further onto her back, still feigning sexiness as best she could. Beads of sweat dropped onto her tucked body, and, still feeling the burn in her cheeks, she made for his belt again, successful this time. He slid his confident eyes over her, and she doubled her efforts to reach at him.

He stopped, nose to nose, and slid his hand to push down her denim jeans. She wriggled her feet to remove them completely. Then he smoothed his hands along her hips, over her panties. Another surge of warmth hit her face when she felt the tingling pads of his fingertips.

"Wait, Reid, I've never..." she tried to relay.

He began to pull back, but before he could she wrapped her elbows around his neck and clung to him. She exhaled slowly, and her legs stopped trembling.

"You're sure?" he whispered.

She returned with a delirious smile and held him closer. He removed the cotton around her waist, the last chance to turn back, and then she helped Reid with the rest of his clothes. She took a few deep breaths to steady herself—anxiety, excitement.

It was impossible to guess how long their bodies worked— each moment was both forever and fleeting—but Reid finally crashed to her lips, panting. She looked at him with a sheepish smile, vacillating between embarrassment and satisfaction. They remained there, feeling each other's hearts thump, until they remembered they were due for dinner.

By the time they opened the door it was dark outside, and the cooler air flowed in without protest. They made their separate ways home.

TIM

The clicking of the scanner and jangle of change was the basis for a successful business, but the primary cause of boredom for Tim. He knew he wore a somber gaze as he stood there asking the same customers the same questions, responding to them with the same ambiguous phrases, day in and day out. More than one might expect, he tuned out what a customer actually said and responded the with the coverall phrase, "I know, right?" He was uncertain how long he could maintain the act, but he would continue doing so until caught. As he saw it, he managed well enough without the customers noticing, or perhaps they were in on the same game as he was, wandering through life avoiding contact as much as possible.

He tried to include Emma in his life, but his attempts were squelched before they could be carried out. She never let them root. If she could only have looked at him just once the way she did the new guy. It felt as if he was peering through a spyglass at somebody else's happy ending, somebody else's future memories of summer. He'd seen her in the store intently browsing everything from latex gloves, to garbage bags to nutrition shakes—*nutrition shakes!*—trying to avoid being seen staring at him. When she came in alone, she would look around for him in a way that was more obvious for her attempts to hide it.

"—Have a wonderful day ma'am."

He really did his best to suppress the moments they'd shared in the past, and how she used to look at him with tenderness, but there was too much undistracted time while he stood there beeping items away. It was impossible to ignore the eroding feeling, layers upon layers of his soul being removed in regular sweeps.

That was once again his train of thought before an amiable, distracted "Hello" broke his concentration. He looked up to china-blue eyes that he hadn't seen in a very long time. Her irises still held those crystalline highlights that could stop a man dead in his tracks.

"Hello," he responded, not really hearing his own words amidst his bewilderment.

She'd gained an insignificant amount of weight, was on the verge of transitioning into full-blown adulthood, but she stood there as sure as day with her piercing eyes and a selfless grin. The shock stunned him. *No way.*

"How about the weather? Hot?" he muttered, his brain still on automatic.

"Yes, quite." She glinted a full set of white teeth. She surely didn't recognize him, probably didn't remember him at all, but remained there with full tenderness all the same. Her easy movements maintained the angelic quality he remembered. As she waited for her two items to be rung up—a bag of marshmallows and two Hershey's bars—she looked down at her phone, distracted.

Tell her. Tell her!

"Hey, so, were you ever a camp counselor at Camp Green? I think it's like Sherman Park now?" He tried to sound casual.

Surprised anyone would know the small footnote of her life, a puzzled smile grew. "I *was*, a long time ago. How did you know?" She rotated her head and squinted trying to recall his face.

"Amy, right?"

She nodded.

"I'm Tim. Used to go by Timothy. You were my counselor at one point, I think…" *Definitely her.*

A pause, and then came the moment of recognition. Her eyes widened, and she slid her head back to scan him like a painting in a museum.

"Timothy! Wow you've grown so much."

"So you *do* remember me?" He fished for the attention.

"Of course! You saved that girl. I'd never forget that. What was her name again?" That amazing smile.

"Emma?"

"Yes, Emma! Wow. What ever happened to her, I wonder."

"She's doing well. We're friends now."

"I can't believe how much you've grown up," another scan, "You were such a little guy when you came to camp."

She was lively as they reminisced; her hands animated each sentence. He finished ringing her items, and she automatically handed him cash. He handed back the change but tried to keep her a bit longer.

"Since then, how've you been?"

"Really good, actually. A few years after that job, I decided to go to college. I finished up not too long ago. Right now, I'm just trying to find a job—typical college grad statement, I know. Going to a barbeque at the moment with some old friends, thus these." She pointed to her purchases and winked. "And you?"

"Great. Just one more year of school and then off to college."

"That's great Tim. I'm positive you'll do great."

"I hope so." An old fat lady with a toad face walked behind Amy and shot him an impatient frown.

Amy hastened their conversation to a close, "Well, hey, it was nice to see you. I still can't believe how you've grown up."

She grabbed her items, and with a small flutter of her fingers she waved goodbye. His smile drained as she moved further away, and by the time she exited his butterflies were caught and had their tiny skulls bashed in. Toad lady stared at him disapprovingly, as if he'd just gotten away with murder.

Still preoccupied in his attempt to catch one last glimpse, he fumbled with toad's items. When Amy was no longer in sight, he returned to scanning, toad giving him the what-in-the-hell-are-you-doing-boy look. Before he could tell her what was on his mind— *fuck off, lady*— he did something absolutely absurd: he darted out of the store, catching Amy just as she was slamming the trunk of her car closed.

"Hey, so..." He ran his fingers through his hair and snorted nervously.

She paused—patient smile, deep eyes.

His back remained rigid. His words came out rushed and coarse, but he managed. "Can I have your number?"

She didn't move, but her face questioned his intentions.

"You know, to stay in touch."

Had it not been so sudden, she might have politely declined, but as it was his boldness startled her and she obliged.

Dazed to receive the key to her gated, exclusive world, he was hardly able to articulate the digits on the back of the receipt. He walked to the store floating, leaving her standing there bashful—arms crossed, grinning downward, rubbing the toe of her shoe on the ground. He hardly minded the toad's scowl as she pointed him out to his store manager, or the stares of his fellow employees watching to see if the unusual events of the day would continue.

When the shift manager called him to the back to talk about what happened, he did his best to conceal his smile. After a stern lecture, his manager decided to write him up instead of firing him because he was such a good, hardworking employee. Tim didn't know whether it was the habit he picked up at the register or if he was too preoccupied to listen to anything the man offered, but with the exception of a handful of key phrases the entire conversation floated past him. He walked out completely and utterly unaffected, still giddy.

For the rest of the day he thought of nothing else but the ten digits scrawled on the back of the receipt, resting uncomfortably in his front right pocket. His fingers, eyes, needed proof over and over again. Between customers he would slide his palm to the unprotected sanctum of denim and ensure the slip of paper was still safely tucked away. As soon as he went to his fifteen-minute break, he powered on his phone and stored the information.

Once the number was digitally secured, he thought for a moment and concluded that three days was the proper time to wait before contacting her. By the end of his shift, however, the number was already down to two.

His mother greeted him when he arrived home, but he brushed past her—shut her down with three or four words—and made his way to the desk in his room. He pulled out his phone and placed it neatly on the desk before attempting to catch up on the summer reading list of his advanced placement English class for the fall. He worked diligently, but every now and again he would glance at his phone, as if it were giving him disapproving looks for lack of attention. He tried returning to his studies, but soon found he was unable to concentrate.

He determined, *fine*, he would pick up the phone, stare at its black screen. Satisfied at his mediation, he set it back down, turned to his book again. His foot tapped impatiently. He picked up the phone and swiped to unlock it. It had won. He resolved to message her.

After a simple sentence, he set the phone in its resting spot and returned to staring at his book. It was just a message after all. He distractedly tapped his pen on the desk until finally the pulsing buzzes came. *Bzz bzz bzz.*

Nice to see you too.

Carefully, he crafted his return. The time between messages was excruciating, but even so they relayed back and forth. Even her neutral responses either excited thoroughly or disappointed severely, but like a hardened sentry he set aside his emotion and sent mild and impassive responses. Hours stretched, drawing out their conversation to the night, not revealing anything of significance but rather providing just enough to continue the conversation. The forced manner of their earlier messages relaxed to a natural rhythm: *BBQ'ing is done. This beer is strong!*

When it approached midnight and his efforts began to dwindle, he made one last attempt to resuscitate the cause by suggesting they spend a day together some time soon. That's when he received the devastating blow. He read it slowly, hoping it wasn't true. She apologized for perhaps mistaking his intentions but hoped he didn't look at her romantically, because she was so much older. She had to be in her late twenties—if not a slightly older—it was true, but regardless he was infatuated. He dug himself deeper by admitting that he was fond of her, careful to omit more suggestive language.

When the buzz announced the reply he wasn't certain he should read it, but with a resigned breath he picked up his phone: *I'm fond of you also, but trust me when I tell you Tim, I'm not what you want. I'll make you a deal, though: Once you finish college, if you haven't fallen in love with some lucky lady and I'm not dating anybody, I'll go on a date with you. No promises you'll enjoy it though ;)*

Everything was immaculately written, suggesting she was serious about the proposal. She would go on a date with him. He reread it over. She would. A peaceful smile crossed his face. The words in his book became clear again, and for the first time he could remember, he was happy to be studying. *Deal.*

REID

September arrived, and summer was losing ground to autumn. The cirrus plumes stretched in high wisps, a reliable sign of the changing season. Soon they would capitulate to creamy, puffed clouds of innocuous shades, before finally giving way to darker forms by the year's end. The temperature during the day was a sliver cooler, and the sun dove under the hills a fraction earlier. By now the new lives that had arrived the previous spring were either strong enough to continue through winter or too weak to continue at all.

Reid became aware, on one of those afternoons, that if he wasn't scheduled to leave there was no telling if he would've succumbed to the same level of passion as he had. His inevitable departure added to the eminence of their relationship, the magnitude of their devotion. He was driven mad waiting to see her each day, to discover over whether she'd portray the angelic innocent or lascivious sinner he'd come to know in her. Half the time she wordlessly slid her fragile frame under his body and tossed her shorts to the corner of wherever they were. Other times, she'd jump onto him, wrapping her legs around his torso until he collapsed, taking advantage of him. She'd straddle him with her strong legs, hold him in place, rock into him. Her lanky forearms never proved heavier than a sheer scarf wrapped around his neck while making love. Afterward, he'd run his palm along her creamy skin.

In his obsession with the moments they shared, Reid found that the only thing worse than the sickly outcome of unreciprocated love was that of actual reciprocation. He no longer had the luxury to brush aside his invented fancies as delusional whims; they'd become physical entities. He'd wake up with a bout of terror at the thought of losing her. He found the scent of privet in the strangest corners of the house. He'd be sitting next to her, and somehow still miss her. Although they slept away from each other except during small naps, he could barely attend to sleep knowing her heavy breaths would soon be removed from his life. Within days he'd forgotten how to talk about normal things, and only grand ideas came to mind.

The world around them seemed to further validate their union. He'd tested the fuel pump, the battery, fuses, and oxygen sensors, even jigga-jigga'd some wires without any luck, but the night after their lovemaking, Reid tried the ignition one last time and found the truck started right up—as if their passions were the solution to its mechanical issues the whole time. The engine spat a slew of sooty black smoke through the tailpipe, and they directed the vehicle down Forester at a steady twenty-five, kissing intermittently to avoid stunting their success.

The achievement with the truck allowed him to check one of the final mental boxes for things to complete before he left. Perhaps as a means to avoid a decision already made, maybe to conceal the dread he felt, but the closer he came to finishing the last handful of tasks around the house the more worked up he became.

He was en route to complete the shed outside well before he was due to leave. Theoretically, it could be considered done whenever he felt like it—they'd already begun resting tools there, after all—but the trim wasn't quite up to Reid's standards.

The wood was still coarse, and it needed a finishing coat of paint.

Emma and Greggory sat outside sipping tea, watching while Reid worked like a madman. Sometimes they'd gesture for him to join, but with a wild eye he often refused. The times Reid came over, beads of sweat dried around his temples while he reclined in the rocker and spoke about summer. When Greggory wasn't around, Reid would sneak light kisses, tender kisses, wet kisses, dusty kisses, neck kisses, and every other type of kisses there were. Emma would survey his face after the last peck, eyes half-closed in her dreamy state, her soft palm lingering on his neck. He'd wait a moment before kissing her again, so he could witness the dreaminess over again. Then, inspired, he'd return to his work.

One day Greggory made a comment about a shift in the two's demeanor, although he claimed not to know exactly what had changed. When presented with the comment they feigned ignorance, but deep down they were quite aware that the last fragments of summer were drifting away. They carried on with their usual tasks as if nothing was out of ordinary, but when they had time they'd venture to Emma's empty house and shed their clothes as if it was their last time, each time. Their trysts began to occur more frequently as the days ticked by, and with each morning his symptoms of longing intensified. With a week left, his chest felt heavy. After Monday a sinking feeling settled in his stomach. Tuesday came and his hands began shaking when Emma wasn't near, like a withdrawal. By Wednesday, he was pale from lack of sleep. Monday, the day of his departure, was a stone's throw away.

He followed her to the hill across his house Thursday afternoon, and together they settled in the dirt. They spoke of their secrets and dreams well into the night. On Friday, they made critical, hastened love in Emma's empty room until the night forced them to separate. On Saturday Reid finished the trim of the shed to his reluctant satisfaction. The two-inch framing couldn't be smoother nor the coat of paint more even; the enamel gleamed. It was still daytime when he finished, so he and Emma made their way down the street, hopped over the rusty barbed-wire fence, and spent the rest of the day at Davvy's.

When Sunday arrived, there was nothing left to do but wait.

EMMA

The sun reigned heavily over the land on Sunday, almost like a last effort from summer. It was early when she arrived, but Greggory had already finished preparing morning drinks. She studied the dark circles around his eyes and his disheveled hair and determined he'd gotten about as much sleep as she had.

That last full day together was spotty in her later memory, the lack of sleep causing her to forget many of the little things. The three reminisced for much of the day, and then ventured to town for dinner as a sort of going-away celebration. Greggory, Reid, and Emma bumped along in the more reliable truck; her thigh pressed against Reid's. She suppressed a flood of loneliness.

When they returned afterwards, they sat outside and whispered amongst themselves. Greggory noted the need to buy a new chair so Emma wouldn't have to grab the one from inside, as she'd grown accustomed to doing. She hadn't the heart to remind him that it would be unnecessary.

Not too long after his comment, Greggory kissed the tops of their heads and made his way to bed. Even after he left, she and Reid didn't speak. Instead, he pulled his chair closer so they could hold hands. She didn't know what time it was, but she felt a tug on her arm, being led to his room, just as she was beginning to drift off.

She did her best to remove her jeans, bra, and shirt as Reid stabilized her with an arm. When she was in her panties, she crawled underneath the thick, cozy layers of blanket. She could feel his body next to her. She wrapped around him, holding his waist and resting her head on his bare chest, and soon her breaths became rhythmic. His soft lips pressed onto her forehead. Right before sleep took her, she mumbled, "You know, you could always just stay if you wanted." Then the void overtook her.

REID

You could always just stay. The words rang in his head and kept him from sleeping. He was unable to shake the sinking feeling. *You could always just stay. Just. If you want. If I want?* The words felt like a last supper before the electric chair. That would be it, nothing left for eternity, if he closed his eyes.

He pulled her closer. Minutes passed. The crickets and toads outside croaked. She stayed woven around him. The smell of her hair lingered. He watched her chest gently rise and fall before his blinks became cumbersome and his body finally relaxed into sleep.

EMMA

She awoke with a sheepish grin, until she realized it was Monday. It had been a deep sleep, and she couldn't shake the feeling that Reid assisted by watching her through the night. Although she was being careful as she lifted herself, the movement caused Reid to stir. His eyes were bloodshot and his cough was stiff.

"Hey," he croaked, still somehow managing a grin.

She climbed on top of him and kissed his warm mouth. If they'd had the house to themselves she would have submerged under the blankets; the idea excited her. Instead she lay on top of him, looking into his eyes, kissing him, listening to the inhales and exhales qualifying their summer.

Pots and pans clattered faintly in the kitchen. Greggory was already awake. She stood, allowed Reid run his hands over her body, and then threw on the clothes she'd worn yesterday. She matted down her tousled hair, and once presentable jumped onto the thick blankets one last time—another kiss—before heading to the kitchen.

Greggory must've been too preoccupied to consider the possible doings between the two, for he offered no word to the fact she'd spent the night.

He greeted her simply, "Tea's almost ready, Em," with a note of fatigue.

She approached the table and realized the chair had been left outside to collect dew. She went out to retrieve it, and upon her return she gave Greggory an apologetic shrug. He shrugged in return before coming over to sit down.

At one point he clicked his mouth to speak but instead let out a long sigh. After a few moments, Reid came from the hallway. She and Greggory simultaneously revolved their heads like two attentive birds reacting to motion.

Even though Reid didn't have to leave until early evening, each moment carried on as if they would have to pick up without warning. Breakfast, lunch, the hours bled both long and quick, all in a haze. Breakfast, tea, hugging goodbye. What had they done that day? Picked up his clothes, packed, hugged, kissed. The rays flooded the carpet through the transom, warm and caressing; the three of them walked outside. She and Reid under the awning, and Greggory patiently jangling the keys near the truck. The two stood close together holding hands, making promises to see each other again soon, perhaps Thanksgiving.

"Hey, Emma," he looked into her, "I'm glad to have met you this summer."

She couldn't speak; it would open floodgates, reveal the parts she tried to hide. Instead, she hugged and kissed him once more. He began to walk to the truck, letting her hand slide out of his—truck door opening—Greggory poking his head over the metal roof.

Then came Greggory, "Hey, I just wanted to say, don't be a stranger. I know your last day was scheduled for yesterday, but," he paused, "but you know you're always welcome."

She nodded, "Of course I'll visit." The words allowed the first droplet to curve down her cheek.

Then Reid's words, "I'll see you soon. I love you."

The first part was unrealistic, *soon*, but the second, that he loved her, she couldn't help but believe.

"Me too. I love you."

The door closed, and a few more tears were pulled from her sockets by gravity.

She walked the rusty truck to the street, and Reid poked his head out to offer a somber smile. She stood watching his features blur, his waving hand blur. The truck bumbled down Forester until it too blurred. In the distance she could make out the composed blinking of the turn signal before it turned right and disappeared.

GREGGORY

The motor of the truck canted as he and his grandson bumped along. They didn't say much. He looked over and saw Reid's thoughts congeal to a grave stare at the glove department. He tried to find the words that could help, but none came to mind. The silence sapped his courage to speak.

The years without filial contact, without *any* contact, weighed on him now that he was reminded what it felt like. Reid's visit gave him a second chance. How long ago it had been when he and his own son lived together, when Paul was little and they all camped as a family in the hills.

He was still uncertain whether Paul would visit after everything that happened those many years ago, but his mind encouraged the thoughts of his son and grandson returning together next time. They could have a barbeque, maybe work on a project together, go camping in the valley. The ideas cascaded. He didn't remember the exact spot from before, but they could come close to finding it. Emma could join as well, the three of them and her. He hoped she would accept his invitation; without meaning to, he learned to enjoy her company. She acted just like Sophia would have in her youth. Sophia.

He missed Sophia.

"Hey, Grandpa?" Reid broke the heavy silence.

"Hmm?" Greggory tilted his head from the road.

Reid looked down at his hands, "I know we've talked about visiting again, but do you think I could—maybe if you'd like—stay out here longer next year?" I mean maybe not live here forever, but—you know—stay awhile?" Reid nodded his head determinedly, to confirm he hadn't misspoken.

"Reid," there was a short pause, "you can stay out here as long as you'd like, even if that means living here. You know I love having you. You know I love you."

"I love you too, Grampa. It means a lot to me."

With those simple words Reid moved his pensive gaze to the passenger's window.

When he was sure his grandson wasn't looking, while Reid watched the road pass them by, Greggory allowed himself to feel an emotion he hadn't experienced in a long time, and a trill of tears found their way to his cheeks.

EMMA

Once the truck left her vision, she was unable to control the welling tears. The stoic trickle became an absurd stream in a matter of minutes. She even told herself how ridiculous it was, he'd be back soon, but whatever logic she tried bent like aluminum to the uncontrollable happenings of her body.

For some time she stood like a beacon, waiting and watching for any indication that he would return, but eventually the valley became more dark than light.

She did her best to refuse the warm amenity of her house, feeling it as a patronizing consolation to her grief, but after a long time standing with her legs aching and her mind utterly exhausted she finally succumbed. Her weighted legs and stiff ankles motioned in the direction of her house. She followed a beeline down Forester, made it to the beginning of her driveway. Before entering, she allowed herself the rebellious thought of turning back around and trekking up the hill, but deep down she knew she didn't have the stamina.

She was resolute as she shuffled down the gravel trail, but upon reaching the fence circling her yard she refused to enter. Sitting alone, sleeping, being inside would destroy her. She marched across the shallow creek bisecting her property and sat on the mottled rock behind their weathered barn. Across the field she looked to the horizon and could barely make out Greggory's home.

Memory after memory flooded her wistful mind. They meant so much to her, but the world around her dismissed them as though they'd never occurred. She looked out at the familiar landscape. The single lonely road that transformed the rolling hills into a neighborhood wound gently to the horizon, the drone of crickets hummed across the land with a mocking aloofness, and the long strands of yellow grass danced idly with the wind. The rabbits in the meadows hardly even knew—let alone cared—that summer was gone. The sun continued its endless journey, and life carried on with its slow-moving, unbridled certainty.

Eventually, her tears exhausted themselves. Even though a sharp spike of rock speared into her back and her inflexible hands became icy, her body remained still—at some point becoming numb entirely. Had she not been anesthetized, she would have recognized the pain and chills diffusing through her body in a dull throb.

In her recollection of summer, in sitting and gazing into something permanent and insoluble, her vision began to falter and she slumped over and fell into something resembling sleep. She believed she was still peering consciously into the distant field when the moon took reign in the sky and the notorious night life began its hymn, but when the truck poked down the road, doing about thirty, she didn't catch the headlights flash in her direction. Later she surmised she had merely missed the truck as it turned left into her driveway. The gentle slam of the truck's door was perhaps too faint to hear. The figure approaching, too stealthy.

It wasn't until she heard the deep voice call her name from behind, "Emma?" that she sat up with a shake of her head. "Hey, are you okay?"

It was a voice, but not the one she expected.

He approached and placed his palm on her shoulder. "Hey Peeks, what are you doing out here?"

Not getting up and not knowing what to say, she blurted out the only thing that came to mind: "How'd you know I was out here?"

From where she sat she could be only barely be visible, at best an outlined figure extending from an outlined figure.

"Well, I always look out here when I get home from work." Her father still had his tie on. "I don't know if you remember," his tone was bashful, "but we went on that trip one time to the ocean and the desert, and when we got back you were so mad, so mad, because we had to get back home and you didn't want the trip to end. You came out here and sat on this rock with your arms crossed. I had to nearly drag you back in. Now I always check over here when I get home. I'm sorry I haven't been there for you lately. At some point I didn't know what to say any more. Are you okay?"

She sat stunned. A sudden necessity to tell him everything pressed her, but instead she stood, her body sore, and crashed into his chest. His warm embrace.

"What happened, Peeks?" His shoes and pant cuffs had gotten muddy crossing the creek.

"Can we go on another camping trip?"

Her chest heaved at the reprieve of his arms.

"Of course." He patted her back

"Next week?"

There was a pause, him considering work, but he rocked her and answered, "Of course."

She knew then that she would tell her father about Reid, but for the moment she leaned on him without a word. It didn't fill all the nooks Reid expertly occupied and then sliced away—nor did she want it to—but she was still grateful he was there to catch her.

She recognized that she'd have difficulty moving forward with her life for some time to come, but in the end she'd be okay.

Her memories of summer, her own devastating love, all the other loves that covered and stained and compounded to cover Forever Road, could only be indications of life. In the end, she'd make it out intact.

Acknowledgements

I would like to thank my grandmother who passed before this book went to publication. I love you Noni, and you will never be forgotten. Every day I carry the moments we shared. Each day I carry your lessons and love within me.

Thank you Papa for being a calming force in my life. When things get a little whacky, I know you're there to re-ground me.

Thank you Alicia and Mom for always providing unconditional love and support.

Thank you Jenny for inspiring this novel, and to your parents who had welcomed me to their property when I was in high school. The property inspired some of the scenes in this novel.

Thank you Heather for letting me read the beginning drafts to you while stuck in a little shack deep in the snowy mountains of Shasta. Don't worry, we weren't in danger! Also, thank you for challenging my writing style and ultimately improving my skills as an author and editor.

Thank you to my friends—there are too many to name— who also let me read the initial drafts to them whilst drunk and inspired.

Thank you to my editor Matthew Ritchie who helped shape the novel to what it is today.

And thank you to my audience members who have taken the risk to pick up this novel and begin reading.

If you would like more information about this novel or about me as an author, please visit my website **ForeverRd.com.** I invite you to write a review, see what's going on with *Forever Road,* or reach out to me personally.